PRAISE F
The Light in the Lake

★ "In Baughman's skillful handling, Addie's memories of her brother and her first-person voice are both heartbreaking and hopeful. The novel offers a gentle, introspective exploration of grief and the wonder and fragility of nature, creating a beautiful and dynamic world in which the scientific method and magic coexist."
—*Publishers Weekly*, **starred review**

★ "Baughman convincingly portrays the varied reactions to the findings as well as everybody's desire for the lake to thrive.... Compassionately told, this compelling debut brings to life conservation issues and choices young readers will confront as adults." —*Kirkus Reviews*, **starred review**

"Haunting, memorable and full of mystery, *The Light in the Lake* is a brilliant combination of beautiful, lyrical prose and a compelling, exciting story."—*BookPage*

"A complex take on science, magic, grief, and family for fans of thoughtful realistic fiction in the vein of Kathi Appelt's, Erin Entrada Kelly's, and Ali Benjamin's novels."
—*School Library Journal*

"Baughman paints with authenticity the grief of Addie.... Addie's unabashed love for science makes her a pleasingly STEM-focused heroine, and her quest to solve Amos' questions about the lake is interesting and admirable." —*The Bulletin*

"Told in prose as luminous as the mysterious creature Addie searches for, *The Light in the Lake* shines with heart, hope, and just a touch of magic." —**Cindy Baldwin, author of *Where the Watermelons Grow***

"*The Light in the Lake* is a moving novel that skillfully balances magic and science, and loss and hope. Sarah Baughman has created a brave, smart protagonist readers are sure to connect with and root for in her compelling debut." —**Supriya Kelkar, award-winning author of *Ahimsa* and *American as Paneer Pie***

"*The Light in the Lake* radiates with heart and hope. As Addie's tender memories of her brother intertwine with the magic she uncovers in her town's beloved lake, we're led on a moving exploration of science, grief, and self-discovery. A poignant, lyrical story that tugs at the heartstrings." —**Mae Respicio, award-winning author of *The House That Lou Built***

"Drawing on the wonder of science and the power of magic, Baughman has crafted a story that plunges readers into the deep places of the heart. In *The Light in the Lake* she reminds us that not even the depths of loss can prevent the rise of light and discovery. A poignant story, filled to the brim with hope." —**Beth Hautala, author of *Waiting for Unicorns* and *The Ostrich and Other Lost Things***

The LIGHT in the LAKE

SARAH R. BAUGHMAN

LITTLE, BROWN AND COMPANY
New York Boston

Copyright © 2019 by Sarah R. Baughman
Excerpt from *The Wild Path* copyright © 2020 by Sarah R. Baughman

Cover art copyright © 2019 by Ji-Hyuk Kim. Cover design by Karina Granda. Cover copyright © 2019 by Hachette Book Group, Inc.

Little, Brown and Company
Hachette Book Group
1290 Avenue of the Americas, New York, NY 10104
Visit us at LBYR.com

Originally published in hardcover and ebook by
Little, Brown and Company in September 2019
First Paperback Edition: August 2020

Little, Brown and Company is a division of Hachette Book Group, Inc. The Little, Brown name and logo are trademarks of Hachette Book Group, Inc.

The publisher is not responsible for websites (or their content) that are not owned by the publisher.

The Library of Congress has cataloged the hardcover edition as follows:
Names: Baughman, Sarah R., author.
Title: The light in the lake / by Sarah R. Baughman.
Description: First edition. | New York ; Boston : Little, Brown and Company, 2019. | Summary: As a Young Scientist, twelve-year-old Addie studies pollution in the lake where her twin brother recently drowned, while secretly continuing his investigation of the creature he believed lives in the lake's depths.
Identifiers: LCCN 2018056973| ISBN 9780316422420 (hardcover) | ISBN 9780316422413 (ebook) | ISBN 9780316422390 (library edition ebook)
Subjects: | CYAC: Grief—Fiction. | Family life—Vermont—Fiction. | Lakes—Fiction. | Water pollution—Fiction. | Vermont—Fiction. | Mystery and detective stories.
Classification: LCC PZ7.1.B378 Lig 2019 | DDC [Fic]—dc23
LC record available at https://lccn.loc.gov/2018056973

ISBNs: 978-0-316-42240-6 (pbk.), 978-0-316-42241-3 (ebook)

Printed in the United States of America

LSC-C

10 9 8 7 6 5 4 3 2 1

To my parents,
who read to me
and saved all my stories

Prologue

Mama says people who think mountains don't move are taking the short view of things. They've been moving, she says. All this time. Doesn't matter that we can't see it.

If we could somehow watch time go faster, I think, or if we'd lived so long we'd felt the glaciers haul through here in the first place, we *would* see it. And then we'd know.

In science class we learned that millions of years ago, our mountains used to stretch up higher than clouds. Sometimes I look at them for so long, I think I can see how they used to be: before my eyes, the rounded green tops rise, sharper than they are now, poking the sky. Then I blink and they settle into place. In those moments, it feels like everything around me—Maple Lake's tossing waves, the sighing wind—is slowly breathing, in and out.

But I'm only seeing what I know was once there. What Mama and my science textbook told me.

Amos saw something else, and he wanted me to see it too.

He loved floating in the lake, surrounded by mountains thick with mossy rocks and tangled cedars. The waves whispered secrets, he said; we just had to listen. He was so certain something lived in that cold water, something ancient and huge and shining.

"You have to look," he'd say, standing on the beach. "*Look*, Addie."

But when I'd squint at the water, at the glowing shape he insisted swelled in the middle, I'd shake my head. "A log," I'd say. "That's all."

It's not that I didn't see the shining, or that I loved the lake any less than he did. I'm the most myself when I'm near the water.

It's just that I had my way to look at the world. And he had his.

People say we look so much alike: fraternal twins with the same leaf-green eyes and bony knees. Same hair, the color of sand and just as wind-whipped and rough.

But what they don't say, because they can't see, is that underneath the eyes and hair and skin and bone, something stronger pulls us close. One side of his heart makes the other side of mine. I'm here because he is, and the other way around. For always. Things that solid aren't supposed to go away.

But sometimes they do. Glacier ice cut through these mountains and pressed down until the hard, sharp rock chipped clean away. And when the weather warmed and the ice went soft, then clear, it left us with Maple Lake, the deepest one in Vermont.

Dad says lake water runs through our veins, and maybe that's true. When Amos and I aren't swimming with Mama, we're casting lines with Dad, hoping for some of that trout and smelt and perch we fish for all year long.

Fished, I mean. This spring Amos tumbled into the lake and slept, down there on the bottom where the stone that used to be mountain now lies flat and unseen.

Now I have to say everything in past tense.

Mama doesn't talk about the mountains anymore. She doesn't talk much at all.

"You want to go skip stones, Mama?" I ask sometimes when I'm feeling brave. We could throw mountain back to mountain. Watch pieces skid across the water.

But even now she can barely look at me when she says no.

Chapter 1

School is all noise and lights—kids yelling, backpacks bumping. We have cinder block walls and metal doors so heavy they take forever to open, then clank shut too fast. Our lunchroom always smells like canned green beans. But I guess that's the good thing about school. It keeps going the way it is, even when nothing else does.

I walk through the hall with my head down, my shoulder bumping Liza's. She's my cousin, and also my best friend. She doesn't care how many times I bump her shoulder. Sometimes she touches her hand to my elbow, lightly steering me in the right direction.

Ten steps, I tell myself. *Ten…nine…eight…* I've been doing this a lot the past two months: staring at my feet, counting steps. I guess I just don't like thinking about all the kids trying *not* to look at me, their eyes full of whispers. My method works pretty well, except one time I walked right into a little kindergartner who had found her way into the middle school wing somehow. There's nine grades in this one building, and we're supposed to watch out for the littlest kids.

We make it to science and I exhale, fast.

Mr. Dale always stands outside his classroom door and sticks his hand out for us to shake as we walk in. I didn't think he'd keep that up past September, but it's the end of the year now and he's still going strong, pumping our hands up and down.

"Addie and Liza!" he says. "Welcome."

"Nice SpongeBob tie," Liza says; she's looking at me, holding a laugh in. We've both tried to figure out if he ever repeats a tie, or if he really has as many ties as there are days of school. This SpongeBob one is new. And pretty dorky.

Mr. Dale just smiles. "I'm glad you have such good taste. My son picked it out; apparently it's what all the Shoreland County preschoolers are wearing. Or wanting to wear."

Since it's almost the last week of school, most of the teachers have stopped giving us homework, but Mr. Dale's been making us chart the phases of the moon since May and he says there's no reason to stop before the full cycle's over. I realize as soon as Liza and the other kids start fishing their charts out of their backpacks that I forgot to look at the moon last night.

As Mr. Dale moves around the room checking work, he pauses just for a second and taps my desk with one finger. When I look down, I see a little yellow Post-it stuck there with a message written on it: *Deep breaths!* Then there's a smiley face with googly eyes, and his signature: *Mr. D.*

Teachers usually walk right by when I don't turn my work in these days, and they don't say anything. Mr. Dale is the only one who leaves little notes that make me feel like maybe someday I'll be okay.

"Your sketches are looking good," Mr. Dale tells the class. He picks Liza's up and puts it under the document camera. On the board, her drawings slide into focus; I can tell she used the dark charcoal pencils she got for her birthday.

"Liza," he says. "Could you please describe the moon you saw last night?"

"It's still a crescent," she says. "Smaller than two nights ago."

"Great," he says. "And why is it continuing to get smaller? It's a—what kind of crescent?"

Waning, I think, just as Liza says it. Waning: getting smaller and smaller until there's barely anything left. Liza's perfect crescent shimmers in the thick charcoal defining her night sky.

"That's kind of weird," I say. My own voice surprises me; the words sounded better when they were just thoughts, but it's too late to go back.

Mr. Dale nods, and I can tell it's the kind of nod teachers do when they want to include you in the conversation but they're not quite sure whether you're going to help it or ruin it. "How so, Addie?"

"Um..." I stall. Mr. Dale waits while the other kids start to fidget. "When you talk about seeing the moon, you mean the silvery glowing part."

"True," Mr. Dale says.

"But when you draw it on white paper, you can't actually *draw* that part." I look at the smudges Liza's charcoal pencils made. "You have to draw the dark part instead, and kind of use the dark part to show the light part." The words tumble out faster than my brain can really think them through. "So you're not actually drawing *the moon*. You're drawing the shadow that covers it up bit by bit until it looks like it was never there at all."

When I stop talking, the room's so quiet I can hear the wind outside, rattling young birch leaves together. Liza's just staring at me, her eyes big as full moons. The other kids stare too—kids I've known my whole life who have been trying really hard *not* to look at me since Amos died. Not wanting to look the wrong way, say the wrong thing. They don't know there *isn't* a right way. They might as well just look.

But Mr. Dale doesn't seem surprised. He just nods. "An excellent point, Addie," he says. "Scientifically and philosophically relevant. Darkness allows us to see light."

Liza sticks her hand up. She knows I don't like having all the focus on me, and she's probably thinking fast, trying to help. "You can sort of *see* the dark part too," she says. "I mean, it has a shape in the sky, if you really look."

"Can anyone predict when that darkness will cover the whole moon?" Mr. Dale asks. "When do you think this crescent will completely disappear and give us a new moon?"

"How about *never?*" In the back corner of the room, Darren Andrews snickers. I roll my eyes. Amos was Darren's friend—one of his only friends—since preschool.

When Darren was little, he'd get in trouble for spinning around in the teacher's chair when she got up to check assignments, drumming on his desktop, tickling other kids during story hour. We've never been close, but he used to at least nod at me in the halls, before. Now he just looks away like everyone else.

Mr. Dale sighs. "Darren," he says. "Let's have a little more faith in the moon. It's been around awhile. Anyone else?"

"A day?" someone asks.

"No way," says Liza. "We've got longer than that."

"Probably not much longer, though," says Mr. Dale. "Keep watching at night. See how long it lasts."

When class ends, Liza stays beside me instead of rushing out to the art room like she used to before Amos died. I zip my backpack—I know I'm taking too long, because Liza's eyes keep darting toward the clock, even though she'd never tell me to hurry—and sling it over one shoulder as I get up to leave.

"Addie," Mr. Dale says, pointing in my direction, "can I quickly touch base with you? I'll write you a pass to art."

I backtrack and stand next to his desk, waving Liza away. "I'll look at the moon tonight," I mumble in his direction. "I just sort of forgot last night. I—"

"It's not that," Mr. Dale says. "I'm just hoping you're planning to apply for the Young Scientist position we talked about."

I think of the crumpled Post-it note Mr. Dale put on my desk. Time to take that deep breath.

I missed a lot of school right after Amos died. So once I came back and Mr. Dale told me about the chance to spend this summer on Maple Lake, learning from scientists about how to study the water, I knew he was just trying to catch me up.

But I haven't known exactly how to feel about Maple

Lake. It used to be the place Amos and I both loved most. Now that he's gone, it feels different. It's a part of me that hurts to look at.

I won't say I didn't listen to Mr. Dale when he first mentioned the Young Scientist position. It's just that everything anyone said that month sounded like it was underwater. All the words gurgled, hard to hear, and most of them drowned somewhere outside me. I just couldn't hold on to them.

I look down at the papers scattered across his desk. "Um," I say slowly. "I've been…"

"…thinking about it?" he asks.

"I kind of have, but—" I twist my backpack strap around my fingers.

"You should consider it." Mr. Dale leans forward and shuffles the papers, then starts working through them with a pen. Maybe he knows I need some time to think.

As the Young Scientist, I would get to work at the biological station, a huge chunk of shoreline owned by the University of Vermont. Scientists go there to monitor water clarity and temperature, chart bird sightings, and study how cutting and using trees can keep the forest healthy. Amos and I used to play hide-and-seek on the nature trails there when we were younger.

"So…it's an everyday thing?" I ask.

"You bet," Mr. Dale says, still checking off papers.

"The researchers are there five days a week, and so am I, now that I'm studying for my master's. We'd like the Young Scientist to be there each weekday too."

Mr. Dale knows I want to be an aquatic biologist someday. The one time I admitted it in homeroom, when we were supposed to talk about what we wanted to do when we grew up, most of the kids just stared.

But before I could figure out how to explain, Mr. Dale cut right through the silence and said that aquatic biologists can study not only the ocean, but freshwater lakes and rivers too, which is exactly what we have in Vermont, in between all the mountains.

"If you're accepted," Mr. Dale continues, looking up from his papers, "and everything goes well, you could join the Science Club next year, in seventh grade instead of eighth. We could make an exception."

That sounds pretty good to me. Science Club members get to ride the bus to the high school once a week to do cool experiments with the freshman earth science class.

"What's the project this summer?" I ask.

"We're looking at pollution levels in the lake," Mr. Dale says. He sets his stack of papers aside and folds his hands. "You could learn about testing water samples, entering data—"

"Pollution levels?" I feel my skin bristle. "Maple Lake's

not polluted. My dad says it's the coldest, clearest lake in the state."

"The water might look clear," Mr. Dale says, "but it's getting to the point where it isn't actually as clean as it might seem. Not according to some preliminary observations. And we want to know why." He looks right at me. "You've spent a lot of time on that lake."

Tears sting my eyes. Most people don't talk about Maple Lake with me anymore.

"It can't be easy," he says, his voice soft. "With...everything that happened."

I look up. *Say it*, I think. *Just say it. Nobody ever says it.*

As though he hears me thinking, Mr. Dale clears his throat. "With Amos," he says. "With your brother."

Hearing Mr. Dale say his name helps somehow. It's like the room had swelled to the point of bursting, a too-full balloon, and his name popped it. Everything settles, calms.

"I don't want to presume, Addie," Mr. Dale continues. "Working at the lake might not sound like the best idea to you. I just..." He trails off, looks up at the ceiling.

I clench the Post-it note so hard my fingernails dig into my palm. He's right, in a way. But the strange thing is—*not* working at the lake doesn't sound easy either.

Mr. Dale turns his palms up and shrugs. "Okay, look. I loved science when I was your age," he says. "When I became a teacher, I promised myself that if any of my students got as excited about it as I did, I'd help them out as much as I could. And this chance to study the lake seemed like an opportunity I should tell you about."

That's when I know for sure I really do miss Maple Lake. I feel it deep down, like water feels the wind pushing up waves. Mama and Dad and I haven't been there since *before*. But I don't think Amos would like it if I stayed away forever. And I realize now, I don't want to.

"If you applied, I think it could work out well," Mr. Dale says. "Scientifically speaking, you're a very strong candidate. You ask questions. And you think about things in different ways, like what you said about drawing the moon. Those are good qualities for a scientist to have."

I stand up a little straighter. "Thanks."

"Take this home," Mr. Dale says, handing me an application. "Talk about it with your parents. See what they say."

"I don't need to talk to them about it." I feel something inside pulling me toward Maple Lake now, even though it's the last place most people would expect me to go. "I'll apply."

Chapter 2

Liza and I line up for the bus together, arms linked, like always. I didn't tell her about the Young Scientist position at lunch or study hall. Not yet.

Liza was born just a couple of months before Amos and me. Sometimes Aunt Mary and Mama called us the triplets, and even though it wasn't technically true, it didn't quite feel wrong either. A lot of times I can tell what Liza's feeling, even when she's not saying a thing.

Like right now, I know she's thinking hard. Worried. She's chewing the side of her lip like she does when she's working on one of her sketches and thinks she messed it up but doesn't know how to fix it. She pulls me a little closer.

"Want to come over today?" she asks, quietly enough that nobody else can hear.

Amos and I used to go over to Liza's a lot after school. Her bus stop came before ours and Aunt Mary was always home by the time we got there, so if we knew Mama needed to sleep before work or Dad was still on a job site, it made sense. But I haven't been going over as much lately. Not since Amos died.

I wish I could explain this to Liza, but I don't even know if I can really understand it myself. Shouldn't I want to hang out with my cousin, the only other person who knew Amos close to as well as I did? The only person who wouldn't just stare at me with big, scared eyes if I started crying out of nowhere, or accidentally talking about Amos like he was still there?

"Um, I can't today." The words feel sharp, even though I don't mean them to be. "I have homework, and I think I need to start dinner because Mama's working…" The rest of the sentence wanders away. I don't need to look at Liza to know she's trying to look like everything's okay, like whatever I want is fine.

"No worries," she says. Our bus is pulling up, and Liza lets go of my arm as the doors heave open. My chest aches.

"Hi there, girls," Barbara Ann says from the driver's seat. "All aboard!" She takes one hand off the steering wheel to motion us up the steps, then winks one blue-shadowed eye.

Barbara Ann's one of Mama's best school friends and even babysat Amos and me sometimes when Aunt Mary couldn't, so I think I know her pretty well. I know you can count on her for a few things. Number one: frizzy brown hair that sticks out in places. She never pulls it back; it just falls all around her shoulders like milkweed fluff. Number two: bright red lipstick. Number three: gum, usually watermelon-flavored, and usually snapped between her teeth while she's talking, which she does a lot.

Snap. I guess there's a number four: the good mood. Barbara Ann really doesn't stop smiling, which comes in handy on days when I don't have the energy to do it myself. It reminds me of being little, learning to ride a two-wheeler: Mama would give me a little push on the back of the seat to get me started. Barbara Ann's smiles feel just like that.

"Hey, Barbara Ann," I say. And I make my lips go up at the corners.

She grabs my wrist. "Wait a second," she says. "Isn't tomorrow—"

"Yeah, I'll be twelve," I say. "Saturday. Guess I got lucky." The words taste sour. Pretending to be happy about a weekend birthday with no school seems stupid this year, but it also feels like a normal thing to say.

The nice thing about Barbara Ann's smiles is they aren't fake. When her lips kind of roll together, like they have to press hard to keep something else out, I can tell she's thinking about Amos and how he'll never be twelve. But her smile's still real. She looks right at me too, which is something people sometimes seem scared to do when they remember about Amos.

"You have a good birthday tomorrow, honey," she says. Then she reaches in her shirt pocket, pulls something out, and presses it into my hand.

"Found this," she whispers. "An early present. Keep it safe." I walk toward the back of the bus and find my seat by Liza just as Barbara Ann shifts into gear and we roll away.

"What did she give you?" Liza leans over, trying to catch a glimpse of my hand.

"I don't know." The thing, whatever it is, is smooth, curved, with a sharp point. I don't want to open my hand, though. When I realize I'm waiting for Amos to come so he can see whatever it is too, tears start and I have to blink hard. Liza hooks her hand through the crook of my elbow, pulls me a little closer on the seat.

I picture Amos across the aisle, leaning over for a closer look. "*Open it!*" he'd whisper, loudly enough for me to know he meant it. But of course if he were here, he'd probably have one too. He would already know what it was because he never would have been able to wait.

I let my fingers open and there it is: white, quarter-moon-shaped. Perfect.

"A tooth?" Liza's nose wrinkles. "Has Barbara Ann completely lost it?"

"It's a white whale tooth." I would know one anywhere; Amos and I love—loved—to collect them. Over ten thousand years ago, the Atlantic Ocean flooded over land pressed low by glaciers, and white whales swam right through it. Only when the land rose back up, filling with fresh water draining off the mountains, did the whales go away. Even so, they left evidence of themselves: one of their skeletons turned up in a farmer's field over in Charlotte a long time ago, and now it's our state fossil. "But it's a really big one. Huge, actually. Almost—" I stop.

"Almost what?"

"Nothing." I shake my head. There are some things I don't want to tell even Liza. Like how if Amos were here, he'd say there was no way a white whale could have this big a tooth, that it had to come from somewhere—something—else. Like the creature, swimming through the deepest parts of Maple Lake.

It wasn't really like Amos to keep secrets, but I know he didn't say anything about the creature to anyone else, not even Liza. He wanted to prove it first. *"You're a scientist, Ad,"* he said. *"You can help."*

But I didn't believe him.

Liza shifts in her seat and clears her throat, a sure sign

she's changing the subject to something brighter, something that won't make my eyes blur and sting.

"So, have you thought about the calf at all?" she asks. "Dad said I should double-check, be sure you still wanted to." She twists her fingers together, waiting for me to say something back. I slip the tooth into my pocket and nod.

Liza always raises a calf as a 4-H project to bring to the Shoreland County Fair. Aunt Mary and her husband, my uncle Mark, have a dairy farm, so every spring Liza has plenty of calves to choose from. This year, a month or so after Amos died, she asked if I wanted to help her take care of a calf and learn how to show it in the ring. She even said I could pick out whichever one I liked best, that she'd wait until I had the chance to come over. She knew I loved the calves, with their big brown eyes and their knobby knees and their tails flicking flies.

After Amos died, so much just stopped in its tracks. But the calves were born, just like they were always going to be. And the fair would still happen. And now, even though it feels weird to keep *doing* things, even though my stomach spins just thinking about it, I hear myself saying "I'm in."

"Good," she says. "You'll already be around anyway, right?"

Amos and I didn't just go to Liza's after school; we spent a lot of time there in the summer too. When we were little, it was so Aunt Mary could babysit us. But as we got older, it became our job to watch Liza's little sisters so Aunt Mary could work more around the farm with Uncle Mark.

"Sure I will." But I remember what Mr. Dale said too, about going to the biological station every day. If I get to be the Young Scientist, I'll need to explain to Liza that even though I can still help with the calf, I won't be able to come as often as she thinks, or stay as long.

Maybe I should tell her about the position right now. I usually tell her everything. "Actually," I say, "there's this thing—"

Liza's eyes get wide, swollen with worry. I know this look. It's the same one she gave me when Amos and I both got bronchitis right before the sixth-grade Spring Fling and I told her, hacking into my elbow when she knocked on my door, that we couldn't go with her after all. It's hard to look at someone's face and see all this hope shining... and then just snuff it out.

"Never mind," I say. "I thought I might need to help my parents out at home, but I don't think I will after all."

"Good," Liza says, and rests her cheek on my shoulder. I tip my head to lean against hers and her brown curls tickle my forehead.

"I'm glad you'll be able to hang out," she says. "It'll just be—lonely this summer, otherwise. If you're not there."

I don't understand how Liza could feel lonely in a house with three sisters. I think about just saying that out loud—I kind of want to—but I hold back and point to the sketchbook on her lap instead. She carries it everywhere. "Can I take a look?" I ask.

"Not yet," she says. "I've been working on most of it at home anyway. Maybe when you come over tomorrow, you can see some sketches. I'm entering the Shoreland Art Show this year and I have a whole portfolio I need to put together."

I feel my eyebrows shooting up before I really want them to. It's not that Liza isn't talented, but the Shoreland Art Show is kind of a big deal.

"Yeah, I know," Liza says, reading my mind as usual. "Not likely."

"I didn't say that." I don't want Liza to think I don't believe in her. I do. But I also know kids from all over the state enter. "Do they have a separate category for middle school?"

Liza shakes her head. "Whatever I enter is going to get thrown right in with the high school kids' stuff," she says. "I'll be at the very bottom of the youngest age bracket. I could use some advice on my entry."

"You can do it," I say. "I'll help if I can."

I mean it too. The last person who asked me for help was Amos, and I wish I had done more.

I remember when he came back from Teddy's store that first Saturday in March, his bike tires slicing through soft leftover snow. I can't believe it was only three months ago now, one of those days that felt like spring but wasn't. The sun shone so bright, it made us all think winter might end early. We had nearly a week of those days. Too many, I know now. The sun that beat on our shoulders and peeled off our coats turned the lake ice weak, brought pockets of melt up to the surface, daring it to crack.

But that day, just about a week before he left me forever, Amos hopped off his bike and let it tip over. He reached toward me, holding a notebook, the kind you can buy for fifty cents at Teddy's, with a cover that flips up and folds back. Small enough to fit in my pocket.

"What's it for?" I asked. But I kept my hands knotted behind my back.

He leaned in. *"Keeping track of the creature."* Barely a whisper. *"Remember?"*

And I laughed. Not in a mean way, but still.

"There's no creature," I said. *"Besides, why are you whispering?"*

Amos looked over his shoulder as though spies were hiding in the woods past our house. *"I just don't want anyone* else to know but you and me," he said. "Not yet. Not until I prove it for sure. So that means I need to keep researching. We need to."

If there really were a magical creature down there in the lake, old as glaciers, moving dark and cold, Amos would be the one to find it. But I didn't believe it existed. There couldn't be any real evidence for something like that, and I told Amos so.

"C'mon, Addie," he said, his eyes soft. Hurt. "You'll see. I've been writing clues down since last fall." He patted his back pocket, where another line of silver coils stuck out.

"Clues about a creature," I repeated. "That doesn't sound very scientific. If you ever wanted to prove it, you'd need actual evidence."

He shook the notebook a little, urging me to take it. "Maybe you could find some of your own," he said. "You could try."

Finally I untwisted my hands and took what he offered and stuck it in my pocket. But not because I actually believed.

I think I did it because of his eyes. They usually glittered, like sun on cedar leaves, and I didn't like the look of them clouded over, all the hope of working together sucked away. So I held out my hand and the sun came back out. Just like that.

I've been telling myself I'll open his notebook tomorrow, on our birthday. It won't hurt to at least read what he had to say. What I never wanted to hear when I had the chance. But now I don't know if I'm ready. Maybe because picking up his notebook and reading it myself, without him there, is only something I can do because he's gone. Forever.

If Amos were here, he'd be running up the bus aisle, breaking all of Barbara Ann's rules, demanding she tell him where she got the tooth. He'd be pulling the notebook out of his pocket and bugging me for a pencil.

I close my fingers back around the tooth. I let it dig right into my skin.

Chapter 3

My birthday starts with emptiness, the kind of quiet that comes from sounds that don't mean anything. I lie on the bottom bunk trying to hear something other than the faucet, water spilling into the sink, Dad clearing his throat, Mama knocking glasses against the counter, the refrigerator buzzing. But there's nothing else. No voices. On the top bunk, an empty mattress bears down.

Mama said she'd get me a different bed. Dad said he'd haul this one away, chop it up. He even promised to burn it, his eyes raw, his voice almost shaking. I believed him. I could almost see his dry, cracked hands tearing the panels apart, stacking them just right, lighting a match.

But they didn't. The top bunk's still here and Amos's clothes still hang in the closet. Sometimes I pull one of his shirts out and put it on, just to feel it. And I keep lying there every night, half expecting Amos to hang his face over the edge and whisper: *"You awake?"*

Silence pours into the space left by the whispers, but all I have to do is wait. Every time that silence starts to feel like it could swallow me up, a warm feeling wraps itself around my body and squeezes. When it's there, I can't move, but I don't want to either. I just press my fingertips into my sides and squeeze back until I can't squeeze anymore.

I lift the corner of my mattress and pull out Amos's notebook. Even though I still haven't opened it, I'm glad I kept it. I threw the one he gave me, blank, into Maple Lake the last time I went there, the day after Mama and Dad and I huddled under weeping cedar trees, staring at that shimmering hole in the ice. It was long gone. But here was Amos's, real as skin. If Dad had lit that match, I might not have found the courage to rescue his notebook from where I knew he kept it under his mattress.

Pain swells but I hold the notebook in my palm. It shakes a little, and I try to make my hands quiet. Opening a notebook should be so easy. Just flip the cover back. But I can't make my fingers do it. I just sit, feeling my head throb, staring at what Amos wrote on the front—CLUES in big block letters crossed out with a black marker, EVIDENCE written above it.

He must have done that for me.

But what kind of evidence could he possibly have found?

I close my eyes and picture Maple Lake shimmering under the sun. There are scientific facts I know about it. I can tell you it's three hundred feet at its deepest point. I can tell you it's full of perch and lake trout. I can tell you that by mid-August, the average surface water temperature ranges from 67 to 73 degrees Fahrenheit.

But I can't tell you why, when I slide into that same water and stand with my toes just touching the sand at the bottom, the waves tipping me lightly back and forth, I feel like I could live there, warm and cold at the same time, filled up and fresh. I can't tell you why the fish I catch look at me with their gold-and-black eyes, why they lie heaving and shining in my palm once I've pulled them out of the water, breathing at the same pace as the waves knocking the boat. And no matter how much I read about the very deepest bottom, about the cliff walls and mineral veins, I can't tell you for certain how it feels at the exact point where the water turns from silver to midnight blue. I can't tell you everything you might see once you've swum past the glacial formations and around every corner of the boulders that slump down, down, down, bigger than houses.

There are things I can only imagine.

And maybe those are the kinds of things Amos counted as evidence. Maybe those are the kinds of things I'll find when I open this notebook.

But I don't. I pull on jeans and slip the notebook in my back pocket. Then I move from the silence hanging in my room to the silence Mama and Dad make in the kitchen.

Dad sits at the table, pressing the fingers of one hand into closed eyes. He doesn't see me.

"Hey," I whisper, a sound so small I think I might have imagined it. I take one step forward. Cough.

Dad jolts then, looks at me. "Honey girl," he says. His hands tremble but he opens his arms and I walk in. I sit on his knee even though I know I'm too old for that, especially now that I'm twelve, and lean against his shoulder. He smells like sawdust and sweat. I press my heels against the tops of his work boots, the hard leather slick and worn. *Say something else, anything.*

Dad holds me a little tighter and whispers: "Happy birthday."

Mama always made pancakes on our birthday, chocolate chip for Amos and blueberry for me. She'd bring out a big jug of the maple syrup we help Uncle Mark and Aunt Mary boil down every spring and for once not even say, "Stop, that's too much!" if we poured a big river on our plates. She knew Amos would eat all the leftover syrup with a spoon anyway. She'd watch him lick the plate and say, "I guess that's how you stay sweet." Like how else could Amos be so kind? Squeezing my hand when thunder cracked, hugging Mama around her neck after she got home from working the night shift at the hospital, on a morning thick with clouds. He really was maple-sweet, when we weren't arguing about whose turn it was to bring in wood for the fire or dry and put away the dishes.

Mama sets the jug of syrup down on the table, then moves her hand from the jug to my head and lays it there, right on top of my hair. She's standing so close to Dad and me I can hear her breath go in and out.

"Happy birthday," she says. Then the fingers leave, so fast I can't remember if I really felt them.

"Are we going to—" I start, but Mama's gone already, looking out the window. All I hear is silverware getting scooped out of the drawer, knives and forks clashing. I wonder how many she's counting out and hold my breath, hoping it's right. The whole first month after Amos died, she kept bringing four sets of silverware to the table. The spare set just lay there, like silver bones. We all tried not to see it.

Until she put her fingers on my hair like that, I wasn't even going to ask if we could go to the beach today. She always took Amos and me out there on our birthday, once the sun had gotten its chance to shine awhile. We'd wear our swimsuits underneath our clothes and dare each other to jump in even though the water is still pretty cold in early June. Mama always said cold was a matter of perspective. She said "melted" was good enough for her. She'd pull her shirt over her head and disappear. When she came up, she was almost always laughing, cold water beads rolling off her hair.

But that was the Mama before. The Mama before sang in the kitchen. The Mama before stayed awake long enough after her night shift just so she could kiss us goodbye when we woke up for school. The Mama before jumped into lakes and laughed.

The Mama after is made of silence and ice.

She brings out the pancakes. Just one kind: blueberry. As soon as I see them my throat closes up. I want to say thank you. I know she probably didn't want to make pancakes, not this year. I know she didn't have to. But the words won't come. I feel Dad's arms tighten around me.

Eat! I tell myself. But the harder I stare, the worse they look. If I take a bite, I think, they'll taste like cardboard.

It's not just mountains that change. If you'd asked me a year ago whether I could ever hate blueberry pancakes, I'd have said no way. But when Dad shifts me off his lap and we all sit down hard in our chairs, I can't stop looking at Amos's empty place. I used to stare at it and tell myself

Amos had just gone out in the woods, picking branches to whittle. I used to pretend he'd stomp in soon, wild, hair sticking straight up with bits of leaf caught in it, and Mama would yell at him for being late but smile and hug him at the same time.

At first, I didn't believe it. But now I know he's gone.

What I haven't figured out yet is who I am without him.

Right then, with all that sadness filling me, I reach behind and touch the coils of the notebook that peek out of my back pocket.

I finally cut a big bite of pancake with my fork so Mama won't regret making them, but when I put it in my mouth I just taste dust. Slippery, syrupy gray ash. I chew and swallow, forcing it all down.

What Amos did when he died is draw a big line into our lives. We all had a *before*. Now it's just the rest of us left with an *after*.

Chapter 4

After breakfast, I sit cross-legged on the bottom bunk and lay Amos's notebook and the whale tooth in front of me. For a while I just look at the front cover. I wish Amos hadn't crossed out his first title. For a magical creature, *Evidence* just doesn't fit. *Clues* seems like the right word after all.

"Open it," I say out loud. *Just open it.* "What's the big deal?"

A fluttering starts inside my stomach. It's not fear, though. It's the feeling I used to get on the boat, that moment when Amos or I would hook what we knew was a big fish. I'd feel the tug on the line and watch how it skidded, how my arms strained to hold it. And I'd know that something in the inky blue deep was alive and rising.

This time too, I don't know what I'll find, but just touching the notebook feels in a way like having Amos nearby.

When we were little, Mama used to read us picture books about Bigfoot and the Loch Ness Monster. Neither of us could stop thinking about creatures that seemed to grow right out of their places, whispering their existence through dimples in the waves and footprints in torn leaves. You had to look closely if you wanted to see them. And you had to believe.

So we used to stand on the beach holding our breath as the sun settled over the water and washed it in pinks and oranges. Goose bumps would rise on our arms the way little arrows of wave would poke up and swirl with glowing tips as we whispered to each other, *Did you see that?*

When I got older, I learned that water reflects light most when the sun is low in the sky, and I stopped thinking there was anything special about those sunset sparkles. But Amos never stopped.

I hold my breath and open the cover with my eyes shut. Then I count—*one, two, three*—and look fast before I can think about closing the notebook again.

The first thing I see isn't very scientific, which I expected: there are no charts, no logs of dates and times.

Instead, Amos has filled the first page with what looks like the beginning of a list, and lots of drawings.

1. On full-moon nights the water makes a different sound. Not scary, just different. Kind of like a really big drum.

It's surrounded by doodles and letters he mashed together to re-create the sound: *Booommp* and *Paaahhhw* and *Sssh-hhhhwahh!* I laugh out loud, hearing Amos making those noises.

But full-moon nights? I didn't think Amos paid much attention to moon phases, and this was before Mr. Dale made us start tracking. Besides, how would he have managed to get out to the lake on a full-moon night without me knowing?

2. Sometimes when I'm out in the boat, especially near the green parts, the water starts moving underneath even if there's no wind. The waves feel bigger then too, more like the ocean than Maple Lake.

A few more pages of doodles follow. He's sketched out our boat, hoisted up on huge waves. A stick-figure version of him in the boat, his mouth a round O. Squiggles and question marks. I keep looking for some sketch of whatever he meant by *green parts*, but he just drew with pencil, so I can't tell what he meant. Maybe he just imagined it. Maple Lake is definitely not green.

I turn the page to find another clue:

3. When I'm near the western edge of the shore, standing on Bear Rock, and if there's enough light out in the middle of the lake to make Sparkle Island, I can see this shape in it. It comes up but just for a second, then goes back down. And it kind of shines. I know it's not a bird because it comes out of the water, not the air. And it doesn't jump like a fish either.

A shape—the one he was trying to show me before.

The next few pages fill with pictures: a smooth lake with different shaded shapes emerging in the middle. In one, a kind of blob of a creature hovers underneath the water with a cartoon word bubble coming out of its mouth. It's saying: "Hello up there!"

4. Once when I went out on the ice—

I gasp and shut the notebook, fast as I can. I don't want to read about the ice. Instead, I press my knuckles into my eyeballs until gold lines flash back and forth in the dark, until they hurt.

⁓

"You should come too," he said. *"Just to check something out real quick, something I noticed last time I went ice fishing just with Dad. This time you'll really see."*

"You shouldn't," I told him. *"Come on. Mama said not this late in the season, not by ourselves."*

I was always the cautious one.

"Mama said, Mama said. Come on yourself, Addie! We're almost twelve. It's only March; the ice is still thick enough. We just fished last week, remember? I promise you'll see."

But all I saw, running down the narrow trail after too much time had passed, tripping over roots and calling his name, was the snow-covered water, the water hard and white as bone, except for the dark space in the middle where it had opened its jaws and swallowed him.

⁓

"You're so stupid, Amos!" I whisper now to my empty room. Then I yell: "Stupid!"

Nothing answers. There's nothing left. I bring my fist down on the pillow, hard, but all it does is give way, sagging under my knuckles. Just like the ice gave way under Amos.

I close my eyes again, tight, willing that hole to freeze over. My mind lets it, and the darkness disappears.

Now a different memory brings Amos and me to hard ice earlier this winter, pulling a loaded-up sled to our favorite fishing spot. Dad's already there, drilling with his auger, ice shavings whirring up around the dark hole we'll fish from. Amos says something I can't quite hear, and I see him throw his head back, laughing. I see his eyes. Green like mountains, like moss.

The sound of Amos's laugh tumbles in my ears and I blink away tears, calm again. The indentation I punched into the pillow slowly crinkles away.

"Fine," I say, at nothing. "Fine. I'll read your clues."

I open the notebook again and force my eyes back to number four.

4. Once when I went out on the ice, I saw something. It was almost dark so I couldn't see much, but every time I took a step, these little flecks of gold spread up from under the ice and followed my feet. So I think the creature sheds scales while it swims. And the scales float up. And they're magic, so they can move through ice. Maybe they're real gold. I think if I could just go out again, maybe with my auger and ice scoop, I could catch them.

My eyes sting, and I shake my head.

But then, warmth settles on my shoulders. I wipe my eyes and take a deep breath. The warmth wraps itself around me and squeezes again, just a little. I squeeze back.

"Addie?" Dad's voice floats just outside my door. He knocks twice. "You okay, honey girl? Thought I heard a yell."

I sniff, wipe my eyes. Slide the notebook under my pillow. "No," I say. "I'm okay, Dad."

"Can I come in?" he asks. "I have something for you."

I get up and twist the door handle. Dad's standing there with a small box. He smiles at me and ducks under the doorframe.

"Your mama had to rest up before work later tonight," he says. "But she wanted me to give this to you. From both of us." He hands me the box.

"Thanks." I slide my finger carefully under one taped fold of paper, then the other. Amos always ripped into wrapping paper, letting it fly out over his shoulder in little pieces. It always made Mama laugh.

The box slips out and I think I must be seeing things. "An iPhone! No way, Dad!"

Dad smiles. "You like it, then. Figured you were old enough."

"Yeah. I guess I am now." Lots of kids in my class have

had phones since last summer at least, but I don't tell Dad that. Maybe he knows Uncle Mark and Aunt Mary got Liza one for *her* birthday and wants to catch up.

"It's—not quite new." Dad scratches his chin like he does when he's embarrassed. "One of the guys on the crew wanted to get rid of his old one, and he always kept it in a case, so—"

"It's perfect." My throat feels thick. I slide the phone out of the box, holding its cool heft. "But wait. Don't you have to, like, pay for a special plan? Doesn't that cost a lot?" I remember how much Amos wanted one of these.

"Don't worry about that," Dad says. "But don't spend a bunch of time on the internet. It'll suck up all the data. And if your mother or I want your attention, put the phone down." His eyes shift down to his hands, the fingers working their way into knots.

"I know," I say.

"We just want you to keep the phone on you all the time," Dad says. "Be able to call, you know. Keep in touch."

"Like—stalk me?" I'm not mad; I just think Dad might be taking this a little too far. "You always know where I am. School, home, sometimes Liza's. That's pretty much it."

"Summer's coming," Dad says. If my snark bothered him, he doesn't show it. His voice stays gentle. "You won't be in school then, and even if you spend all your time at the farm, a lot can happen."

I feel my cheeks redden. It's so hard to keep anything from Dad. "Well," I say slowly, "I might not always be at the farm. I…might be at Maple Lake too."

Dad's forehead wrinkles and his eyes change, going from soft to piercing. He crouches down, his elbows balanced on his knees, so he has to look up at me. "Maple Lake?" he repeats. His voice sounds like one big question mark.

I can't look at him, so I look at my pillow instead, hiding the notebook underneath. "I want to apply for a summer thing out there," I say. "A Young Scientist position. My teacher told me about it."

Dad looks up at the ceiling for a second, sucks in a breath. "Have you talked to your mama about that?"

I shake my head. "I will," I say. "I'm going to soon."

"You know, Addie," Dad says. "Things are just different now."

I look down at the phone, so quiet and heavy in my hand. Like it would have saved Amos, stumbling into dark water. I thumb the icons that pop up when I turn it on.

Messages, one says. I wish I could send a message to Amos. "Yeah," I say softly. "I know."

Dad reaches out and wraps both of my hands in his

big ones. My skin sticks to the iPhone. "Addie." He looks straight at me. "They'll *always* be different."

Ice takes shape in my mind, spreading fast. I shiver. I know he's right.

Then Dad leans over and kisses my forehead, like everything is settled.

"But Dad," I say. "I really want to do the Young Scientist position."

Dad just smiles sad and slow. That means he doesn't know what to think yet. "We'll see," he says. "Hey, it's about time to get ready to go to your aunt and uncle's. I've got to load a few things into the truck. I'll call you over when I'm done."

He shuts the door so softly I don't even hear it click into the latch. When I know he's gone, I pick up the whale tooth and open the notebook again. Right below number four, Amos wrote 5. But that's all. There's no sentence, just the number.

"Number five," I say. "What was number five, Amos? What were you going to write?"

I dig through my desk drawer for a pen and sit back on the bed. Dad's words echo in my head: *Things are just different now. They'll* always *be different.*

I bite my lip and rub the whale tooth, letting it poke my thumb.

So much is different. I thought Amos would be eating pancakes right beside me on our twelfth birthday, but he's not. I thought Maple Lake was clean, but it isn't.

And I thought Amos's idea about the creature in the lake was crazy. I still think that. But maybe—

The notebook doesn't make actual sense to me, not one bit, and the clues aren't real evidence at all. It's not the kind of evidence Mr. Dale will show me how to collect. I could never put it in a spreadsheet.

But when everything's upside down anyway, it's easier to see how what doesn't make sense could still be worth looking at.

Suddenly, I know exactly how to finish number five. I move the pen across the paper before I can think too hard about it, writing down the date and taking some measurements with my ruler.

Barbara Ann found a white whale tooth on the beach, I write. *But it's so big. Too big.*

The next part is harder, and not like me at all. But I don't have an explanation for it right now, and this is Amos's notebook after all.

It looks like it came from something else.

Chapter 5

Dad drops me off early at Liza's, he says so he can check on a job and Mama can get enough sleep before work, but he's probably also thinking I might have the best chance of enjoying my birthday if I'm with Liza.

And it does always feel good to open Liza's door. There's noise—Bumble barking, Liza's three little sisters babbling and yelling, her mom telling them to hush, music playing from the radio in the kitchen—and it's thick and warm, spilling out of the farmhouse where my dad and Uncle Mark grew up.

"Sissie! Addie!" Two of Liza's sisters, DeeDee just about to finish preschool and Sammie just about to start, tug Liza's and my sleeves with sticky hands. "We're making a store, and we're selling raisins and marbles and crayons and everything's two cents. Come *ohhhnnnn!*"

I let them pull me into the living room and my aunt Mary rounds the corner from the kitchen, holding Baby Katy.

"Addie, honey," Aunt Mary says, and pulls me into a hug with one arm. The baby pats my shoulder with her fat fingers. "Happy birthday." Aunt Mary's voice catches. *Please don't cry*, I think. *Just let it stay noisy and normal.*

She pulls away and I smile, relieved. She's not going to cry, even though her eyes glisten like everyone's do when they look at me.

"I'm glad your parents can make it for dinner and cake," Aunt Mary says. "If you want to stay the night—"

"That's okay," I cut in. Spending my birthday night without someone to talk to on the top bunk won't be easy, but staying at Liza's might hurt even more. There's something about being around people who remember Amos that makes me miss him harder. The same goes for Mama and Dad, but at home, it's easier for me to close my door and just be alone. At Liza's, I can't hide.

I watch Aunt Mary as she shifts Baby Katy to her hip, lifts a big bowl out of the refrigerator, and tucks a stray piece of hair behind her ear. She and Liza have always had the same thick, curly brown hair and freckles across their noses. Aunt Mary catches me looking at her and winks. When I was little, she used to rock me to sleep when Mama was working late. I still remember the sound of her voice singing lullabies: *Say good night, close your eyes, and the stars in the skies will keep shining....*

"Come on," Liza says. "Let's hang out in my room."

Aunt Mary wraps me in another hug before Liza can pull me toward the stairs. "It's good to see you, sweetie," she says, and her arms are strong enough for both of us, warm and close around the parts of me that might break.

Liza's room seems too small somehow, the walls pushing in. I pull the whale tooth out of my pocket and roll it in my palm.

"Can I see that again?" she asks, reaching for the tooth.

My hand feels cold without it.

"Cool," Liza says. Her forehead wrinkles as she turns it around, holds it up to the light. "It really is big, like you said." She hands it back to me. Her eyes have a searching look, like she can feel the shape of the things I'm not saying. I can feel it too, and it makes my heart pound. I quickly shove the tooth back in my pocket.

I need to say something. But talking about Amos's notebook feels like too much. "So," I say, "Mr. Dale told me I should apply for that summer thing."

"Huh?" Liza asks. "I don't remember him saying anything about a summer thing."

"You probably just forgot. Maybe he posted it on the bulletin board." Liza's not usually forgetful.

"Maybe?" Liza chews her lip.

"Anyway, it's this Young Scientist position out at Maple Lake," I explain. "Mr. Dale says the lake's polluted, and he and some other scientists are researching it. He says if I apply and get picked, I can learn how to help them."

Liza gasps. "What?" she says. "Wow. That's..."

"Crazy?" I finish. "I know. I mean, Mama will probably freak. She doesn't want me going out on the lake anymore."

Liza looks at the wall. When her eyes move away from me like that, I know she's got bunched-up words inside that she wants to say but won't.

"Honestly?" she finally says. "I know you want to be an aquatic biologist and all, but would it really be that weird for your mom to freak about it?"

I open my mouth, then close it again, like a fish struggling for air. My face feels hot. Okay, maybe it's not *weird*, exactly, but is my best friend really supposed to be siding with my mom?

Liza's voice drops low. "Sorry," she says. "I just mean... do *you* actually want to go out on the lake now?"

Words stick in my throat again. Deep inside my head, I can hear a tiny voice saying "Yes!" as loud as it can.

My out-loud voice is quieter. "I kind of do," I whisper. "Sometimes."

"Okay..." Liza says slowly. I can tell she's trying to make enough space in her head for what I'm telling her. Sometimes doing that means rearranging all the ideas that used to be there, kind of like moving furniture into different places around a room, or giving away what doesn't fit. "But also...polluted? That doesn't make sense. Maple Lake's the cleanest one around."

I shrug. "I thought so too," I say. "But they're scientists. They must be onto something."

Liza doesn't look convinced. "But you'll still be able to come over?" she asks. "To help take care of the calf?"

"After I'm done out at the lake some days, I can come over," I say. "It's not like the calf needs us eight hours a day, right?" I try to make my voice light, but Liza's forehead is wrinkled up like a Kleenex again and she's biting the right corner of her lip.

"I do still want to help you raise the calf, Liza." I lean over and nudge her shoulder with mine. "But I want to go back out on Maple Lake too. I know this might sound weird, but...I miss it."

"You miss it?" she says. Then she shudders. "I don't."

"It's hard to explain, I guess." How do I make her understand that the lake is part of me? No matter what it took from me?

"I just want you to be okay, Ad," Liza says.

"I will be," I say. "And hey, I haven't forgotten about the Shoreland Art Show either. That's a big deal. I'll help you with your portfolio."

Liza's eyes brighten. "You promise? I'm super nervous about it."

"So where is it?" I always love seeing Liza's art. "You promised I could take a look."

She blushes. "Okay, this is totally dorky, but you know how Mr. Dale has been making us draw the moon? I got super into that."

"You're submitting what you drew in class?" It's not that I don't think her moon drawings were good—they were beautiful even though they didn't have to be. It's just hard to imagine a school science assignment turning into an art project.

"Not quite," Liza says. "I redid them to be bigger, more detailed. But yeah, I wanted to show the phases of the moon."

She reaches over to her desk and hands me a folder thick with paper. Her face looks almost shy, which is strange for someone who knows everything about me, even that I'm a little scared of lightning and like to wear mismatched socks.

I open it, and like always when I see Liza's drawings, I take a sharp breath in. Her moons shimmer in dark night skies. But at the same time that I know she's done a good job, I can also feel something missing. I just don't know what it is.

"These are really beautiful," I say. I know she wants me to say the next part, but I pause, thinking of just how.

She leans in, encouraging me. "But..." she says.

"Well, it does feel like there's something missing," I say, shuffling the papers. "What's here is good, but I think there should be more. More than just the moon. I wish I knew what."

Liza nods, her brow furrowed. "I know you tell it like it is." She takes the folder back and sets it on her desk. "I'll work on it more. There's time."

I swallow hard. I *am* supposed to tell it like it is. We both are. That's the agreement. I don't keep secrets from Liza, and she doesn't keep them from me. Not when we were six, and I was scared to go in the barn because of ghosts, and she gave me a flashlight and we brought Bumble with us every time we went in there, for months. And not now either. Maybe because we've known each other forever, we know it doesn't make sense to bury words. They just come out sideways later. That's why the secret of the notebook and the creature sits like a lump in my stomach, but nothing can make me talk about it. Not yet.

"You'll figure it out," I say.

"You know what's actually kind of funny?" Liza says softly. "Your mom probably would have wanted to do this Young Scientist position too. I mean, if she were still a student."

I laugh. "Doubt it," I say. "Mama likes the lake—*liked* it—but..."

"Well, *my* mom says your mom was really into science at Shoreland High," Liza says. "She got all A's back then."

"Really?" I knew that Mama had to learn something about science to become an aide at the hospital. I took for granted that she knew a lot about where we live just from growing up around here. But I didn't know she might have been as interested in science as I am.

"Yeah, back when you first decided you wanted to be an aquatic biologist, I was telling my mom and she said— 'Sounds like the apple doesn't fall far from the tree.' Doesn't your mom ever talk about it?" Liza's eyes dig into mine.

I look away and shrug. "Maybe," I say, even though Mama's never told me anything like that. About what she was good at once upon a time. It's strange that Liza knows something about Mama that I didn't.

"Makes sense when you think about it," Liza says. "How'd you think she knew about glaciers and freshwater ecosystems and all that other stuff she kept telling us about even when we were, like, way too young to understand?"

I see her point, but thinking about Mama young, in school, and happy, just feels too strange.

"Anyway," Liza says. "She might let you do it after all. If you're *really* sure you want to."

Down the hall I hear the door opening, boots stomping the mat. Uncle Mark's and Aunt Mary's voices rise and fall but I can't make out the words. I hear Grandpa's laugh too—rough and kind, ending in coughs. Grandpa technically retired, but he still likes to come over and help out in the barn. He says farmers have a hard enough time making ends meet, the least he can do is help. And Uncle Mark says the only place you'll ever find a dairy farmer who's *really* retired is a cemetery.

"C'mon," I tell Liza. "Let's go out there."

Bits of straw hide in the creases of Grandpa's neck and scratch my cheek when I hug him. "My Addie Paddie," he says in a voice that's not even a little sad. "Twelve doesn't make you too old for a nickname now, does it?" He lays his big hand, all knuckles and gnarls, on my head.

"Nope," I say. Uncle Mark leans over to kiss my forehead. "Happy birthday, Favorite Niece," he says. He always calls me that, even though I'm his only niece. "You got a second? Want to come out to the barn and choose a calf to help Liza train? I know she's been waiting." He looks over at Aunt Mary, and a little smile blooms on her face. She squeezes my shoulder.

The calf pens smell like sweet milk and sawdust. I take a deep breath and close my eyes, just for a second. When I open them, I see the calves, staring quietly back at us with wet brown eyes.

By this time in June Liza's usually already been working with her calf for a month, getting it accustomed to her hands and voice, teaching it how to wear a halter so it will behave well and obey her in the show ring. This year, while the calves stood on their shaky legs and grew and grew, she's been waiting for me instead. I picture her standing in the barn with her hands curled into fists at her sides, forcing herself not to just walk right up to one of them and reach out her hand.

I know she'll wait as long as I need her to, which makes me want to choose faster.

"How will I know which one to pick?" My voice feels thick and strange, but Liza closes her fingers around mine.

"They're all really cute," she says. Her eyes settle on me, steady and strong, but moving too, like they're still searching for something. "And Dad, of course, is convinced they all have perfect conformation. You can't really go wrong."

"She's right," Uncle Mark says. "I'd say you could pick just about any of them."

But I'm already walking toward one of the calves. I can't stop looking at the pattern on her coat. Like most Holsteins, she's a mix of black and white. But I've never seen quite as many splotches, especially on the legs, as she has. It looks like someone dipped a brush in a can of black paint and flicked it on snow-white legs, over and over. When I get to her pen, she doesn't skitter away but walks right up to me, her nostrils flaring as she sniffs my fingers, her tongue curling out of her mouth.

"This one," I say. But then I remember this is really supposed to be Liza's calf, that I'm just helping, and I look back at her. She flashes a thumbs-up.

Uncle Mark laughs. "That was quick," he says. "You sure?"

He scans the little calf, runs his hand along her back. "Nice topline," he says. "Straight legs, long neck."

"I'm sure," I say.

"Okay, then." Uncle Mark puts his arm around my shoulders and I lean into him a little. He reminds me a lot of my dad, actually. They have the same straw-colored hair that sticks out under their caps, and the same big shoulders. They're always right where I need them to be, standing still and strong.

"Plan to come back in a couple days," he says. "I'll give you girls some pointers. Liza could use a refresher."

Liza rolls her eyes. "I've been doing this forever, Dad," she says.

"*Forever*, or for two years?" Uncle Mark asks. Then he winks at me. "It's never too late to learn something." Liza grimaces, but she lets him pull her into a side hug.

I reach out and scratch the hard spot on the calf's forehead, between her eyes. She nods her head up and down, pushing against my hand.

"Hey," I say, laughing. Amos would have laughed too. This calf has a good sense of humor.

Uncle Mark smiles. "Typical rascal!" he says.

I turn my palms up and feel the calf's warm breath. Then she sticks her tongue out again and tries to lick my sweatshirt sleeve.

"She's got a personality, that's for sure," Uncle Mark says. "You'll want to handle her plenty, get her used to being touched. And you'll want to think of a name."

"You called her a rascal," I say, pulling my sleeve away and wiping it on my jeans even though I don't really mind the slime from her tongue. "That works for me."

"It fits," Uncle Mark says, laughing.

Rascal bobbles on her skinny legs, then stands still. She

looks right at me and blinks. "Bye for now, little Rascal," I say. "See you soon."

One day she'll join Uncle Mark and Aunt Mary's herd and graze in their pastures and give milk every morning and evening. But for the next two months, she'll be ours. Liza's and mine.

Back in the house, Liza and I drag a few folding chairs up into the dining room and squeeze them between the spots where she and her sisters usually sit. Aunt Mary brings out her slow cooker full of my favorite: barbecued beef. That bowl she pulled out of the fridge earlier turns out to be a salad full of spinach and lettuces she seeds in trays under fluorescent lights when it's still too dark and cold to think about gardens.

Mama and Dad arrive just as Aunt Mary's wondering whether or not she should plug the slow cooker back in. "Sorry we're late," Dad says. Mama smiles stiffly.

"Oh, stop," Aunt Mary says, kissing Dad on the cheek and wrapping Mama in a hug. It looks like she's hugging a tall, hard tree. "Come on over here, Laura. I'm putting you right next to Baby Katy. She could use a little auntie time." Mama's older than Aunt Mary by five years at least. It took her and Dad a long time to have Amos and me, and when she looks at Baby Katy, her eyes get soft and glittery.

I squeeze between Grandpa and Dad and watch Mama tenderly wipe Katy's little fingers as she bangs her spoon over and over again on the high chair.

"Happy birthday to our Addie," Grandpa says, and Mama clears her throat. I shrink against my chair because I know she can't help but add "and Amos" in her head. I don't blame her; I do it too.

Silence only hangs for a moment before DeeDee and Sammie start fighting over a fork and Aunt Mary tells them to hush, and Uncle Mark starts spooning beef onto buns and handing them around the table. There's chewing, and talking, and passing salt and salad and lemonade.

And I don't know what makes me say it right then. Maybe it's the noise DeeDee and Sammie make yelling over each other and over Baby Katy's spoon banging; my words feel easy to slip in underneath.

Or maybe it's that warmth I feel wrapping around my shoulders again, that feeling that whatever I'm about to do or say will work out after all.

"My science teacher asked me to apply for a Young Scientist position at Maple Lake this summer," I say. "And I'm going to."

Suddenly, everyone's looking at me. Liza's mouth drops open. I keep talking.

"It's going to be great," I say. "Mr. Dale says the lake's polluted, but they don't know why. Not yet, anyway. That's what we're going to figure out."

Mama's eyes flash but she doesn't speak.

"Well," Aunt Mary says. "Doesn't that sound interesting."

"Polluted?" Uncle Mark laughs. "Wrong lake for that. Everyone knows Maple Lake's cleaner than soap."

"I guess it isn't," I say. "But I'll keep you posted." Uncle Mark shakes his head, but he seems more shocked than mad.

Dad's eyes find mine. His lips turn *just* up at one corner. "Well—" he starts, but doesn't seem to know where to go from there. If he's surprised about the pollution, which I didn't tell him about before, he doesn't let on.

"You've always done good in school, honey," Grandpa says, nodding.

Mama's eyes fill. A lump swells in my throat. I'm probably not the only one waiting for her to say something.

Instead it's Aunt Mary who speaks. "Time for cake?" she yelps, and scoots her chair back, racing into the kitchen.

Mama puts both her hands flat on the table. "I don't want you on that lake," she says.

Dad shifts in his seat. He clears his throat but doesn't speak.

"She could learn a lot," Grandpa says. Then he turns

58

to me. "And you'll still be able to give Liza a hand with her calf, right, Addie? I know she's happy for the help."

"I won't be here all the time like before," I say. "But I am definitely still helping with the calf."

"She's going to be the one to show it too," Liza says. "I want to take a break from that this year. I need to focus more on my entry for the Shoreland Art Show."

Grandpa smiles, and I can see Liza's trying to, but she's chewing her lip again. And the air around Mama is so hard words just bounce off it. I hear Aunt Mary stacking plates in the kitchen. *Hurry up with that cake*, I think. *Please.*

"Maybe so," Mama says slowly. "But Addie..." She looks at me then, and I can tell she's only half angry. The rest of her is just sad. "I can't let you."

Baby Katy bangs her spoon on the high chair tray and says *ba ba ba*, like she agrees. Everyone else is frozen, even DeeDee and Sammie, their eyes darting back and forth from Mama to me.

"Mama—" I say, but when I look at her eyes, gray-blue like the lake in a storm and just as wet, I can't keep going. Mama knows I love the water, but I've never told her I want to *work* on it someday.

And sure enough, Mama shakes her head. "No, Addie," she says. Then softer: "Honey, no. You don't need to go out there. You just stay close. Stay right here with us."

"Cake!" Aunt Mary calls, scurrying in from the kitchen with a big plate balanced on her hands. If she can tell how hard the air in the room got, how everyone froze up like icicles dripping halfway off a too-hot roof while she was gone, she doesn't show it. She puts the cake right in front of me and lights a match. The candles catch and burn.

I blow all twelve candles out in one try, but as Mama wipes her eyes and everyone claps, I realize I forgot to make a wish.

Chapter 6

So you talked to your parents?" Mr. Dale asks, glancing over my application essay.

"Um—yeah," I say. I mean, technically, I did. We just didn't totally agree.

Mr. Dale's dark eyes narrow, and he runs his hand over his buzzed black hair. "Hmmm," he says. "You know I'll be calling them, right?"

"Calling them? Oh yeah—sure," I say. "Obviously." I look at the wall.

Mr. Dale leans back in his chair, crosses his hands over his chest, and smiles. "You know, Addie," he says, "when I was your age, I was really into skateboarding. You know what my parents weren't into?" He looks at me, waiting.

"Um…skateboarding?" I ask, glancing quickly in his direction.

"Bingo," says Mr. Dale. "So guess how they felt when they found out I was sneaking over to the skate park in Bridgeport after school instead of staying for basketball practice like I'd been telling them." He sucks a quick breath in through his teeth.

"Probably not so great," I say.

"Bingo again," says Mr. Dale. "What I'm saying, Addie, is that your parents need to be on board for this."

"On board. Definitely. They will be. I mean, they are." I look back at the wall.

"Ohhhkay," he says slowly. "Terrific. I'll give them a ring later today."

"Thanks, Mr. Dale," I say.

He shakes his head. "Not a problem. And Addie—I'm glad you applied. It's a great opportunity."

You have no idea, I think. I know from Mr. Dale's stories in class that he goes home to a wife and three little kids, two dogs, and a very old, cranky cat that meows too much. He probably hasn't heard silence in years. He doesn't know how loud it can feel in a house.

"Thanks," I say. "I, uh—I really hope I can do it."

Mr. Dale just smiles. "Fingers crossed," he says.

The next day after school, I'm only half listening as

Mama and I drive a mile past the mountains and rolling pastures until we get to town, where Teddy's store and the post office and bank and library sit in a short, pretty row. I wish I could find the right words to talk to her about the Young Scientist position again.

Since the Walmart came in farther down the road, Teddy's is one of the only little town stores left around here. You can't get the kind of stuff they sell at Walmart—they butcher all their own meat and sell milk and yogurt from farmers like Uncle Mark. Teddy's also has free coffee in a pot that's always on, and a basket of candies for little kids.

What's probably most important is that we all know Teddy, and we know Teddy Jr., who took over after his dad retired. We know their whole family. I'm pretty sure we're third cousins once removed or something.

"Well, look at the lovely Lago ladies!" Teddy Jr. exclaims as soon as we walk in. He's made it his personal mission to expand the store by bringing in more local produce.

Mama smiles. "Oh, stop, Teddy," she says. "How's business?"

"Booming," Teddy says. Then his forehead wrinkles up and his voice drops. "And how are you?"

Mama sighs and looks at him. For a while, she doesn't speak. "Oh, you know," she finally says. "We're going to be okay."

Teddy gives her a hug, then looks at me, his eyes glistening. "You're not too old for candy, are you?" he asks, and grabs the basket from the counter. I focus on choosing a caramel so he can't see my eyes.

Every time we go to Teddy's, we can count on running into someone we know. Probably more like five people. Which is why, when Mama sends me to the deli counter for sliced ham, it's not surprising at all to find Barbara Ann in line ahead of me, picking up a package of chicken drumsticks.

"Hello there, Addie," she says. Her hair's sticking out every which way like usual and she's wearing a big flowy shirt that looks patched together from about a hundred different-colored cloths. Then she leans in close enough for me to smell her watermelon gum and whispers: "How's the tooth?"

I look over my shoulder before answering and sure enough, there's Mama heading down the aisle. I don't feel like explaining why Barbara Ann's talking to me about teeth of any kind. But at the same time, my insides kind of sparkle just thinking about the tooth, stashed in my desk drawer next to the notebook.

"It's good," I whisper back. "I carry it around a lot, but right now it's in my bedroom. I'm keeping it safe."

Then Mama reaches us, carrying two jars of pasta sauce.

"Barbara Ann!" she says, and her eyes light up. Mama puts the jars in the shopping basket I'm holding and reaches around Barbara Ann's shoulders for a hug.

"Laura," Barbara Ann says, squeezing Mama extra tight. Even though they don't see each other as much as they used to when Amos and I were young enough to need babysitting, Mama says there will always be certain people in life who make it easy to just pick up where you left off, and Barbara Ann is one of those people for her.

Barbara Ann pulls away, gently touching Mama's elbow. "Addie and I were just catching up. She was updating me on her birthday gift."

"Birthday gift?" Mama asks. "You mean the phone?"

I flush hot, willing Barbara Ann not to say anything else.

Mama doesn't know about the tooth, I think. *And she can't know.*

But I should have known Barbara Ann better. It's not like she'd ever lie to Mama, but she also doesn't tell her everything. She used to sneak us packs of gum when she'd come to babysit and as far as I know, Mama never found out.

"The Young Scientist position," she says, winking at me. "I heard all about it from Mr. Dale at school. And it certainly is a *gift* to let Addie do that."

Mama sighs. "Well," she says. "I got a message from Mr. Dale on my voice mail. But it's not really a sure—"

"A wonderful thing for your girl," Barbara Ann says, her eyes kind.

"Wonderful?" Mama asks. "That wasn't exactly my first thought."

"Joining the Science Club a year early is a great opportunity too," Barbara Ann continues. "It'll give Addie experience at the high school. Could open up some doors for college later on."

"College," Mama repeats. "It's gotten pretty expensive, you know. And besides, I'm not sure we want Addie that far away."

Barbara Ann's eyes twinkle. "You thought about going once too," she says. "Back when you—"

"That was a long time ago." Mama's biting her words off at the end. I can see her stiffening as she speaks, turning away from her friend.

"You know," Barbara Ann says, "I like to think the ones who learn the most about Shoreland County might be the likeliest to stick around."

"Really," Mama says. It isn't exactly a question. She's cocking her head now, looking at Barbara Ann as though she can't quite decide what to think.

"Sure," Barbara Ann says. "The more they know, the more they'll care enough to stay. Think of Jake Alderson's son, the Agency of Natural Resources officer. Spent all day long in the woods with his dad growing up, and I guess he couldn't get enough of it, so after he went to school and learned what he needed to know, he came back."

"Well," Mama says. "I'm not sure that *caring* more about Maple Lake is really the point."

"But staying could be," says Barbara Ann.

Mama's eyes get wide and she looks from Barbara Ann to me. Hurt and hope fly over her face like birds.

"And you know what else," Barbara Ann continues, snapping her gum as though she hasn't noticed Mama's reaction at all, "the best way to step clear of a fear is to walk right through it."

In the car on the way home, Mama stays quiet. It isn't a far drive, but I roll down the window so I can feel the June air and watch our mountains, soft and green, sliding past. When we pull into the driveway, Mama turns off the car but doesn't move to open the door.

"She sure was acting a little loopy today," Mama says.

"Barbara Ann?" I ask.

"I mean, there's nobody calmer in a snowstorm, even with thirty wild kids in her rearview. But what she said about the lake—" Mama chokes back the word. "What she said about knowing a place. Did that make any sense to you?"

I shrug. "I don't know," I say, even though I think Barbara Ann probably had it right. "I mean...you and Dad grew up on Maple Lake too."

Mama and Dad know Maple Lake better than anyone. Better than Amos or me. Definitely better than these scientists who are coming to study it. And *they* stayed.

"We did," Mama says.

"And you're still here." I wish Mama could see things a little clearer sometimes.

"We are." Mama looks straight ahead, her knuckles tight on the steering wheel.

I shrug again. "I want to learn about it, anyway. The lake." Then I stop. Mama sighs and leans her head back against the seat.

I reach out and, before I can stop to think about whether she'll want me to or not, I touch Mama's shoulder. It's the kind of thing Amos would have done. I'm surprised to find her skin warm, soft. I think of her heart, pumping so hard under her loose cotton shirt.

Mama turns, cups my face in her hands, and looks hard into my eyes. All of a sudden I have this memory from *before*—Mama, in the shallows, splashing water at me while

I splashed back, laughing. Amos and Dad were tying up our little boat. It was really hot that day, I remember, and I loved the feel of the water raining in bright pellets against my face. After one especially big splash, Mama took a few jumps through the water and cupped my face just like this. *"My little girl,"* she said.

She doesn't say it now. But from somewhere deep down, I hear the words again, clear and true, and I know the Mama from before is still there, underneath this new one. Finally she pulls the key out of the ignition and tugs the latch, giving the sticky door an extra push. As she gets out and leans over into the back seat to grab our plastic grocery bags, I hear her mumble: "Maybe it won't hurt."

And that's the last I hear about it from her. Later that week, at school, Mr. Dale shakes my hand and congratulates me on being the Young Scientist. At home, Dad puts his arms around me and reminds me I'll need to carry my iPhone when I go out to the biological station, as though I could have forgotten. He even gives me a thin plastic case for it—"Hundred percent waterproof," he says, slipping the phone inside and handing it over.

But Mama doesn't say a thing.

Chapter 1

On the last day of school, in homeroom, Mr. Dale sneaks in some extra science time and puts Liza's moon sketches under the document camera again. He says something about nature and patterns repeating and tells us to look for those patterns when we're outside.

Amos was looking for where the patterns changed instead. Where things didn't look the way they were supposed to. If he could see the whale tooth, I know he'd say it was too big to be a whale tooth, that the creature it came from would have to be something altogether different.

I turn over my moon chart and start sketching what I remember of white whales.

What if—

I remember Amos's clue number four, about the flecks

of gold, and as I sketch in the whale's tale and blunt nose, I begin adding tiny scales, all over its body. Liza would be so much better at this, and I think about sliding the sketch onto her desk, asking her to help. But I still want Amos's notebook to be just mine.

I add a long, winding tail, and more scales. It's not that I actually believe Amos was right. But aquatic biologists don't just study the water; they study what lives in the water. And I know they're finding new species all the time.

What if they didn't all leave? What if some stayed behind—and grew—and changed?

"What is *that*?" Darren's voice pops behind me and I can feel him bouncing on his heels just over my shoulder. I cover the drawing with one hand and look up fast. I must have zoned out, because the document camera's off and all the kids are milling around, cleaning out their desks and cracking dumb jokes.

"What is *what*?" I mumble, flipping the paper back to moon phases. I just don't feel like dealing with Darren right now.

Hurt sparks in Darren's eyes and he shakes his head. "You never used to be so weird," he says.

I don't look up at him. "You never used to be so annoying."

Mama used to bring Darren home from school with

Amos sometimes on her days off. She'd feed them crackers and apples and lay her hand on Darren's head like she was a little bit his mama too.

In school teachers complained he couldn't sit still, but he and Amos would sit together for hours, up in the maple tree in our yard or at the kitchen table with Legos spread out around them, and I never knew what they were saying, but I would watch them, their heads bent toward each other, their lips moving.

Once we started middle school, Darren didn't come over so much anymore. But at lunch I would see Amos take his tray over next to Darren, who usually sat alone. And I would see their heads bend just like they did when they were little, and Darren's lonely look would slip away.

Now I feel Darren's eyes on my paper, and I sit as still as I can. But he doesn't move away. Instead, he comes around to the front of my desk.

"So," he says, "you doing the Maple Derby?"

The Maple Derby is this fishing competition for Shoreland County kids that happens at the end of June.

I don't say anything at first, and Darren keeps talking, looking down at his shoes. "I know it's kind of weird timing," he says, "since the other derbies happen in the fall or spring, or winter for ice fishing."

I think of Amos, clapping Darren's back at lunch, telling

him jokes. "Yeah," I say, trying to muster the energy to keep talking, not shut him down completely. "They probably made this one up to keep kids busy once school gets out."

Amos and I never signed up. We were always out on the lake anyway, and Amos said he didn't like competition when it came to fishing. All those boats crowding the water, vying for spots. He didn't even *want* to know if anybody else knew about Dad's supposedly secret spot for perch. Besides, Darren won the contest just about every year, and I kind of had the feeling Amos didn't want to risk taking that away from him.

"You can do it, Ad," he'd tell me. *"If you want."* Still, I could always hear hesitation in his voice, and I didn't really want to fish without him anyway.

But for some reason, today, I say "Maybe" to Darren. His eyebrows go up.

"Maybe not," I continue. "Haven't decided. I'm helping Liza with her 4-H calf this year."

"Well, let me know if you need some tips on fishing," he says. Inside, I grumble. Darren knows Amos and I have been fishing our whole lives. I don't need fishing tips from anyone.

But as he rocks back and forth, kicking his heavy boot heels, one after the other, I know Amos would say, *"He's just excited, Ad,"* and let it go. Amos would remind me that

Darren spent most of the summer haying and cleaning calf pens at his neighbor's farm, and we both knew that the money they gave him for helping out went right to his Gram. That the Maple Derby was a big deal to him, and he was a skilled fisherman. Maybe it felt good for him to think he could help someone.

But Amos isn't here, and my heart feels all bottled up. "I'm good," I say, and look back down at my paper until Darren moves away. I watch his shoulders hunch, his head hang, as he twists a plastic bag full of stuff from his desk in his right hand. It hits me that I've never seen him with a backpack. Maybe he doesn't have one.

Later, I think about finding him and—I don't know. Asking him for some tips after all, even though I don't need any. Maybe even showing him my drawing. But by the time I clean out my locker, he's gone, and Mr. Dale's telling me when to show up at the biological station next week, and to be sure to pack a lunch. Liza waits outside the classroom door; I catch her eye and she mouths "Come on!" The buses won't leave for another five minutes, but Liza likes to pick her seat early.

"I'll be there at nine," I tell Mr. Dale. "My dad says he can drop me off."

"Perfect." Mr. Dale holds out the bowl of wrapped

peppermints he always keeps on his desk and nods at me to take one.

"Thanks," I say. "See you next week."

On the ride back to her house, Liza's quiet. I feel the same urge to say something to her that I felt too late with Darren. So I try asking about her art portfolio, about Rascal, but she doesn't say more than three words at once. She leans against the window like some kind of weight is pushing her shoulders down.

But she still waits for me to get off the bus and walk up the lane, and after we drop our backpacks off, she hands me a granola bar to take to the barn.

By the time we get into the calf stable, Liza seems a little lighter. She brings me to Rascal's pen and hands me a small halter with a rope attached.

"She's pretty adorable," Liza says as Rascal wobbles over. "And not afraid, at least not compared to a lot of them. You picked a good one."

"What should I do with the halter?" I ask.

"Nothing yet," Liza says. "Just hang it on the hook there. Try petting her instead."

Rascal lets me scratch her neck, but when I rub her ears she tosses her head up and skitters away. Liza laughs. "It just takes time," she says.

I hear the barn door creak open and Uncle Mark appears. "Thought I'd check how everyone was doing," he says. "Looks like she's getting used to you, huh?"

"She's kind of shy," I say. But as though Rascal can understand and wants to prove me wrong, she walks over and sniffs my hands with quick breaths.

Uncle Mark laughs. "That's pretty normal for a little calf. Have you tried putting the halter on yet?"

Then he shows us—well, me, really, though he says it's a good reminder for Liza too—how to slip the halter over Rascal's nose and head.

"Just leave it like this awhile," he says. "She'll get used to it by and by."

Uncle Mark moves his hands gently across Rascal's coat. She shakes her head and rubs her nose against his jacket, but she seems to sense he knows what he's doing. Dad always says you can see how much Uncle Mark loves animals because he treats his cows almost like people. They all have names, and he even stores pictures of them on his phone.

"It'd be a good idea to brush her a bit today too," Uncle Mark tells us. He grabs a soft bristle brush from a ledge on the barn wall and lets Rascal smell it, then touches it lightly to her side.

"So, Addie," he says. "Your dad told me you'll be working with the scientists out at Maple Lake."

"I haven't started yet," I say. "But soon."

"I gotta tell you, it's hard to believe that lake's polluted." Uncle Mark runs the brush along Rascal's side and back. "You want to try brushing?" he asks.

Uncle Mark's a patient teacher. He taught me how to use a bow drill to send smoke curling up without a match, how to build a campfire from tinder and coal. We'd sit around those fires and he'd tell stories about all the constellations in the sky, pointing to them one by one: Ursa Major, Ursa Minor, Orion.

I take the brush and follow Uncle Mark's lead. But I can feel Rascal's skin kind of shiver under my touch, and she scoots to the side, away from my hand.

"A little more pressure," Uncle Mark says, "and breathe slow. If you're calm, it'll help her be calm."

I take a deep breath. "I don't think the scientists would just say Maple Lake was polluted for no reason. And if it is—I kind of want to know about it. So we can fix it."

"I just hope they know what they're doing," Uncle Mark says. "That lake's spring-fed and deep and, since before my great-grandparents were kids, clean as can be."

I want to ask Uncle Mark if he's tested the water, if he really knows for sure. But it doesn't feel right. Instead, I just say, "I hope I can learn more about it."

Uncle Mark puts his big hand on my shoulder and

queezes gently. "You're a good kid, Favorite Niece," he says. "If anyone can help those scientists figure out what's going on, it's you."

Then he gives Liza and me a kiss on the tops of our heads and waves, walking out the door. Now it's just Liza and me and Rascal, who already seems to be getting used to her halter, at least a little. She's not tossing her head so much. And she's actually standing still. I pass the brush to Liza so she can have a turn.

"So, you start that Young Scientist thing next week, right?" Liza asks, putting her hand up by Rascal's tail and walking slowly around her back end.

I know right away this is why she didn't say much on the bus. School ending means summer starting. The first summer Liza and I won't spend mostly together.

Rascal's halter has slipped to the side from her rubbing her head against the stall, so I work on adjusting it while Liza takes the empty grain bucket off its hook. "Honestly, Ad, I'm just kind of nervous for you," she says.

I feel my hands shake a little. "Nothing's going to happen."

Liza looks up at the barn ceiling, at the cobwebs strung in the rafters. "I just . . . still don't see why you would do it," she says. She opens her mouth again, then closes it. But I can tell what she wants to say next. *Instead of hanging out here. With me.*

It's strange how someone who knows me better than almost anyone can't understand something I want so much. If Liza can't see why I need Maple Lake, how can I ever explain?

I shake my head. "I just feel like I have to do this."

"Because of Amos?" she asks. She kind of chokes on his name and I'm worried she'll start crying. But she doesn't. She walks over to the grain bin and I follow her to hold the cover open while she measures out scoops for Rascal.

"Not just because of him," I say. Which is true. But she's not wrong either; it's partly for him. Of course I want to learn everything I can from the scientists there, and if the lake's polluted, I want to figure out how to help it. I also have Amos's notebook in my pocket. Keeping it nearby makes me feel like a piece of him is nearby too.

Liza turns to me. "Well, I'll be here, Ad," she says. "Rascal and I will be here."

I reach out to squeeze her hand, and she lets me. But her eyes look like clouds hanging over the mountains. She blinks twice, like I've seen her do before when she's trying to keep tears from falling. And then she looks away.

Chapter 8

The morning the Young Scientist position begins, I wake up after Mama's already come home from work and gone to bed. The smell of coffee wafts in from the kitchen; Dad's probably already filling his travel mug, packing it into the truck with a turkey sandwich and a bag of chips. When I come out to pour some cereal, I see my backpack, laid out on the table with a water bottle and a brown paper sack next to it.

"Thanks, Dad," I say, pointing to the bag.

"Don't thank me," he says. "That was your mama."

"Really?" I ask. "When did she pack it?"

"After work, I guess," he says. "Left it out there for you."

I picture Mama's hands, her fingers knobby and strong, shaking open the paper bag. I peek inside.

"No way!" I say. "A Fluffernutter!" I hardly ever get

these. Mama always freaks out about all the sugar in Marshmallow Fluff. Filling cavities costs a lot, she used to tell us, and ruining baby teeth doesn't help the adult ones. "I think the last time she made them for us, we were, like, five." Then I cover my mouth with my hand, realizing I've done it again—said *us*.

Dad wipes his eyes with the back of his hand, but so quickly, he might just have been blocking the sun.

———

And then I think about Amos. For just this one perfect second, his skinny tanned legs swim into focus, and they're running away from me. I *see* him, I really see him, holding his Fluffernutter, racing along the beach. *"Can't catch me!"* he's screaming. I'm laughing, stumbling after him, my Fluffernutter squished in my palm. *"Can too! Can too!"*

Then I'm tripping, falling, knees hitting sand. The Fluffernutter flies out of my hands. Tears come as I scramble to the sandwich and find it covered in grit. Ahead of me Amos stops, turns. Sunlight catches his hair and turns it golden. His eyes darken and he begins to run back toward me. I'm wiping at my sandwich, crying. *"Addie,"* he's saying. *"Addie."*

Then he kneels beside me while I cough and sob. He holds his Fluffernutter out.

"It's okay," he's saying. *"You can have mine."*

I can still smell it, half sweet, half salty. I still remember how it felt to take it, soft and warm, from his hands. I remember how I tore the sandwich in half, sniffling, and handed one half back. How we ate it in five bites each, listening to the waves.

I close the bag and put it in my backpack.

"Ready to go?" Dad asks.

As we drive up the road to the biological station, Dad's fingers softly tap the steering wheel.

"So I'll pick you up after," he says. "And take you over to the farm so you can keep getting acquainted with that calf. Rascal, right?" It feels like he's talking more to himself than to me.

"Okay," I say. I haven't talked to Liza since we brushed Rascal. I know she's been helping Uncle Mark feed her and the other calves, probably staying at Rascal's pen for an extra minute to rub her ears.

But Liza feels far away now, here, where thick trees near the shore mostly hide the lake. If I watch carefully, I can see flashes of blue between the shivering green leaves.

"You'll be careful," Dad says.

"Yes, Dad."

"You can change your mind, you know," he says. "Just

call me. Or your mother. Don't worry about waking her. Use the iPhone."

"I'm not going to change my mind, Dad." But I can feel my heart pounding.

"Okay, okay," he says. "I know."

He pulls up to the biological station. It looks the same from the outside as I remember it, kind of like a big log cabin, set so far back in the trees it almost looks like it grew right out of them. Inside I know there's at least one lab, because Mr. Dale told me about it, and different rooms where the researchers can have meetings or give presentations. There's even a mini-museum open to the public with pictures and dioramas and explanations about Maple Lake's history from the time of the glaciers till now. Amos and I used to sometimes go look at the displays after we were done hiking the trails.

As we walk up the path leading to the biological station, my phone buzzes. It's Liza.

You still coming over later?

My chest tightens, just for a second.

4-ish, I text back.

Mr. Dale opens the door before we get a chance to knock. "Addie!" he says. "Welcome." He sticks his hand out to Dad, who waits for just a second before shaking it.

"Hello, Mr. Lago."

83

Dad nods. "Hello," he says.

"Did you want to come in?" Mr. Dale asks. He steps aside just a little, and sunlight from overhead cuts through the dark doorway behind.

I look up at Dad, who swallows hard and puts his hand on my shoulder. I know, and he probably does too, that if we go inside, we'll see the windows that open out onto Maple Lake. I don't know if Dad wants that.

But he nods. "Sure. Wouldn't mind taking a look around."

Mr. Dale motions us both inside. Dad hesitates, like he might take back what he just said, but he stays right behind me as I walk in.

"Here's the main lobby," Mr. Dale says. "It's a great spot for visitors who want to learn a bit about the lake. We've got some informational pamphlets over here, a topographical survey of the geographic region, hiking trail maps, camping tips, a diorama of the lake and surrounding mountains—" He points to each item.

I follow Dad's eyes as they travel up the walls to the wooden ceiling, skipping over the windows that look out on the lake. I don't know if Dad's ever been in here. Usually when he's anywhere near Maple Lake, he's *on* it, fishing.

"The lab's just down this hallway," Mr. Dale explains. "But maybe you want to see the beach first? It's not too far from the public one, but we have our own boat launch. It's helpful for collecting water samples and traveling to farther points on the lake."

From Dad's favorite perch spot, we can see the biological station, but I've never been on this beach, just the public one where Amos and I would wade in the shallows after we hiked.

"I know you're quite an expert on Maple Lake," Mr. Dale says as he opens the door. "I should probably be asking you for fishing tips." Mr. Dale fishes too; our boats have even crossed paths, and when they do, we always wave. Of course, it's been a while.

Dad stuffs his hands in his pockets and clears his throat. "Don't know about that."

"It's true," I say. "Dad doesn't even need one of those fish-finders people rig onto their boats. He knows right where to find them, any month of the year." I'm talking fast, trying not to look out the window at all that blue.

Dad shakes his head, embarrassed, but Mr. Dale's already leading us out. As I step through, I'm hit with the smell of water, clear and cold, and gritty sun-warmed sand. My hands start to shake, so I ball them up into fists.

Maple Lake is five miles long and a mile wide. Two big mountains—Mount Mann to the west and Bevel Mountain to the east—run almost the whole length of the lake.

Between Mount Mann and the shore, there's a narrow road that twists and turns, but on the other side, Bevel Mountain plunges straight into the water; there's no room for a road. Because of those mountains, boating out into the middle of Maple Lake makes me feel closed in, like I'm in a big, open-topped tunnel filled with blue. I've hiked the trails up above, on skinny paths that twist into narrow outcroppings flanked with cedar and pine. The lake folds out below, flat and smooth as a blue bedsheet from all the way up there, where birds swoop and dive.

Mr. Dale keeps looking at Dad and me like he's worried. I bet he can guess that for us, seeing Maple Lake rolling in, wave after wave, might feel like too much. I remember Barbara Ann saying it was good to walk right through fear. But at this very moment, I don't like how tight my chest feels. I see Dad's jaw clench as he looks toward Mount Mann, jutting up from the lake in hard slabs of granite and trees tipped sideways, their roots hanging on rock.

Breathe, I tell myself. *Just breathe.* Mr. Dale's talking again, but I can't hear. I reach back with one hand and tap the pocket that holds Amos's notebook. As soon as I touch it, I *do* breathe, shakily at first, then steady. *It's okay*, I say. *It's Maple Lake.*

Dad shifts back and forth on his feet, checks his watch. "Time for me to go," he says, right in the middle of Mr. Dale saying something about the prevalence of cedar trees along the shore.

Mr. Dale looks surprised but recovers quickly. "Of course," he says. "We'll see you later, then, Mr. Lago," and he reaches out his hand again. Dad takes it but looks sideways at me, his eyes asking, *Are you sure?*

I nod. You don't have to *be* sure to *say* you're sure. And sometimes saying it helps it come true. I reach up and hug Dad, my forehead pressing into his neck. "See you later, Dad," I say. And then I watch him go right through the door without looking back even once. The lake murmurs behind me. The waves tickling the sand sound like little whispers, telling me to stay.

"Ready to see the lab?" Mr. Dale asks.

"Sure," I say, then: "I mean, yes. Yes."

We walk back into the main building and down the narrow hallway ending in a door that Mr. Dale pushes open.

"I'd like you to meet Dr. Li," he says, gesturing to a slim woman with long, straight black hair pulled into a ponytail at her neck. She rises from a table with papers spread out on it and smiles gently.

"You must be Addie." She speaks with an accent, her voice clear and bright as music. "I've heard so much about you. I understand you want to be a scientist too someday?"

I nod. Suddenly I'm feeling shy.

"Well, I'm so glad your teacher was able to bring you to the station this summer," she says. "We have a lot to work on, and from what Mr. Dale has told me, I know you'll be a big help."

I feel my chest swell just a little, imagining myself peering over Dr. Li's deskful of papers, studying them closely. Somehow I can already tell that working with her is going to help me a lot.

"You know your teacher, of course, but these are a couple of my other graduate students, Jake and Tasha." Jake, red hair cut close to a pale, freckled head, waves from his desk next to the wall. "Hey there, Addie," he says. Tasha, standing next to Dr. Li, sticks out a brown hand ringed with silver bracelets and smiles. "Welcome to the club," she says as we shake.

Then Dr. Li looks around. "Hmmm," she says. "I seem to have lost that boy. Again."

Just then, past the window, I see the boy she must be talking about, black hair flapping as he leaps over dead logs and stones on the shore, clutching a soccer ball under one arm. Then he stands still, holds one arm up high, and spins the ball on a fingertip. Dr. Li narrows her eyes. "It will be a miracle if we ever get him back into this lab," she says.

"That's Tai," Mr. Dale tells me. "Dr. Li's son. He's your age, actually. Right, Dr. Li? Twelve?"

"Twelve indeed," she says, frowning.

Even from inside, we can hear as Tai whoops and laughs, now juggling the soccer ball with his knees as his feet make deep prints in the sand. Then he sets the ball down, runs right into the lake, and starts to shriek. I cover my own giggle with one palm. *Well, yeah*, I think. *Of course it's cold.*

Dr. Li shakes her head and looks up at the ceiling. "I'm sure there aren't too many local residents who would run into Maple Lake in mid-June," she says. "Right, Addie?"

"Pretty much right," I say. "Then again, my family's a little crazy. We go ice fishing when it's fifteen below. We swim even when it's raining. And my brother—" I gulp, letting the word sit in my mouth. I gesture out at Tai, now hopping away from the lake, hugging his shoulders. He picks his soccer ball back up and runs past the window. "My brother's kind of like him." Mr. Dale doesn't flinch at the present tense, and neither do I. If Dr. Li knows about Amos, she doesn't show it.

I hear a door slam, then a ball bouncing on hard tile, and footsteps running fast. "Towel!" Dr. Li yells.

"Oops, forgot!" says the voice on the other side of the wall. It's a quick voice, bright like sunshine. More footsteps, a loud clang, then: "Coming!"

Tai bursts into the lab wearing swim shorts, not-quite-dripping wet. He rubs the towel hard over his face and hair, then lets it drop from his shoulders onto the soccer ball while he fumbles around in a bag on the floor and grabs a T-shirt featuring what Liza would probably call abstract art on the front. I'm staring at the mass of lines crisscrossing all over it when Dr. Li's voice cuts in: her tone has shifted, sharpened.

"Tai, this is Addie, the Young Scientist from the local middle school," she says.

Tai grabs the soccer ball with one hand and my palm with the other. "Hey, Addie," he says. "I'm Tai Jiang. The… Young Stowaway from Brooklyn? That has a nice ring to it." Then he lightly sidesteps around the center table and gives Jake and Tasha high fives; I see Dr. Li cringe as a few papers flutter to the ground. But I can't stop smiling.

"Sorry, Mom," Tai says, shuffling the papers together. Then he stands up straight and runs his fingers through his wet hair. "Cold out there."

"It just feels cold because you got wet," I say. "Besides, the lake won't really warm up until later in July. And even then, you'll want to be good and hot before jumping in, or else you'll freeze when you get out."

"Hey, it's refreshing," says Tai, shivering. "And my mom says it's still fine to swim in, even if it's probably kind of polluted. Right, Mom?"

Dr. Li shakes her head slowly, reorganizing the papers

Tai scattered. Then she looks up. "I don't want to alarm Addie," she says carefully. "But yes, we are noticing some harmful algal blooms popping up in the shallow, warmest parts of the lake. Have you ever seen any, Addie? Kind of a bluish-green color on the surface of the water?"

I try to remember if I've seen anything like that in Maple Lake. "I'm not sure," I say. Maybe I should ask Dad when he picks me up, but then again, I don't think he wants to talk about the lake any more than Mama does. Dropping me off and picking me up most days is probably more than enough for him.

"The blooms often don't show up until late summer, early fall," Dr. Li says. "But people began reporting them this past year, and we're on the lookout for more so we can confirm their presence and investigate causes."

"I mean…I know that every time we put our boat in or take it out, we have to check for milfoil," I say. I've never paid much attention to it, but I think Dad has to remove it from the hull sometimes. "Is that what you mean?"

"Eurasian watermilfoil," Dr. Li says. "That's what we call an invasive species—a plant that is not native to this area that is likely to cause harm to the economy, the environment, or human health. It's different than the algal blooms I mentioned, but yes, it is still a problem."

"Could the milfoil be causing the algal blooms?" I ask.

"Or, I mean, could the pollution in the lake make it easier for an invasive species like milfoil to grow?" Even though I don't know exactly how it all works, it feels like these different problems with Maple Lake could be connected, like the fine threads of a spiderweb.

"Good question," Dr. Li says. "A debatable question, actually. Milfoil wouldn't necessarily be connected to pollution the way harmful algal blooms are, but it does indicate an ecological imbalance caused by human actions."

Imbalance. I picture the lake teetering on one side, about to slide away; I guess I never thought of Maple Lake as being able to balance or not. I never thought it could be anything except what it was—blue and deep, fresh and cool. And sometimes cruel.

Mr. Dale claps his hands together. "Great start," he says. "Addie, I'd like to sit down and talk with you a bit more about what you'll be learning this summer, and how you can help. Care to join us, Tai?"

"Go with them," Dr. Li says before Tai can answer. She pokes him lightly and he squeals, clutching his shoulder.

"Owwww, Mom, my *arrrrm!*" he yelps. Then he looks at me and smiles, but he stands still, not moving toward Mr. Dale or me at all.

Dr. Li pries the soccer ball away. Her movements are slow, even gentle, but her mouth is set in a hard line. Tai squeezes the ball a little tighter against his hip at first, then gives up and lets it drop into her hands.

"Fine," he says. "I'll go." He falls into step with me and leans toward my ear.

"No offense," he says. "I'm just not a huge science fan."

"No worries," I say. This is my thing anyway. I tuck my hand into the back pocket that holds Amos's notebook, fighting the urge to pull it out right away and write *harmful algal blooms* and *imbalance* and everything else Dr. Li was talking about—it's all evidence of *something*. I'm not quite sure how it could possibly fit with Amos's clues, but I want to find out.

Chapter 9

Mr. Dale leads us into another room with a refrigerator, sink, and table. "You can stick your lunch in the fridge if you want, Addie."

I do, then sit next to Tai in one of the chairs Mr. Dale pulls out for us.

"Okay," he says. "So, Addie, we talked about earning some credit this summer that would allow you to join the Science Club early. In order to do that, you need to demonstrate that you can think like a scientist. And that means following certain steps."

"Like scientific method steps?" I ask.

Mr. Dale gives me a thumbs-up. "Care to summarize?" he asks.

I shrug. "I'm a little rusty."

"I'm not," Tai says. "You can thank my scientist mom for that. But I can condense it down for you, like way down. There's what, six steps? I can explain it in three words, guaranteed."

"I'm intrigued," says Mr. Dale.

"Okay," Tai says. "Ready? Here they are: *Wonder. Learn. Share.*"

"Wonder, learn, share?" I repeat.

Tai nods decisively. "You got it."

Mr. Dale laughs. "Nice," he says. "It kind of works, and it's so succinct. Perhaps I should be changing my curriculum." He gives us each a handout anyway, filled with the actual steps we have to follow: make observations, ask questions, form and test a hypothesis, then analyze and communicate what we learned. I like Tai's version too.

"So what are we wondering?" Mr. Dale asks. "What do we need to learn?"

I straighten up in my seat. "We're wondering if Maple Lake's polluted," I say. "Or I mean, *why* it's polluted. I guess we've observed it is, because of the harmful algal blooms."

"And we need to learn how bad the pollution is and where it's coming from," Tai says.

"Exactly," Mr. Dale says. "Tai, from what I understand, your mother believes you are quite capable of participating in this project with Addie."

Tai leans back and plunges an imaginary dagger into his

heart. But then he pops up. "I'm not big on science, Mr. D.," he says. "But I'll tag along with my buddy here." He holds clenched fingers in the air, and I bump mine back. As soon as our knuckles hit, I feel my throat catch and my eyes burn, just for a second. I look away, trying to forget the last time Amos and I fist-bumped.

Mr. Dale pulls out his laptop and shows us a spreadsheet. "Here's a water sample log," he says. "It's important, because this is where we keep track of the nutrient levels we find in different parts of the lake. We'll be asking you and Tai to practice entering numbers every week, plus travel around the lake with us to help take samples."

"Are we going to start that today?" I ask.

"You bet," Mr. Dale says. "But before that, I want to show you one of those harmful algal blooms Dr. Li mentioned, so you know them when you see them."

Blooms sound so pretty, like some kind of water flower. I picture pink and white lilies nestled on their green pads. But that word *harmful* reminds me it's probably not a flower at all.

When Mr. Dale takes us outside and points at an almost-slimy green spot in the water, I wrinkle my nose. I wouldn't describe these as blooms at all—little chunks of near-fluorescent green ripple with the waves. "There aren't many," he says. "Not yet, at least. But wherever they exist, we know the water quality isn't perfect."

"It looks pretty gross, honestly." Tai sticks his tongue out in a grimace.

"Yup," Mr. Dale says. "But how it looks is the least of our worries. These harmful algal blooms can take over almost an entire lake. Did you know beaches elsewhere in the state have been shut down because of it?"

"Uh, I can see why they'd shut down," Tai says. "Who would want to swim in that stuff?"

"Nobody," Mr. Dale says. "It's bacteria. Cyanobacteria. It's dangerous for people to be in water with harmful algal blooms like this because of the toxins that might be in there—not just in the water, but in the air too."

"But that couldn't happen here." My words just blurt out and as soon as I've said them, I know they sound foolish, especially for someone who wants to be a scientist. I lower my voice. "I mean, *how* could it?"

"I know it's hard to imagine, Addie," Mr. Dale says. "But we need to determine what's causing this pollution if we want to keep it from spreading any further. All part of the *learning* step, if we're going by Tai's method. As we collect water samples, I'll also be asking you to note on the map where you see harmful algal blooms. That will help us determine how far-reaching they are. In some parts of the lake, they might go away, but in the shallower areas, you'll see them more often."

I look again at the patch of greenish-blue sludge, trying

to remember if I've ever noticed anything like it before. I don't think I have.

But all of a sudden, I realize—Amos did. This must be what he meant by *green parts*. He just didn't know what they technically were called, or how they got there.

Amos wondered. He tried to learn, the best way he knew how. And he definitely wanted to share, first with me and then, he said, once we were sure, with everybody.

I feel something in my chest break open.

I didn't help Amos. Mostly, I made fun of him for even thinking about a creature.

His clues aren't very scientific, but he *was* following the scientific method. And the mystery he wanted to solve feels important. It's the job he never got to finish.

Mr. Dale, Dr. Li, Amos—they all see something in Maple Lake. Something other people don't want to see.

But that doesn't mean they'd agree. Dr. Li and Mr. Dale might not see a magical creature, and Amos might not have seen that Maple Lake was polluted.

I decide right then that my job will be to investigate it all. If I see any other evidence of pollution that could help the scientists, or any clues that remind me of Amos's, I'll keep track of them.

Mr. Dale sends Tai and me to start researching Maple Lake's history on the computers in the lab. I know some of the facts already, but some are new. Like how the ice that used to cover Vermont was almost a mile thick. How every time the glaciers moved, they took chunks of earth and trees with them. How they made valleys, shaped mountains and lakes.

"So, did that Mr. Dale guy blackmail you into this Young Scientist thing or what?" Tai asks, scrolling through web pages.

He says it so casually, I almost burst out laughing. "Uh...*what?*"

"You know," he says. "Like, did he promise you eternal A's? Or like, 'Addie, I'm desperate, I need a student to help me this summer, and if you don't, you'll fail science forever'?"

"Well, he won't be my teacher forever, so that would be kind of pointless," I say. "But seriously, I do want to be a scientist. Like your mom." Saying it out loud feels big somehow, like I can't back out. But it feels good too.

"Well, you're in for it." Tai rolls his eyes, but his voice doesn't sound mean. "My mom's crazy. You've already decided you want to be crazy too?"

"I guess," I say. I might as well own it.

"I have to admit, though," Tai says, pointing to a picture of a white whale on the computer screen, "my dad would be totally into this whale thing. When I was younger, he used to take me to see fossils at the Museum of Natural History."

"Where is your dad anyway?" I ask.

A cloud seems to pass over Tai's eyes. "He's back in New York."

I feel heat creep into my face; maybe I shouldn't have asked. "Your parents aren't together anymore?"

"Oh, they are," Tai says. The laugh that tumbles out of his mouth has a bitter sound. "Usually when my mom has a summer project somewhere, my dad and I stay in the city together. But he made me come this time."

I wait. I can tell there's something more there, but if Tai doesn't want to say it, I'm not going to ask. At least not now. I know what it feels like not to want to talk.

But then Tai takes a deep breath and spins his chair away from the computer screen. He's had his foot on a soccer ball this whole time, and he rolls it under his toes. Now he lobs it in my direction and I have to react fast to trap it with my foot. "How do I put this," he says. "My dad thought it would be a good idea for my mom and me to spend the summer together because…well, let's just say things get kind of tense at home."

"With who?" I ask. I lightly kick the ball back toward him.

"My mom and me," Tai says. "She's super intense about my grades. I mean, my dad cares about them too, but it's not, like, the *only* thing about me that matters to him. With my mom, well—let's just say I'm not the child scientist she dreamed of."

"Maybe we should switch moms," I say. "Mine's not too happy about me being here."

"Really?" he asks. "Why?"

"She's just kind of paranoid." Right now, I don't know how to explain it more. "So if you're not the child scientist, that's okay. What are you instead?"

Tai stands up and starts hopping over and around the ball, tapping it back and forth, showing off his footwork. He looks around before he answers. But there's nobody in the room except us.

"Promise not to talk about this while I'm around my mom?" he asks.

"Of course," I say. I wonder what the big deal is.

"So...I made the soccer team at my school last fall," he says. "Practices were every day, and I just told my mom I was staying late to get homework done."

"Wow," I say. "How did you keep the secret for a whole season? Didn't you have games and stuff?"

"She was working so much," Tai says. "My dad took me to the games. He probably told her what I was doing eventually. But I think this summer he wanted me to figure out how to talk to her about it myself."

To me, soccer doesn't seem like it should be some big secret. Tai would be a natural. He's bouncy and bursting, like a coiled-up spring. Whenever the soccer ball's nearby, it's spinning under his feet like a charm. If there's something you're that good at, I think, should you really be worried about showing it?

"Why wouldn't your mom want you to do soccer?" I ask.

"Maybe for the same reason yours didn't want you doing this Young Scientist thing?" Tai shoots back.

He's right. It's not like talking to Mama about spending the summer on Maple Lake was easy, even though science seems as natural to me as soccer does to Tai. "Point taken," I say. "Moms can be weird."

"For real." Tai shakes his head a little, like he's trying to shake off water. "Whatever. Here I am. I'll leave it at that."

We both go quiet then, and through the open office windows, I can hear the waves. That's what I love about water. It fills in all the empty places.

"You shouldn't feel bad, though," Tai says suddenly. "I think it's cool that you're doing this Young Scientist thing. You're into it. Go for it."

I picture Liza's eyes. I hear her voice in my head. *Would it really be that weird for your mom to freak about it? . . . I just want you to be okay, Ad.* Her words stick, but I pry them away. Tai's sound better right now.

"Thanks," I say. "And you're into soccer. You should go for that too."

Tai sighs. "Guess we'll both have to remind each other. Anyway, maybe this summer won't totally suck after all."

"Yeah," I say. "Maybe not."

Chapter 10

After we've had enough of research, Tai and I head to the beach, carrying life jackets, water bottles, and a cooler out to the boat. It feels good to get outside; my eyes hurt from staring at the computer screen for so long, scrolling through web pages about glaciers.

I set the cooler down next to the boat and wipe my forehead with one hand; it's getting hot already, and my sunscreen's melting.

"So," I say. "What would you rather be doing this summer?"

"Besides awesome science in Vermont?" Tai smiles, and I know he isn't being mean. "Oh, wandering the streets."

I snort. "What does *that* involve?"

Tai pulls a phone out of his back pocket. "Here, look,"

he says. "My friends and I have a group text. Check out what they're doing while I'm gone."

I lean over and squint at the little screen, full of pictures of kids squished together on what looks like a bus seat, linking arms on a busy sidewalk, balancing ice cream cones while they sit on benches. There's even a group selfie where they're holding up a soccer ball with a sign stuck to it: MISS YOU!

"Cool," I say. "Looks like they're having fun." Then I feel bad for reminding Tai he's not with them. A new text pops up:

How's life in the woods? Bored yet? Tai scrolls faster and tilts the phone just a bit so I can't see it. I want to explain that I already know it's easy for people from somewhere else to poke fun at how rural our little corner of Vermont is, that I still love it here and always will. But Tai looks embarrassed, so I let it go. I don't want him to feel bad.

Tai thumbs a quick message. I crane my neck a little farther and my heart jumps when I catch what it says: **Not really.**

I hear the *thunk* of a door closing at the biological station and look up to see Mr. Dale walking toward us through the sand.

"Hey, guys," he says. "All set for the boat?"

I knew it was coming, but as soon as he says the word

boat, I catch my breath. This will be my first time on a boat since before Amos died.

Of course I want to go. Of course I *don't* want to go.

Tai tucks his phone back in his pocket, turns toward the dock. Tiny splashes of water against the shoreline fill my ears, getting louder and louder.

I'm shaking under my skin. Every bone vibrates.

Then, just when I think I might rattle to pieces inside, the warmth comes back around my shoulders and squeezes. I squeeze back and feel my bones go quiet. One more deep breath and I'm walking toward the boat.

Tai's already on board, buckling a life jacket. Mr. Dale's untying the rope that tethers the boat to the dock. As I walk up, he looks at me with worried eyes.

"You going to be okay, Addie?" he asks.

I clear my throat. "I'm good." I put my life jacket on and gesture at the boat wheel, trying to hold on to that warm feeling. "I actually know how to drive a boat. I learned two years ago."

"I thought so," Mr. Dale says. "I was pretty sure I'd seen you at the wheel when you guys went fishing last summer. Do you know how to use Navionics?"

"Navi—what?" I've never heard of that.

"I'll show you," he says, and points to the GPS on the

boat. "Tai, you might also find this interesting. Basically, Navionics is an app that provides charts of lakes. You can preprogram your locations and find them using your boat's GPS the way you'd find an address." Mr. Dale hits a few buttons and shows us a list of locations around the lake that Dr. Li has picked for us to sample.

Then he starts the engine and the familiar smell of sharp, sweet gasoline mixed with churning water fills my nose. My heart lifts with the boat as we curve away from the dock. The hull bounces lightly against the waves and I keep my feet steady. I always get the same feeling on our boat, like I'm part of the lake and the lake is part of me.

The fear that shook my bones has slipped away. I can almost imagine that Amos is standing right behind me, leaning over my shoulder. *Mama and Dad should come out here again*, I think. *Maybe it would help.*

"Addie," Mr. Dale says as he slows the boat to idle, "would you like to finish driving us to our first location?"

"Really?" I ask. Mr. Dale smiles and moves aside, gesturing toward the wheel. I step into place and I don't feel even a little nervous as I guide the boat toward the spot on the GPS. I feel like I'm doing exactly what I'm supposed to do. Tai watches with wide eyes.

"All right," Mr. Dale says. "Cut the engine and let's

drop anchor. I want to show you and Tai how to collect a sample here."

I haul the heavy anchor and watch as it tumbles through the water, first through the clear part I can see, and then into the dark deep I can only imagine, where it takes hold. Mr. Dale lifts three clear plastic bottles out of the cooler and hands one to each of us.

"So this is called a sample bottle," he says. "Today's are already labeled, but you'll have to do some labeling later on. First, you want to rinse it three times in the water." He demonstrates by holding the bottle by its bottom, lowering it into the water, then flipping it underwater so it fills. Then he tips it out and repeats the process. "Just in case there's any dirt or dust in the bottle, rinsing helps clear it out."

I dip my bottle down and shiver as my hand hits the cold water. But the lake feels gentle, holding my fingers as I hold the bottle.

"After you've rinsed, then you need to slowly submerge the bottle again," Mr. Dale says. "Be really careful not to touch the inside of the cap, because you could accidentally contaminate it." Once he's filled his bottle, he pours the top inch or two of water back into the lake and tightly twists a cap on. Finally, he puts the bottle into its own plastic bag and onto an ice pack in the cooler.

"Why do we have to take so many different samples?" I ask. "Wouldn't the water be the same all over the lake?"

"Not exactly," Mr. Dale says. "Different tributaries—smaller streams and rivers—flow into Maple Lake, and testing the water at different points can help us figure out where runoff from different sources might be contributing to pollution. Then we can look at what's happening higher up in the headwaters to see what people are doing that could cause trouble."

After Tai practices taking his water sample, Mr. Dale pulls up the anchor.

"Wait, that's it?" Tai asks. "We're done?"

"Yup," Mr. Dale says. "All set."

"No way," Tai says. "I totally want to see more of this lake. It's pretty cool, actually."

"Wait a second," I say, peering at him through squinted eyes. "Are you saying we're having fun?"

Tai smiles and shrugs, surrendering. "Possibly."

"I appreciate your interest, Tai," Mr. Dale says. "I'll take you guys for a little spin before we head back." He turns the boat farther north in the lake, away from the biological station.

Tai cranes his neck up to look at Bevel Mountain's sharp granite face, plunging straight down into the water, where waves kiss its edge.

"So there's no beach on this side of the lake?" he asks. "Just mountain, all the way down?"

"The glacier that came through here cut through mountains too," I explain. "Then it melted. But that's what makes Maple Lake so cool. Unless you're in a boat, you can't really visit this whole side of it, because of the mountain. My brother—" I stop. Shoot. I don't really want to talk about Amos yet. But I've already said it.

"Your brother what?" Tai asks.

"My brother liked to row to that side and anchor the boat. Then he used to swing off the tree branches into the water, where it wasn't rocky anyway." I try to stay calm, not let anything into my voice. My mind races, trying to think of something else to say. But Tai's staring hard at me.

"Used to," he says. "He doesn't anymore?"

Mr. Dale glances at me as he turns the boat. I can tell that if he had Post-its, he'd be slipping me another one. *Deep breaths.*

"What? Oh—" I bite my lip. *Please don't cry*, I tell myself. "My brother actually died." The words fly out like little birds and hover in the air. They have their own wings now, and even though part of me can't believe I set them free, I couldn't take them back now even if I wanted to.

"Whoa," Tai says. "Whoa, I'm—how did that happen?"

I just shake my head. Mr. Dale turns quickly to look at

109

me again as he lets up on the throttle; we're getting closer to the dock now. *I can tell him if you want*, his eyes seem to say. But if anyone should explain about Amos, it's me. I just don't want to.

"Okay," Tai says softly. "Okay, I—I'm really sorry."

I nod. I don't feel like I have to say anything, which is nice. Tai's a really easy person to just *be* with. Still, I feel the weight of glaciers pressing on my heart. I blink back tears.

Mr. Dale docks the boat quickly, and I hop off to loop the rope around the piling. "Nice work, Addie," he says, his voice ragged. "You certainly know your way around boats."

"Thanks," I say.

"I've got to head back to the lab," Mr. Dale says. "You two are welcome to a lunch break."

Tai and I carry the cooler and life jackets inside and grab our lunches from the fridge. Then we head back out toward the same big rock and sit down, spreading napkins on our laps.

"I gotta say, my friends in New York would not know what to do with this place," Tai says, gesturing at the lake. Then he looks down at the sand, traces loops in it with his finger. "You probably saw them asking if it was boring here, when I showed you those pictures."

"I know why they'd ask," I say quietly. "But I don't think it's boring."

"Me neither," Tai says quickly. He's blushing. "But I think they just mean—look around. There's nothing here. I mean, besides a lot of water. Mountains. Trees. That's basically it. You can stare at one spot forever and it doesn't change."

"If you don't know what you're looking at," I say.

I look out at the lake, the waves moving and moving. Sunlight dances on the water, sparkles colliding. A loon floating about twenty-five yards out suddenly plunges into the water, tail straight up, then comes back, a silver smelt thrashing in its beak. I point fast, and Tai raises his head just in time to see the loon fly away, beads of water sailing from its wings.

"That's not nothing," I say.

"True." Tai crunches an apple. "I think if my friends actually came here, they'd be impressed. It's different, but it's kinda cool. It's super calm. You can like, *think*."

Then this idea just comes up out of nowhere, bubbling into my brain like a fish wriggling up through the deep. "Hey," I ask, "have you ever gone fishing before?"

"Not really," Tai says. "Maybe once or twice on vacation."

"Do you want to learn a little more about it?" I ask. "There's this fishing contest we have here every June. The Maple Derby. We should totally enter."

Tai laughs. "Not sure you'd want me on your team," he

says. "The words *fishing* and *competition* don't go together so well for me."

But I still feel those bubbles popping up and flying around inside, and I just know that I'm signing us up. I rub my hands together and look at Tai. "That's not an actual no, though, is it?"

He smiles. "Guess not."

"Besides," I continue, "you've fished before."

"We're talking *rarely*," Tai says. "But yeah. At least, I like being on the water. My mom's parents were from this city in China, way up near the border with North Korea. When we go back to visit, she sometimes takes us there, because she used to visit all the time when she was a kid. We go on day trips to this really beautiful lake called Lake Tianchi."

"Really?" I ask.

"It reminds me of Maple Lake because of the mountains." Tai stands up, brushes his hands off on his knees, and hops over to the soccer ball he left in the sand. He starts working on a few foot patterns, then kicks the ball my way. "They look kind of different than here, but yeah, there are mountains all around Lake Tianchi too. And it's super cold. There's actually ice on the lake until, like, mid-June. There might be ice on it now."

"Maybe it was made by a glacier too," I say. I just manage to stop the ball, then kick it back.

"Yeah, maybe," Tai says. "I'll have to check with my mom. She'd know for sure." He holds the ball still and picks up some small stones, then tosses them into the lake one by one. "There is one difference, though."

"You mean like how they're on opposite sides of the world?" I wish I could go to Lake Tianchi and see it for myself.

"That's obviously true," Tai says. "But that's not what I meant. I was talking about the monster."

"The what?" I feel the back of my neck prickle, like a cold wind's blowing against it. There's no wind, though.

"Yeah," Tai says. "Everybody thinks there's this lake monster in there. Of course every year there are these sightings of it. It could be legit. I mean, a lot of people have said that they feel something bump their boat, or they see some strange-looking shape in the water from shore."

"Maybe your mom should look into that," I say. My voice wobbles. I hope Tai doesn't notice.

Tai snorts. "Yeah right," he says. "She doesn't buy it. If Lake Tianchi had pollution issues, though... Well, she'd be right on that."

Amos's notebook presses into one of my pockets, the tooth another. "What about you?" I ask. "Do you think there could be a monster in that lake?"

Tai throws another stone, then looks at me. A smile tugs one corner of his mouth up. "I'm open. Never say never, right?"

I guess not, I think. But I don't want to tell Tai about the creature yet.

My phone buzzes; it's an up-close photo of Rascal, her tongue stuck partway out and curled toward her nose. This cutie says hi, writes Liza. I smile, but my thumb freezes over the screen.

My mind is stuck on a lake on the other side of the world and the silvery shape that might move through it.

And I don't text Liza back.

Chapter 11

I can't stop thinking about Lake Tianchi. I know I shouldn't use too much data, but I figure I can look it up really quickly on my phone while Mama and Dad get dinner ready.

A sparkling blue lake fills the screen, ringed by gray mountains. I read that it's nearly seven hundred feet deep, over twice as deep as Maple Lake.

And in English, it's called Heaven Lake.

I bite my lower lip, scrolling as fast as I can. There's not quite as much information on the Lake Tianchi monster as I want to find. Some people say there might even be more than one, that they swim together, rippling across the water.

"Addie!" I hear Mama call. I hit the home button on my phone and shove it under my pillow.

"Coming!" I say. I open the notebook to a fresh page and record as much as I can remember about the Lake Tianchi monster. I'll have to go back later when I have an Internet connection and add more notes.

"Addie, food's hot!" Mama calls again. I rush out my door and down the hall to dinner.

"So how'd things go with Rascal?" Mama asks, setting bowls of pasta and sauce on the table. Dad brings in a pitcher of water and we all sit down. From outside, a breeze pushes through the window screen and the curtains flutter.

"Good," I say. "She's really cute. Liza and I fed her and brushed her again. She's getting used to the halter."

"You've got a way with animals, Ad," Dad says. "Guess you got it from me." He winks in my direction. "I used to love raising those calves."

"And Liza?" Mama asks. "How was she doing?"

"Fine." I remember laughing together when Rascal tossed her head and knocked a brush out of my hand. It felt good to laugh with Liza, even though we didn't say a whole lot otherwise.

But Rascal and Liza were such tiny parts of my day, and I'm wondering if Mama's going to ask about the bigger part.

Dad does it for her.

"Now, what did you say they found in the lake, again?" he asks.

"Harmful algal blooms," I explain. "They're apparently really bad."

Mama stops chewing. "What?" she asks.

"Harmful algal blooms," I repeat. "They're these plants, kind of, but—"

"I know what they are." Mama shakes her head. She looks almost nervous. "It doesn't make sense. That lake's always been so clean. Are they sure about the blooms? Where did they find them, anyway?"

I didn't know Mama even knew what harmful algal blooms were. She told us so much about how Maple Lake came to be a lake, and about the trees and plants that grow around it and the fish that swim in it, but she never told us about those. It's weird to hear her talking about the same kind of science I've been studying.

"They were by the boat launch at the biological station," I say. "But there are other places that we're supposed to check too. The lake just *looks* clean. Something's going on."

"What do you think it is?" Dad asks.

"Not sure." I shrug. "Something's got to be coming into the lake from somewhere, though."

Mama looks up from her plate, and her look suddenly changes. Her eyes have this pretty shine to them, like sparklers on a dark night. "You know what can sometimes happen?" she says, then keeps going before we can respond.

117

"Construction projects can create a lot of runoff. The Walmart went up two years ago, and that new string of condos on the shore—couldn't that be something?"

I'm frozen stock-still, just listening to Mama say more about my work at the biological station than she's said to me in weeks. I'm afraid if I move, she'll stop. She nods to herself.

"Construction," she says. "Something to look into for sure."

All her brightness and talking fills me with something I barely knew I was missing anymore. "Mama, do you think—" I start. Then I close my mouth fast. There's no way this is going to work.

But Mama's listening.

I get brave. "Do you think you—maybe want to walk the trail?"

Mama sighs. "The Mount Mann trail," she says. She knows that's the one I mean. It's the one she always walked with Amos, the same way she always skipped stones with me.

At least she's not angry. She's something else—sad. Maybe just tired. The wrinkles around the corners of her eyes look so deep, like ruts in a road.

"We don't have to go all the way up," I say. If I could just get her *on* the trail, where she always used to go, maybe—just maybe—she'd start coming back. The Mama Before. "Just to the lookout. That would be enough." I'm talking too fast, trying to get all the words out before she can say no. But I can feel the silence coming back, the sparklers fizzing away to darkness.

Dad clears his throat. "Be good for you maybe, Laura," he says.

Mama's shaking her head. "I don't think so." But then she touches one finger to my wrist. I freeze, hoping she'll leave it there. For a moment she does; then it slips away. "Maybe later."

"It's okay," I say. Too fast again, but the words keep tumbling, trying to cover up the ones I shouldn't have said. "No problem—I'm really busy anyway. Mr. Dale wants us to keep researching all this stuff about the lake. I'll go to the library so I can use one of their desktops. I think they're only open another hour, though, so I'd better head over. You don't have to drive me, Dad—I'll bike."

Dad opens his mouth, but I push my chair back and take my plate to the sink before he can say anything. I squeeze the tooth for good luck.

"Take your phone!" Dad calls as I open the door.

Once I'm out, I just concentrate on the pedals of the bike, my feet pushing up and down, up and down. I listen to my breath. I push my front tire into one of the ruts on our dirt driveway, wobble back and forth a little. Mama's "Maybe later" loops in my mind. I see her eyes, glistening and empty. *Forget the trail*, I tell myself, but even when I close my eyes for a second, the bike moving underneath me, all I see is the hard-packed ground that twists up, up to the lookout where Maple Lake spreads out underneath.

Liza's face swims into my brain too, her eyes hopeful as she hands me her folder of drawings. I see her reaching for my hand, singing "Happy Birthday" with the rest of the family around the table at Aunt Mary and Uncle Mark's.

But those pictures of everybody I know best make me feel suddenly closed in, hot, like I'm shut in a tiny box with no way out. I just want to go back to the biological station, where I can dive into my questions and my research with Tai, who never knew Amos. Who met me before he knew that I'm supposed to be part of someone else.

I'm breathing hard by the time I pump uphill to the library, but I stop with my hand on the door handle. *Calm down, Addie*, I say. *Just chill.* Another deep breath, and I duck into the cool quiet.

Ms. Allen, the librarian, looks up from the cart of books she's shelving. We have a really tiny library, just one big room crammed with so many shelves and books it's almost claustrophobic, but in a really good way. There's even a brick fireplace Ms. Allen keeps going all winter. "Hi there, Addie," she says.

"Hi, Ms. Allen." I smile at her. "Can I use a computer?"

"Of course," Ms. Allen says. "You know the password, right?"

I don't even have to think. "*Mountain*. Every time. Right?"

"You got it," Ms. Allen says.

"Actually," I say, "maybe you could help. I have some research I need to do for my summer project out at Maple Lake. Mr. Dale wants us to look up information about the lake's history."

Ms. Allen's eyes brighten. "I do know we have a book or two about Maple Lake. Let me see what I can find."

Just then a *whoosh* of air sucks the swinging foyer door open; someone must be coming in.

Footsteps pound, and then I see Tai, one hand running through his stick-straight-up hair, the other balancing a soccer ball against his hip. He spots me. "Hey! Addie!" he calls.

Ms. Allen smiles and gets up from her desk. "Well, hello there. I don't think I've seen you before. I'm Ms. Allen."

"Sorry," Tai whispers, flashing her a smile. "That was probably a little loud. I'm Tai."

Ms. Allen laughs. "We're the only ones here, Tai. The books don't mind."

Even so, Tai tiptoes over to the computer, gently places his soccer ball on the floor, and holds his hand out for a low five. "What's up, Ad?" he asks, still whispering. "Mom dropped me off here. Told me to explore. So I figured dribbling a soccer ball around that sidewalk outside would be a good workout."

121

"I was just doing some more research about the history of the lake," I say.

Ms. Allen comes over with a book that looks like it hasn't been checked out since probably 1990. She even has to wipe a little dust off the cover before handing it to me.

I read the title aloud: "*A Glacial History of Shoreland County.*" I bet Mama's read this book; she must have learned about glaciers somewhere. I let it fall open to a photo of the white whale, then reach back and carefully remove the tooth from my pocket, hiding it in my palm.

Tai leans over to look. "Cool picture; I can't believe there used to be white whales around here. Kind of makes you wonder what else could be in that lake, right?"

My grip on the tooth loosens. I think of the way Tai barreled into the library, just like Amos used to do in muddy boots, and I know I want to tell him.

I let my hand open and hold the tooth out in front of Tai.

His eyes get wide. "Is that a dinosaur tooth?"

"Sort of," I say. "It actually looks just like a white whale tooth. The thing about it is that this tooth is big. *Really* big. Like, almost three whole inches, maybe—bigger than any white whale tooth I ever saw."

"So what are you saying?" Tai asks.

And then I tell him what I haven't told anyone else. Not even Liza. Maybe it's Tianchi, or maybe it's that Tai's new, and safe, someone without the kind of history that could get in the way of me trying to do something different. I just let the whole story pour out—Amos's theory about the lake creature, the clues he found, the notebook he left.

"When we were little, we used to talk about there being a creature living in Maple Lake," I said. "I mean, it's not hard to see why. If you spend enough time on the lake as a kid you're bound to come up with some stories like that. But I started getting more and more into science and trying to figure out why things were the way they were in nature, and Amos just wanted to think about what *might* be there instead."

"Hmmm," Tai says. "I think I might be with Amos on this one. It's neat to think about what might exist."

"I just like figuring out what I can know for sure," I say.

"Well, what do you know for sure about this tooth?" Tai asks. "You said your bus driver gave it to you, right? Where'd she find it?"

"I...don't know." I guess I never asked.

"We should find out," Tai says.

"I don't know her number," I say. "My mom does. She's known her forever. But I don't really want to ask her." Mama and Dad would obviously wonder why.

I look back toward Ms. Allen's desk and see a phone book perched on the corner.

It's not too heavy; there aren't many people in Shoreland

County. I know Barbara Ann's last name from hearing Mama say it so much, and when I open the book to the *L* section, it doesn't take me long to find her entry: *Leddy, B. A.*

I punch her number into my phone and hold my breath while it rings.

"Um, hi, Barbara Ann?" I say when she answers, her voice sliding in slow and clear. "This is Addie. Addie Lago. I just wanted to thank you for the tooth. It's really...cool."

Is it weird to say I hear her smile? Her voice stretches up at the corners. "I'm so glad you like it, Addie."

"I just had a question, though," I say. "What I wondered was...well...where did you find it?" *Please don't tell me you just bought it at the Bluewater Museum for a buck*, I silently beg. I want so much for it to be real, mysterious, to deserve its spot in Amos's notebook.

The tooth stares up at us, colossally big, bigger than the heads of the perch swimming through Maple Lake.

Barbara Ann doesn't say anything at first. For a second I think she's hung up. "I found that on the beach," she says finally. "Walking just before sunset. It was sticking out of the sand."

"What made you pick it up, though?" I ask. Our sand is full of stones, left over from all the mountain pieces that chipped away. A half-buried tooth would just blend in.

"It was shining," Barbara Ann says softly. "Shining like

you wouldn't believe. I guess people would probably say it was just the way the sun hit it, but—"

Her voice falls away. Then it comes back. "But I don't think that's it," she finishes. "I don't think that's it at all."

Part of me wants to say something else. But most of me just wants to stop the call and let this sink in. "Thanks, Barbara Ann," I say. When she finishes telling me to have a great summer and to take care of that tooth, I hit the red End button and stare at the phone and the tooth, side by side.

"So?" Tai asks. "What did she say?"

I tell him about the shining tooth, and I watch his eyes. They get wide, but they light up too. I haven't really seen them do that until now. Tai leans back and chews his lip. He's really thinking.

"I kept telling Amos that if he really wanted to convince me there was some creature living in the lake, he'd have to produce evidence," I say. "So that's what he started doing. He kept a list of clues. And I think this tooth is just the kind of clue he was looking for."

Tai leans forward in his seat, his elbow resting on a jiggling knee. He's looking at me so hard I have to look away. "So your brother was trying to use science to prove that the creature was real?" he asks.

"Basically," I say. "But I didn't believe him."

"And you do now?" Tai asks.

125

"It doesn't really seem possible," I say. "But I do have the notebook where he kept track of everything."

"Don't you see, though?" Tai stares at me, his eyes wide, urgent. "This is just like Tianchi."

"Same idea, I know. That doesn't mean *either* creature is real." Tai looks disappointed. I rush to explain what I want to do. "Amos saw the harmful algal blooms. He wrote about them in one of the clues. It makes me wonder what else he recorded that we could explain."

"He saw the blooms?" Tai's forehead scrunches up. "What did he say about them?"

"Nothing, really. I don't think he knew what he was looking at." He really just mentioned the *green parts* in passing, but the fact that he noticed them at all makes me curious about the rest of the clue. "I was thinking—or, I just *wonder*, I guess, if we're using your scientific method—that . . . maybe whatever Amos was talking about could actually be part of what your mom is trying to figure out."

Tai nods slowly. "I'd buy that."

My phone buzzes; this time it's a text from Dad. I stiffen.

You still at library

I punch letters with my thumb, rushing to finish.

Yeah tell Mama don't worry. Be home later

"So," I say. "I came here to do some research. Guess I

126

should probably start that." And I'm not just curious about Maple Lake's history; I want to know what might be happening now too. I type *lake pollution* into the search box and words float onto the screen. *Watershed. Runoff. Sediment.*

"Eh," Tai says. "Mr. Dale gives us time during the day to research that stuff. I kinda care more about your brother's clues right now. Do you have his notebook?"

"I always have it," I say, reaching into my pocket. I'm actually really glad Tai seems to care about Amos's clues. I know Amos would have appreciated it too. But when I touch the notebook's edge, I stop for just a second. Part of me doesn't want to pull it out. Amos gave this to *me*. He wanted *me* to see it.

But then I feel it again. A big squeeze around my arms, like someone's pressing them into my sides. It's not Tai; he's just sitting on the chair in front of me, waiting for me to say something.

Go ahead. Did I say that out loud? Or did I hear it? Think it?

Show him. My arms relax; the pressure's gone. And where the pressure was, there's just warmth now.

I've never really let myself think this before, not clearly. But these things that don't quite make sense—the too-big tooth, the notebook with its strange clues—tell me that even though I can't explain it scientifically, the warm feeling that squeezes me so hard sometimes I almost gasp is Amos, telling me he's here. That everything's okay.

The truth is I feel him everywhere. Not just here in the library, surrounded by dusty books we checked out over and over again when we were little, but also on the lake, wind slicing through my hair and waves rolling at my feet.

And if Amos—who isn't really here, who *can't* be here— is all around me, what else might be real that I can't see? I owe it to Amos to find out just how real his clues are. If I do, I can help him the way I never did while he was alive.

I hold the notebook out for Tai, like I did the tooth. He looks at me softly, not saying anything.

"Go ahead," I tell him. "It was my brother's." The warm feeling stays, swirling around me. "I signed up for this Young Scientist position so I could research pollution on the lake. But I have to research the clues my brother left too."

Tai looks up at me fast, his eyes wide. But I nod, and he lifts the notebook out of my hands. Now we're sharing it.

Chapter 12

I pull on pajamas and sit in bed, thumbing through Amos's notebook. Last week at the library, Tai told me that based on what Barbara Ann said about the whale tooth, I should add to clue number five, and I did: *mysteriously shining*. But just as I take the tooth out to look at it again, hoping for the millionth time to see some of that shine, the doorbell rings.

Then I hear Dad down the hall. "Liza!" he says. "Come on in. You too, Mary. Where you headed?"

Oh no, I think. I was supposed to go help with Rascal yesterday, but I forgot and went to the library again to read about harmful algal blooms.

Still, why is my stomach flip-flopping on itself like this? I should *want* to see Liza.

I hear Mama telling Aunt Mary to come sit down,

have some tea, and then, sure enough, she calls my name: *"Addie!"*

I can't quite read the expression on Liza's face when I walk down the hall.

"Hey," I say. Seeing Liza feels so normal, but strange too, even after only a few days. It reminds me of when I broke my arm in fourth grade. All those weeks in a cast, I forgot what this really important part of me looked or felt like. When the doctor finally cut the plaster off, I remember staring down at my arm and feeling like I didn't even know how to move it anymore.

"Let's go to my room," I say, and reach out. Liza hesitates, then lets me pull her down the hall.

She doesn't have much time to prepare for the Shoreland Art Show, and I should have invited her over before. I meant to, I really did. But it also feels like the only things I have enough energy for are Maple Lake and the notebook.

Liza goes in ahead of me, and when I turn back after shutting the door, she's staring at me, her eyes pooling.

"I haven't been in here," she says. "In—in a long time." She wipes both eyes and looks up at the ceiling.

I know right away what she means. She hasn't been in here since...Amos. She walks over to the bed, reaches up to the top bunk, and just rests her hand on the wooden railing.

I look around my room, at the emptiness that grew there. The desk with no papers or comic books or pencils piled on it. The bed with no blanket or pillow. Mama and Dad boxed all those things up and put them in the closet where his clothes still hang. And then they shut the door.

Liza knows how this room is supposed to look. It feels like she knows too much. Like she can't look at me without seeing him.

"Where were you yesterday?" she asks. She blinks fast, wipes her eyes.

"Um," I say. "The library." But I can feel my stomach twisting up in knots. I'm not telling Liza the whole truth, and she knows me well enough to know that.

She squeezes her lips together, then lets out a breath. "Rascal missed you," she says.

I stare at the wall only so I can avoid her eyes. "I was just there," I say. "I mean, it wasn't that long ago that I was there."

"Every day counts with a calf," she says. "I led her around the barn. It wasn't so bad. She's basically gotten used to the halter. But she needs to get used to you too."

My mouth suddenly feels super dry. "I'll come over tomorrow. For sure."

Liza runs her hand across the bunk bed railing and looks up at the ceiling. She smiles, but it's a sad smile.

"Remember when you and Amos helped me make those baloney sandwiches?"

"Of course," I say.

"It was just supposed to be for DeeDee and Sammie," she says. "And we made that assembly line."

"You had the bread, I had the mayo, Amos had the baloney." I can see us standing there in the kitchen. It's like I'm looking through a window at a different version of myself. The one that could still grab Amos by the shoulder for support when I started laughing too hard.

"And whose idea was it to pair a movement with each part of the line?" Liza asks.

But she knows. We both know. It was Amos.

Liza lets out a laugh. "What was mine again? A hip wiggle? Then I had to give you a high five."

"And then I had to do a pirouette and give Amos a high five," I say. "And then—"

We both snort at the same time, which happens a lot when we laugh.

"Break dancing!" we both yell, and the fact that we say *that* at the same time too makes us laugh harder. I don't think either of us will ever forget Amos spinning on the floor, popping up into a handstand, then twisting back up again to slap baloney on a piece of bread. Pretty soon Liza is wiping tears from her eyes again. This time, I'm not sure if they're laughing tears or the other kind.

"And we made way too many sandwiches," I say, "just because the assembly line was so fun. Didn't we end up with like ten before we realized how many we had?"

Liza nods, sniffling.

Those were our days. More baloney sandwiches than we needed and doubled-over laughs. Teaching Baby Katy how to clap and Bumble to shake. The silence between us now is weird. But I don't want to tell Liza about anything I've been dealing with this summer. Why do I feel fine about telling Tai instead?

I want to reach out and grab Liza's hand, but at the same time, I don't. "Do you want me to take another look at your portfolio?"

"I don't have it," she says. "Mom and I were just driving by, and I asked if we could pull in. You definitely should come over tomorrow. I think I figured out how to fix the problem you told me about. I found something to add."

"Oh yeah?" I say. But even I can hear the distraction in my voice. I *want* to help Liza, but I keep thinking about everything else.

"I need to help you more with Rascal too," she says. "I wanted you to be the one to show her in the ring. But you don't know anything yet. Like, what stuff the judge will be looking for or anything."

Guilt pricks me all over, a million tiny needles. "I know," I say. "I'll come."

After Liza leaves, I shut my door and go back to thinking about Maple Lake, and Amos's notebook. There's no way Amos would have wanted me to tell my teacher and another scientist about his clues, not until we could really prove what they meant. But I think I've figured out how to get out on the lake alone, without Dr. Li or Mr. Dale right there, so Tai and I can investigate.

I pull out the notebook and record everything I can about what Dr. Li told me, plus descriptions of the harmful algal blooms and where we saw them. I make sure to write dates and times, just like a scientist would.

It feels a little strange to put data about pollution next to information about the creature, but I'm starting to think there might be more science in Amos's magic than I thought.

Chapter 13

At the biological station, Mr. Dale asks us for a research update. Tai and I run through different possibilities— logging, lawn chemicals, traffic, and the construction Mama talked about.

"There's a lot going on in the Maple Lake watershed," I say, hoping Mr. Dale will be impressed I used that word.

"Good point," Mr. Dale says. "Watersheds can cover quite a distance, so there's a lot that could affect Maple Lake. Nice work, you two. It sounds like you have some hypotheses about what could be causing the pollution."

"*Great.*" Tai pumps his fist. "What's next?"

"I'll bring your mom in," Mr. Dale says. "She has some ideas."

As Mr. Dale leaves, I lean over to Tai. "My mom had ideas too," I say. "She's the one who brought up the construction."

"That's cool," he says. "She sounds smart."

"She is," I say. I can feel something deep in my chest swell just a little. "She was the best science student at her school." I don't say *high* school. Mama might not have gone to college, but she knows a lot just the same.

"We need to get cracking on our secondary investigation, you know," Tai whispers, even though nobody's around to hear.

"I know," I say. "I've got the notebook. We should try to get them to send us out on the lake by ourselves."

"That's what I was thinking," Tai says, pulling out his phone. "Hey, I was doing some more research on white whales after I saw you at the library. They're pretty cool-looking. Did you know that when they're born, they're actually dark gray? And they talk more than any other whale. I guess they have a whole language."

I lean over and look at his phone, even though I know exactly what white whales look like. They have kind of cone-shaped heads with blunt, stuck-out noses, and their faces look almost human, like they're smiling.

"Nice research," I say. "For someone who isn't into science." I poke him lightly.

"Yeah well," Tai says. "It's actually pretty interesting. Did Amos think the creature looked like this?"

"Maybe." I push past the pang I feel at hearing Amos's name. "I don't think he thought of it as a regular white whale, though. He thought it might have started that way but grown and changed over time, since the glaciers."

"Like evolution?" Tai asks.

"Kind of like that, but maybe with some magic that would make it different from regular whales," I say. "You know, it's funny. These whales are related to narwhals, which some people call unicorn whales because of their tusks. And unicorns are magical too." I can't bring myself to add *and also not real.*

Mr. Dale comes back in with Dr. Li. Tai rolls to the other side of the table and sits up a little straighter.

"I'm pleased with the start you've made," Dr. Li says. "You've come across some of the same information Jake and Tasha have been researching. We've run some initial numbers based on the water samples you took with Mr. Dale along with the ones we had, and it's clear that Maple Lake has a phosphorus problem."

Phosphorus. I saw that word in my research. It sounded like a lot of different things could cause too much phosphorus to get into the water, and harmful algal blooms were definitely a major symptom. I wonder how we'll figure out a solution.

"I'd like you to collect some water samples from different points on the lake," Dr. Li says. "Just to confirm what we suspect."

Mr. Dale tosses the boat keys in his hand. "I'm ready when you are," he says. Then he looks toward the biological station and sighs. "Though I've got a lot to do in there too. Dr. Li, do you think you could put off the conversation with Dr. Rush at UVM until we're back?"

Dr. Li winces. "You're right, we are cutting it a little close," she says. "Maybe we should postpone the sampling, though I really wanted the kids to get a few this morning."

I clear my throat. "Um, I could drive the boat," I say. "If that would help." I try not to show how much I *need* to drive the boat by myself. My plan to get out onto the lake to investigate Amos's clues kind of relies on it.

Dr. Li cocks her head to one side. "Drive the boat?" she asks. "Addie, that seems a little"—she pauses, and I can see she's trying to find the right word—"risky?"

"Well, it's just that...I've been driving our boat since I was ten," I say. "My dad taught me. And I took Boater's Safety too; I've had my license since last year."

Tai smiles and sticks his hand out under the table for another low five.

Dr. Li's brow wrinkles, and Mr. Dale steps in. "She does know how to drive a boat," he explains. "But Addie, we'd need to speak with your parents about this."

"I actually talked to them about it," I say. The lie slips out more easily than I thought it would, but it leaves me light-headed. I hope Mr. Dale can't tell. I hand him the letter I typed and printed at the library:

> Dear Mr. Dale,
>
> Addie has told us that she's interested in driving the boat during her research. We feel comfortable with this, and think it's a great way for Addie to keep her skills up since we haven't been out on the lake in a while. Please contact us at the phone number noted below if you have any concerns.
>
> *Laura and Bruce Lago*

Signing the letter in a way that looked like a grown-up and not like a middle schooler who was too careful with her cursive wasn't easy, but I just made my signature a little messier than usual. It was risky including a phone number too, but I figured if I did, Mr. Dale would be more likely to believe the letter and less likely to actually call my parents. Dad barely ever answers his phone on the job anyway.

Dr. Li turns to Mr. Dale. "What do you think?" she asks. "Are you sure this is safe?"

Mr. Dale gives me a careful look. "I've seen Addie driving the boat when she was out fishing with her family," he says. He doesn't mention he also let me drive it the other day, when we took our first water sample. "I know she's been learning since she was very young."

Dr. Li nods. "Well, this isn't exactly conventional," she says. "But I suppose it could work."

"You're required to wear life jackets, of course," Mr. Dale says to Tai and me, his voice suddenly stern. "And to stay in the boat at all times. That's clear, right?"

We nod. Mama and Dad always make me wear a life jacket anyway. And as for staying in the boat, well—that shouldn't be hard.

"Mr. Dale will set you up with more sample bottles," Dr. Li says. "And Addie, I have a map of the lake with about ten collection spots." She hands me a piece of paper. "Each of the spots has been assigned a number, and these correspond with what's programmed into the Navionics. We'll send you to the ones closest to shore so you're not too far away. Does that make sense?"

I study the map and the numbered spots where we have to take measurements. Dr. Li pulls out a highlighter and swipes it across the numbers closest to the biological station.

"Yes," I say. "I've been watching my dad navigate to his fishing spots practically since I could walk." I take another look at the map. "I think you've actually found a few of them."

"Let's hope they remain good for fishing," Dr. Li says.

"You know any kind of pollution can have a negative effect on aquatic life."

"You mean the fish could die?" I ask, picturing Amos casting a line, his eyes squinting out at shining water.

"They might already be dying. Jake and Tasha are working with Vermont's Agency of Natural Resources to crunch some numbers on fish populations." Dr. Li ticks off a list on her fingers: "Sample bottles. Labels. Marker. Data sheets and pencil. Life jackets. Phones in waterproof cases. Cooler. GPS. Anything else?"

"Nope, sounds good," Mr. Dale says. "C'mon, scientists. Let's head out to the boat."

Maple Lake stretches before me, blue and silver in the sun. Every sparkle pierces me, but the beauty also feels so familiar, I want to move toward the water and through it, stepping clear of fear, like Barbara Ann said.

Mr. Dale helps us get set up, then waves goodbye. I push the throttle forward and raise the motor out of the water so the boat rides on a smooth, even plane.

The mountains close in on me, dark and beautiful. I've seen the lake this way a million times, but now with Amos's notebook, it feels new too. It's not what I thought it was. Or, there's more to it than I ever saw before. In the distance, a heron rises from the water and soars into the sky, its wings dripping silver. I have to catch my breath, even though I've seen herons fly a hundred times before.

If there's magic anywhere, I think, it's here.

I know exactly where we're heading first, and I don't need the GPS to get there. The closest spot Dr. Li marked on the map isn't too far from Bear Rock. The huge, rounded top part that sticks out through the water looks just like a bear's back, and people always dare each other to jump off it. I guess it's not that scary—as long as you can swim, you're fine—but I've never really had the guts to try it. Amos did, and I remember how my heart would pound when he crashed into the water. He always came up smiling. I catch myself smiling too, just thinking about it.

I cut the motor. There's not much wind, so I'm not worried about drifting.

"Sample bottle?" I ask. Tai pulls one out, along with a permanent marker. I write the date, time, and place on the white label, then add a number matching what Dr. Li wrote by this spot. I rinse the sample bottle, then hold it under the surface, cap it once it's full, and hand it to Tai, who stores it in the cooler.

No wind means even the leaves on the trees stay quiet. Water bumps softly against the boat. I close my eyes and breathe in deep. And I don't only smell things—I feel them, without having to touch. Spicy cedar branches, flaking bark, warm dirt mixed with sand. Clean, hard stone. The faintest trace of fish. I've always loved this lake.

But I shiver too. Maple Lake has never just been what I can see on the surface. There's so much more to it, plunging dark and unknowable beneath me. I thought I knew what there was to know, or at least that with enough time I could figure everything out. But now I'm not so sure anyone can.

"It's nice out here," Tai says. "Really quiet. But nice."

"My brother was only ever quiet on the lake," I say. "Every other time, he needed to be making noise. Banging around. Out here, in our boat, he just sat still and watched."

A lump rises in my throat. I want Amos to be here so badly it makes my ribs ache.

And then the boat rises. I grab the steering wheel before I even understand the fact of it, that the water actually moved beneath us on such a still day.

"Hey, did you feel that?" I ask. And then it rises again.

"I felt *that*!" Tai shouts.

Water surges underneath now, again and again, like it's getting pushed from somewhere too deep for us to see. A sheaf of wave slaps the side and splashes over the edge, drenching my knees.

The boat heaves toward Bear Rock, the water pushing it higher, higher—

I fumble with the key, the steering wheel, trying to get the motor started and keep us turned toward the middle of the lake before we smash into Bear Rock or, worse, the sharp face of Bevel Mountain. Tai's scrambling up from the bottom of the boat, reaching for the sides. The regular sounds of water and birds slip away, replaced by crackling static. A scream locks in my throat.

And just then, as quickly as it started, it stops. The water shrinks, stills. Quiet comes back.

Tai's face is pale, the muscles in his arms popping as he clings to the side of the boat.

I'm shaking, my fingers still on the key. Finally, I let go and drop my face into my hands.

"What *was* that?" Tai asks.

"I—I have no idea." I stand opposite Tai to keep the boat balanced and stare into the water, shimmering and dark at the same time. *Deep breaths.* As air fills my lungs, I stop trembling. "Actually—I do have an idea."

I fumble for Amos's notebook, zipped into a plastic bag just in case. "Amos wrote about this," I say. I flip past the doodles and sketches to clue number two, just so I can read it again for myself. Amos described it exactly the way I would. I quickly check my watch and record the date and time on the back of the page. *Significant disturbance in the water,* I write. *Unexplained ocean-type wave.*

144

"The waves," Tai remembers, touching the words on the page. Amos's handwriting. "You're right. Did those feel like ocean waves?"

"They really did. That big, anyway." I've only been to the ocean once before, when we went camping in Maine a few years back, but I still remember how huge those waves felt, how they rolled underneath us. *By Bear Rock*, I continue writing. *Almost smashed the boat but stopped just in time.*

I look up at the cedar branches hanging over our heads. They aren't moving even a little bit. *No other wind*, I write. Then I shove the notebook in Tai's direction. He reads my entry and nods. "Something's going on for sure," he says. "Your brother knew what he was doing."

I don't know what to think.

"Let's go to the next spot," I say. My hands are steady but my head's still spinning, and I want to move on.

Tai studies the map. "Two, three, and four are really close together," he says.

I start the motor while he finds the coordinates in the Navionics app. "Know where to go?" he asks.

"Got it." I turn the boat and push the throttle hard, then stand tall at the wheel, trying to clear my mind. I love the hard push of air against my face when I drive fast. The air alone feels tough enough to push through a wall, erase anything it touches.

We take our next three samples quickly—I'm in charge of labeling the sample bottle; then after I rinse and fill it, Tai packages it back up in a plastic bag and puts it in the cooler.

He takes a deep breath. "Was your brother scared of the creature?"

It's a good question, and I realize I don't know the answer. "It didn't seem that way," I say. "He never seemed scared when he told me about it."

"Man," Tai says, shaking his head. "He must have been brave."

"He was," I say. "But you know, if what just happened was what he wrote about—which it kind of seems like it was—it didn't hurt us."

"That was a pretty strong wave, though," Tai says.

"Yeah, but it stopped," I say. "And we're still in the boat."

"True," Tai says. The water's gentle now, barely moving, and I can sense both of us relaxing along with it. "It's pretty cool, actually, when you think about it. Maybe the creature knew we were here and it decided to show itself to us. On purpose."

"Interesting hypothesis," I say. Tai is way more on board with the idea of the creature than I am. "But just because the water moved, doesn't mean a creature moved it. We still didn't really *see* anything." I'm trembling, though. I have to admit, I have no idea what caused that wave.

"We felt it, though!" Tai's voice presses through, louder than before. "I could ask my mom about it. If there's any kind of scientific explanation, she'll know."

I shake my head. "I know part of the scientific method is sharing," I say, "but this feels different to me. We should keep track of it in the notebook, but that's it. I'm—still trying to figure out what's going on."

Tai nods. "Okay. It'll be our mystery." Then he looks over the side of the boat, down at the water, resting his chin on his folded arms. "Hey," he says, "aren't we supposed to be able to see fish swimming around?"

I laugh. "Usually it's not that easy. They stay pretty deep."

"It'd be cool to catch one." Tai looks so hopeful it's kind of heartbreaking.

"You'll need a few tips before the Maple Derby, anyway, if you want to have any hope of placing." I smile to let him know I'm kidding.

But he already seems to know. "Sure," he says, laughing. "And by the way, I'm only doing that derby thing because you and I will be in the same boat. *Literally.* So however you want to cram twelve years of fishing into a few tips works for me."

"Okay," I say. "Might as well start now." There's an old rod and reel on this boat with a jig still stuck by the hook.

Must be Mr. Dale's backup equipment. It's not the best, but it'll do for a lesson.

I hand it to Tai and show him how to hold the rod. "Now what you want to do is to drop the jig straight to the bottom."

"How will I know I'm at the bottom?" he asks.

"The line will go slack," I explain. "You'll see it start to swirl up. Now, once you're there, reel up just a little to create some tension. Then start to jig the line, like this." I demonstrate flicking the rod up and down, gently, then stopping, waiting. Jigging again. "As you go, you can pull the jig up higher too. Then bring it back down."

Tai does well. His wrist moves easily, not too jerky and not too soft. "Why exactly am I doing this?" he asks.

"Perch are bottom-dwellers," I say. "They like the mud, and they get food from it too. Bugs. When you knock against the bottom, it stirs up all the silt and makes them think something interesting is going on."

I steer the boat away from the center of the lake closer to shore, where the Pine River spills into Maple Lake.

"So, fish like structure in the water," I say. "A place where things shift and feel different. Where there's a big drop-off in depth, for example. Or here, where a river comes into a bigger body of water."

I cut the motor. "This is one of our favorite spots," I say. "One of the first Dad showed us."

Tai peers over the edge of the boat as though he'll be able to see fish clustering below. "It's still not going to be that easy," I say.

But Tai's eyes darken. "It's not that," he says. "I'm just pretty sure I see some of those harmful algal blooms my mom was talking about."

My heart sinks, a heavy anchor. "You sure?"

"Look," Tai says, and reluctantly, I lean over too. Greenish-blue slime pools near the mouth of the river. I've never noticed those here before. I wonder if it's even a good fishing spot anymore. I stick the handle of the boat's emergency paddle into the middle of the sludge and try pushing it away to see if I can spot the wild celery and waterweed that give the water oxygen and the fish hiding places. But all I can do is swirl it around, like I'm stirring paint.

"Ugh," I say. I still see plants, but the slimy algal blooms feel thick on top. I pull the paddle away.

Tai's already taking out his phone, snapping a picture. "I'll show my mom."

"We should put it on the map too," I say. "It's probably not a coincidence that those vacation condos are right across the lake, huh?" I look toward the shiny buildings, perched so close to the water they look like they could fall in.

"When were those built?" Tai asks.

"Last year," I say. "And come to think of it, the Walmart's upstream of the Pine River. My mom might really have been onto something."

"Seems like it," Tai says. "But it's also just two buildings. Do you think they really could've thrown the whole lake off so quickly?"

"Maybe the logging that happened here before started it," I say. "Then the construction pushed it over the edge." Nobody's logged the woods around Maple Lake in decades, not since it got turned into a state forest, but there could be logging somewhere else in the watershed that's causing erosion. I shiver a little, realizing that just a few weeks ago I didn't think there was anything wrong with Maple Lake. Now that I know about the problem, I really want to help fix it.

I think Amos would too, if he could be here, though I wonder what he would have thought about Dr. Li's evidence. Would he have believed it, or just seen in Maple Lake what he wanted to see?

I point to the fields beyond the lake. "My cousin Liza's house is up there," I say. "See her barn? Top of the hill?"

"Is it the red one?" Tai cranes his neck.

"Yup. Her dad—my uncle Mark, my dad's brother—is a dairy farmer." I pull the steering wheel, letting the boat arc. "You know where milk comes from, right?"

Tai rolls his eyes. "We're not *total* idiots in the city," he says. "I even went to a farm once, on a field trip."

I laugh. "Okay, okay. Bet you've never milked a cow, though."

Tai holds his hands up. "You got me."

"You should come over sometime," I say. "We usually have a family dinner on the Fourth of July."

"That would be kind of awesome," Tai says. "Could you take a video of me milking a cow?"

"Uncle Mark uses machines," I say. "You just fit them over the cows' udders and they do the milking themselves. But I bet he could show you how to milk by hand too, if you really wanted."

"Okay, you're on," he says. "You're *so* on."

"You can even meet the calf I've been helping my cousin raise," I say.

"You and your cousin have been raising a calf?" Tai asks. "What exactly does that mean?"

Tai's so easy to get along with, I sometimes forget how different our lives are in lots of ways. "It's for 4-H," I explain. "There's a dairy show at the fair every summer. So we feed the calf, and brush it, and teach it how to be led with a halter, and to stand in a certain way for a judge."

Tai's forehead wrinkles. "Sounds interesting," he says, but it comes out like a question.

"You'll see when you get there," I say. "You'll love the calf. She's super pretty, and…kind of annoying, but in a cute way, I guess?"

"Annoying but cute," Tai repeats. "Great sell. Just let me know what time I should be ready."

"The Fourth of July isn't too long after the Maple Derby," I say. "Which, of course, you're totally ready for now."

"I mean…if by *ready* you mean ready to watch *you* fish?" Tai asks, then nods his head firmly, up and down. "Then *yes*, I *agree*."

The rest of the time we're out on the water, it's still and smooth as glass. Dad sends me a text: Mama asks how's it going

And I just write All good

No need to tell him about the wave that almost threw us into Bear Rock. No need to tell him about the boat at all. If I did, he'd probably tell Mama and she'd haul me out of here so fast Mr. Dale's head would spin. And then I wouldn't be able to come out and breathe in the Maple Lake smells that fill me up to the brim with something I can't name. I wouldn't be able to hang out with Tai. And I wouldn't be able to finish what Amos started.

When we finally head back toward shore with a cooler full of sample bottles and a secret, I feel that pressure circling my arms again. That warmth. *Hi, Amos*, I whisper, so soft not even Tai can hear.

Chapter 14

The morning of the Maple Derby, I wake up in the dark and dress in jeans and one of Amos's cotton sweatshirts to cut the early chill. I had to rush to Liza's last night to squeeze in some time working with Rascal, even though I was really distracted thinking about the derby and the harmful algal blooms. I did okay, but Liza kept chewing her lip while she watched me work. I probably wasn't doing the best job of focusing, and Rascal was living up to her name.

I tiptoe into Mama and Dad's room and tap Dad softly on the shoulder. "Time to go," I whisper. In the pale light brimming from the hallway, Dad sees my sweatshirt and smiles. I've already packed a cooler with Fluffernutters, apples, carrot sticks, and chips. Dad hooked our boat trailer up to the truck last night and I've got my rods and reels, life jackets and sunscreen, minnows and lines, nestled in one of the seat boxes.

It's still pitch-black when we pull out of our driveway and head to the cottage where Tai and Dr. Li are staying, not far from the biological station. Their place is surrounded by evergreens, perched on a hill that looks out over the lake. Tai's still rubbing his eyes as he gets in the car.

"Hi, Mr. Lago," Tai says, sticking out his hand. "Thanks for the ride."

My dad's smiles come and go fast, but he doesn't waste them. So when he flashes one at Tai, I know he likes him right away. Tai's all angles and blushes, but sweetness too.

"You two ready?" Dad asks, pulling into the boat launch at Maple Lake.

"Definitely," I say, and Tai holds his fist out for a bump. It's too early to head to our actual spot—we're not allowed to start fishing until first light—but getting here ahead of time lets us slide the boat into the water and make sure we have everything ready to go. A few other boats have already arrived too.

Dad's jaw tightens when he gets out of the truck. I watch him carefully, but he doesn't wipe his hand across his eyes like he did when he first saw the lake at the biological station.

Tai's on the other side of the truck, tightening his

shoelaces, so I step a little closer to Dad. "Thanks," I whisper, "for letting me do the derby."

Dad puts a hand on my shoulder. I heard him tell Mama that there were so many boats out it would be pretty impossible to get in trouble without someone being seconds away to help. Of course I couldn't really explain that I'd been driving a boat by myself at the biological station for a while anyway.

Dad helps me check the motor and gas, makes sure the cooler's set snugly next to the seat box, and hands me two water bottles. He checks the straps on our life jackets, even though we're twelve.

"I told your mama I'd superglue that life jacket onto you if I needed to," he says.

"Instead you just tightened the straps so much I can barely move my arms." I twist stiffly at my waist, from side to side, exaggerating the effect.

"Perfect. That's what I was going for." Dad winks, then pats my shoulder. "Sorry I can't cheer you on. You know how work goes. I'll be here to pick you up, though."

"No worries, Dad." If anything, I'll feel less nervous without him watching me.

On his way out, I see Dad almost run into Mr. Cooper, the Maple Derby organizer, who's walking toward us.

"Bruce," Mr. Cooper says. They shake hands, and Mr.

Cooper claps Dad on the back. "It's good to see you out here. Real good."

"You too, Jerry," Dad says.

After Amos died, Mr. and Mrs. Cooper started bringing meals over to our house twice a week. They left them in an orange cooler outside our door and came back the next day to get the cooler and refill it again. And again. For weeks. I think there were probably nights when if it hadn't been for their chicken broccoli casserole or enchiladas or potato soup, we wouldn't have eaten anything at all.

"So glad you're joining us this year, Addie," Mr. Cooper says.

"Thanks, Mr. Cooper," I say. "And I brought my friend Tai too."

"Welcome to both of you," he says, smiling and shaking our hands.

Plenty of boats have gathered in the shallows by now. Littler kids have their parents with them, but a lot of the older kids, like me, are driving on their own.

As the sun pushes its way up over Bevel Mountain, Mr. Cooper heads up to the dock with a megaphone.

"Welcome to the Maple Derby!" he says, his voice muffled. "As in previous years, this is a small-fish competition. Whoever catches the biggest and heaviest out of five fish, wins."

I lean over to Tai. "I know the best perch spot on the lake," I say. "We have a good chance."

The sun bathes Maple Lake in gold. We put on our sunglasses. Mr. Cooper gives the green light, and people start their motors. The water churns, and it's a little chaotic watching everyone scramble to start, but this is a big lake. Before long, we're scattering in different directions.

I point toward the spot where Tai and I found the harmful algal blooms, because it's always been Dad's secret spot and I'm not giving up on it yet. Out of the corner of my eye I see Darren steering in the same direction, but then he veers off to the right, a splash of white curving in his wake.

After dropping anchor far enough from the blooms that I don't have to stare at sludge, but close enough that I know it's still the right spot, I open my minnow bucket and remind Tai how to hook a little silver minnow so it will stay.

"It's so weird that fish eat fish," Tai says. "Can you think of another animal that does that?"

"Not off the top of my head, I guess," I say. "But minnows aren't really *the same* as perch." Minnows are tiny and silver, like slippery nails. Perch are pale green, with dark green stripes and sharp, tall fins.

"Still weird," Tai mutters, but he easily hooks a minnow onto his line.

I've never jigged at this spot without catching perch.

But Tai and I sit there for an hour, trying worms, different-colored jigs and speeds, and slightly different spots, and—nothing.

"Think it's the harmful algal blooms?" Tai asks.

I look up at the Pine River, spilling all the way from high up past the mountain in the fields by Uncle Mark's farm.

"Maybe," I say. "But how can it be this bad? How can they just be gone?"

Then, all of a sudden, the boat starts to move. I feel the anchor scrape and pull against the bottom. "What the—" Tai says, grabbing the side of the boat.

There's no time to think; everything's moving too fast. It's like we're the minnows on a line and some giant on the opposite shore is reeling us in. The boat skids so fast toward the middle of the lake, far from the mouth of the Pine River, that I can barely breathe until, without warning, it stops. And everything stills.

I turn around, look at the other boats dotted across the lake. *Did anyone see that?* Nobody seems alarmed. Tai and I just stare at each other, breathing hard.

"What. Just. Happened." Tai's voice feels as heavy as a stone.

I just shake my head. My throat feels so dry, when I finally speak, it's more of a croak. "Anchors don't just—move like that."

"I figured." Tai reaches out to put his hand on mine, and I realize I'm shaking. "What do you think it was trying to do?" he asks. "Why would it pull us away from that spot?"

I shake my head. "I don't know yet. But there's no *it*, Tai. We still don't have proof."

Amos never wrote about anything like this in the notebook at least. This clue is all our own.

"Well, proof or not," Tai says, "it's something. Aren't you going to write it down?"

I pull Amos's notebook out of my back pocket and begin writing. *Something pulled us away from the harmful algal blooms. It even moved the anchor.* I eyeball the distance to our old spot: two hundred yards, maybe?

I lean over the side of the boat and look down in the water. I can only see so far before it disappears into mystery. Bits of sunlight swirl just below the surface. Gentle waves glisten. Yet I keep looking down, down, as deep as I can, then deeper. For one second, I imagine I'm there at the bottom, sitting on soft sand, watching water plants wave dreamily, where all sounds fade, where quiet fish slide past.

Then I'm back up, staring at a surface that twinkles so brightly it's like stars fell right into it.

Tai starts baiting another hook. "Well, I don't know about you," he says, "but I'm ready to try this spot."

I can't exactly argue.

Tai casts his line and jigs like I showed him. "It feels deeper here," he says.

Then I see his rod jerk. He flinches back, starting to reel. "Got one!" he says. "I mean, I must have one, right? Right?" The rod bends hard, curving over the water. I leap up and race to help him, but he doesn't need it. He's reeling steadily, and when he pulls the fish out of the water, my jaw drops.

It's huge. I help Tai unhook it and grab my hanging scale. "Two pounds!" I yell. "Whoa, Tai!"

"Is that good?" Tai says. "I mean, it looks big, but—"

"Uh, *yeah*," I say. "That's really good for perch."

I toss the fish in the boat's live well, where it can swim until we get back to shore.

We fish for the next hour, and I catch a few, but it's Tai who's on a real roll this morning. He catches six more perch, none as big as that first one, but all good size. I have to say, even on our best days, I'm not sure Amos and I ever had this great of a haul, that fast. I wish Amos could have been here to see it happen. I can almost hear him clapping Tai on the back and whooping into the air.

When we pull in to the dock, I see Dad, grinning, his hands stuck in his pockets.

"What are you doing here?" I ask. "I thought you were supposed to be at work."

"A dad has his reasons." Dad puts his arm around my shoulders. "You did good out there, honey girl," he says.

If Dad was watching me, does that mean he saw us race to the middle of the lake?

"Um...so, how'd the water look?" I ask.

"Like glass," Dad said. "Must have been a smooth ride."

There's no way Dad would be standing here so calmly if he'd seen what just happened. So he must not have seen anything. I look over at Tai, and he's looking at me too. He raises his shoulders in a little shrug, but my heart's pounding.

If nobody else saw it, did it happen? In science, it wouldn't be right to claim that something was true if other people didn't see it too. I don't know how to explain this. But I know what I felt, and so does Tai.

After getting everybody's attention, Mr. Cooper shakes Tai's hand and declares him the winner of the Maple Derby. He not only caught the biggest perch for sure out of five, but his others were heavier than pretty much everyone else's too, mine included. Tai's blushing, and his smile stretches all the way across his face. He looks in my direction, and I give him two thumbs-up. It feels like the sun sparkles aren't just shining on the lake; they're in me too.

I start packing up our gear and hosing off the boat while Dad goes to the truck. But then I look over my shoulder and see Darren, his hands on his hips, his eyes stormy.

I glance back at Tai, try to concentrate on the pride filling my chest like a balloon. He holds up his winning fish and the ribbon Mr. Cooper gives him as I snap a picture he can send his friends, who are "definitely *not* going to believe this, like no way, not ever," he tells me.

Turns out Tai's pretty great at fishing. But I think whatever force brought us out to the middle of the lake ended up helping too. Today's clue makes six total. If we investigate clues one, three, and four and find they're real too, I'll feel like I'm doing what Amos wanted me to do when he was alive. I'll be tracking his evidence. But will I believe in his mystery? I still haven't *seen* a creature yet. I haven't experienced anything that anybody but Tai can see.

I shiver, looking back out over the lake. Tai and I both know what we felt. And if it was Amos's creature that pulled us away from the harmful algal blooms and toward the cleaner, deeper water, maybe there was a reason.

So why didn't it help Amos? If it has enough power to pull us halfway across the lake, how could it let him drown?

I don't understand everything I'm seeing. But looking for Amos's clues, and finding my own evidence, also makes me feel that what I can't know for absolute certain isn't exactly scary. The closer I get to it, the more I feel it's just a part of things, a mystery that needs to be there.

"Oh man," Tai says, coming up behind me, waving the

ribbon he got from Mr. Cooper. "I'm starving. I could really go for some *jiaozi* right about now."

"*Jiaozi?*" I ask. "What's that?"

"They're these amazing dumplings," Tai says. "I look forward to eating them whenever I go back to China, especially where my dad grew up in Beijing. I mean, there are great dumpling places in New York too, but there's something about the ones I get there that's just extra delicious."

"What do they taste like?" I don't think I've ever had a dumpling.

"So, there's this dough," Tai says. "It's kind of thick and really good, and it's wrapped around these pickled vegetables and meat, and boiled or steamed. Then there are sauces for dipping."

"Sounds great." Tai's description is making my stomach growl.

"Oh, it is," Tai says. "The food in China is my favorite by far."

Thinking about all the dishes I've never tasted makes me itch to go far away. Not forever, just long enough to taste new foods and see new places. "I think right now, you're probably going to have to settle for ice cream."

Tai sighs, then smiles. "I can deal with that."

Dad promised he'd take us to Swirls & Scoops to celebrate. It's definitely the best ice cream around, and it's only open in the summer. If you don't know what you're looking for, you might miss the little hut set back in the trees, with picnic tables spread out in the grass.

Dad parks the truck and walks ahead of us so he can catch up with Mr. and Mrs. Lafayette, sitting at one of the picnic tables. Mr. and Mrs. Lafayette are really old, and Dad's known them since he was a kid, hanging out with their grandkids.

While he talks, Tai and I stand off to the side of the line, checking out the menu, a list of flavors painted on a whiteboard.

"So I was asking my mom about Lake Tianchi," Tai says. "I wanted to figure out if it was formed by a glacier too. If it was, I thought maybe the creatures might be similar. Like they came from the same kind of magic."

"What'd she say?" I ask. I don't even need to look at this menu. I know it by heart.

"Get this," Tai says. "It used to be a *volcano*. So the actual lake is in this thing called a caldera. It's this big hole that gets made when a magma chamber in the volcano gets emptied out."

"Wow," I say. "That's crazy. How did a volcano turn into a lake? I mean, with the glacier, it kind of makes sense—it just melted—"

· "Yeah. So volcanic lakes get made when it rains and snows a bunch inside the hole left by the volcano," Tai explains. "And boom, there you have it—Lake Tianchi. No pun intended."

Amos loved puns. "Boom," I echo. "Sounds intense. It kind of happened all at once—the hole anyway. That's really different than a glacier."

"That's not the only difference," Tai says. "The monster—or monsters—in that lake sound kind of mean. They attack boats and fight with each other and stuff."

"The lake's actually twice as deep as Maple Lake, so who knows what's in there?" I say. "You should try to find some evidence of your own, next time you go visit your grandparents."

"Maybe I will," Tai says.

For just a moment, I picture myself on a different shore on the other side of the world, staring into a lake that used to be a volcano.

"So what are you getting?" Tai asks.

"My usual," I say. "Lemon sherbet with rainbow sprinkles."

Tai decides on Maple Moose Tracks. "Seems like as long as I'm in Vermont, I should try the most Vermont-y flavor available."

Just then, I see someone farther up ahead in line turn around and look right in Tai's direction: Darren. Then he looks at me. I can't quite read his expression.

We grab our cones, piled super high as usual, and find a spot at one of the picnic tables, not far from the Lafayettes.

"Yum," Tai says. "This is good stuff."

"It was made right here in Shoreland County," Dad says. "One of the bigger dairies started an ice cream business a few years ago."

That's when I see Darren standing up, moving slowly toward us.

"Hey," he says when he reaches our table. "Hi, Mr. Lago."

Dad pats the seat next to him at the picnic table. "Have a seat, Darren," he says.

For a while, Darren doesn't say anything, and it's kind of awkward. For me, at least. Dad and Tai don't seem too bothered; they're concentrating on their ice cream.

But then Darren breaks the silence. "You won the Maple Derby," he says to Tai.

"Beginner's luck," Tai says.

"Nice work," Darren says. But it doesn't sound quite like a compliment.

"Thanks." Tai slurps his Maple Moose Tracks.

"You know," Darren says, "that contest is supposed to

be for kids who are from here. Kids who have been fishing the lake all year. I don't know why you had to come up here anyway."

Dad looks sharply at Darren. "Watch it," he says. "Tai is a guest in Shoreland County. He's living here for now, and he has every right to do the derby."

Darren looks away, and I see his cheeks flush, his hands ball into fists at his sides. I can tell there's more he wants to say, but he won't. He knows he's already said the wrong thing. Tai just watches him warily, calm but coiled tight.

"I guess when you're spending all your time at the lake," Darren says, sneering just a little, "you don't have anything to do but practice fishing anyway."

Tai looks right at Darren, his muscles still tense, his jaw set. "There's actually a lot of other things to do," he says. His voice is low, measured, completely strong. "There's something wrong with Maple Lake, and people like my mom and Addie and I are trying to keep it healthy enough to still even have events like the Maple Derby."

I open my mouth to show Darren whose side I'm on, but Tai gets there first. "We've been researching pollution in the lake," he says. "Have you ever seen a harmful algal bloom?"

Darren looks away. "I don't know what that is," he says. His eyebrows wrinkle in confusion. He unclenches his fists and stuffs his hands in his pockets. "But how can the lake be polluted?"

"It just is," I say. "We're trying to figure out why. And by the way, a harmful algal bloom sort of just looks like green slime on the water."

"I don't get it," Darren says, looking at Tai. "You haven't even been here a month. How could you know anything about our lake?"

When Darren first started talking to us, there was a sharpness in his voice. Now that's gone, replaced with something else. Something uncertain and maybe kind of sad.

"Well, you just haven't met my mom," Tai says. "She knows about *all* bodies of water. Everywhere. I'm not kidding. We're talking serious nerd alert here." The words Tai says sound like him, but the voice doesn't. There's an edge I'm not used to hearing. He's shifted over to the end of the bench, his shoulders hunched, on guard.

Darren's face shifts. The pinched look melts away. "I guess I should look for those blooms," he says quietly.

"I know we just got here," Tai continues. "I'd never been to Vermont before this summer. But now we're just trying to figure out how to help Maple Lake."

It's easy to tell when someone's being totally honest. And Tai just always is. Maybe even Darren sees that.

"Look," Tai says. "I didn't even *like* science when I got

here. Thought I was in for the boring-est summer ever. Is *boring-est* a word?" He hooks his finger and thumb around his chin and purses his lips, thinking. Darren's lips turn up at the corners.

Tai shrugs and smiles. "Anyway, now even *I'm* kinda roped into this Maple Lake stuff, thanks to Addie. It's practically as addicting as this ice cream." Tai crunches into the cone and closes his eyes. "Mmmm," he says. "Science."

Then Darren laughs, and I have to hand it to Tai. I'm not sure anybody else could have made Darren Andrews go from half mad and super confused to laughing in less than five minutes. Maybe not even Amos.

Dad, who's been licking his ice cream, keeping a close eye on Darren, looks off in the distance, toward the mountains.

"Sometimes," he says to nobody in particular, "you just have to look past your own nose."

Chapter 15

When I get to the biological station, Tai's waiting at the door, rolling a soccer ball around under his foot. "Mom wants to talk to us," he says. "She wants to explain about that chemical that's polluting the lake. Starts with an *f*?"

"*Ph*," I say. "Phosphorus. But where's Mr. Dale?" Usually he's the one who walks us through the science of what we're doing on Maple Lake.

"He's around," Tai says. "Mom just said *she* wanted to tell us some stuff too. Be 'involved' in our 'education' or something."

Tai stays behind me as we walk inside. I can hear the soccer ball spinning on his finger and feel him lunge to catch it when it falls. Just before we get to Dr. Li's office, he stashes it behind a chair in the hallway.

I can feel nervousness, like a current, coursing through Tai as we open the office door. But whenever I see Dr. Li, I feel calm inside. Her voice is so steady, even when she's explaining complicated things. She moves quickly, but smoothly and quietly too, like there's a clear purpose for everything she does. I'm pretty sure there is. For someone who just got here, like Darren pointed out, she sure is working hard to help Maple Lake.

"Your next research assignment will build directly off our recent water sample results," Dr. Li says. "Repeated analyses distinctly show high levels of phosphorus, particularly after rainstorms when a lot of sediment has washed into the lake."

"That makes sense," I say.

"We'll be working hard to determine some root causes," Dr. Li continues. "There are many possibilities."

"I've read about some of them," I say. "How are we going to figure out what's causing the problem?"

"Well, one of the tricky things about science," Dr. Li says, "is that even though we can try our best to figure out the exact answer, sometimes we have to make some guesses too. It's a little bit of a mystery."

I'm definitely with her on that, even though I never realized it before.

"I'd like you to do some research specifically about

possible causes of phosphorus pollution based on what you know about industry and activity in this area," she says, "and present hypotheses to me. Mr. Dale can help as needed. Of course, Jake, Tasha, and I will be doing our own work with this, but it's good practice for you to give it a try also."

"Sounds good," I say. Tai looks at the floor.

"Tai?" Dr. Li says. She looks at him sharply. "You need to be involved as well. You're more than capable."

Tai nods, but he doesn't look at his mom. I watch his cheeks redden, and I think of the soccer ball hidden out in the hall.

I clear my throat. "Um. Dr. Li?" I ask. "Tai's been super involved. I'm—glad he's helping."

Tai looks up at me, surprise flashing in his eyes.

Dr. Li looks a little surprised too. "I'm glad to hear that," she says.

"He's really smart," I continue. "He was researching Maple Lake on his own the other day. He keeps track of all the water samples and helps me find testing sites on the GPS."

Dr. Li looks at Tai, and I see the beginnings of a smile around the corners of her mouth.

"Plus," I say, "did he tell you he won the Maple Derby? He caught the best fish of anyone on the lake."

"He did not tell me that," she says, obviously startled.

"But...keep up the good work." She puts her hand on Tai's shoulder, just for a moment, before walking out.

"Thanks," Tai whispers as we head to the break room to talk about our plan. "You want me to go give your mom a speech about your awesomeness? I totally could."

His words pierce a little. He probably doesn't realize how useful that might be. "I might hold you to that," I whisper back. "Why didn't you tell your mom about the Maple Derby?"

Tai shrugs. "I didn't think she'd care."

"I think she kind of did," I say.

In the break room, instead of discussing causes of phosphorus pollution, like we're supposed to, we end up deciding we need to plan our investigation of clue number one first.

Tai's pretty excited about it. When I think about my first glance at him—hopping around in freezing Maple Lake when most people wouldn't dare go in—I can kind of see why. This clue is all about adventure.

"Are you good at sneaking out at night?" he asks.

"Well...I don't know," I say.

"C'mon, you know everything," Tai says.

I laugh. "I guess I don't have enough evidence to draw a conclusion."

"Is that your fancy scientist way of saying you've never tried?" Tai asks.

"Um, okay, yes." I'm definitely a little nervous about that. But clue number one has to happen with a full moon, and thanks to Mr. Dale and his charts, I know we're finally coming up on one tonight.

And I need to know whether Amos was right.

I look over the dates, times, and locations for each of my observations and review our data about harmful algal bloom sightings. If there really is a creature, why would it suddenly try to be seen after hiding for so long? And why by *me*?

I wonder: Is magic evidence the same as scientific evidence? Could there really be some magical creature trying to tell us what science can't? Or help us understand what we're seeing? If Maple Lake stays polluted and we can't figure out how to fix it, will the creature die?

—

The day at the biological station seems to drag on while Tai and I wait for darkness and the full moon and clue number one. We make a plan to meet on our bikes at eleven p.m., and I promise Tai a headlamp. Apparently you don't really need one in Brooklyn, because of all the lights even at night. Finally, after dinner's over and I've washed and dried the dishes and Dad's moved away from the stack of bills on the kitchen table and Mama's left for work, I lie in bed, watching darkness settle outside the window. I'm too excited to fall asleep.

I have no idea how Amos snuck out as quietly as he must have when he researched this clue; maybe he did it on a night I was sleeping over at Liza's.

When I'm sure Dad's asleep, I push the window up, then carefully remove the outside screen before pulling the window back down. It squeaks— *shoot*—and I pause, holding my breath, waiting for Dad to rustle around, call my name. He doesn't. Everything's silent, except for the crickets singing their tinny songs.

By the time the full moon comes, night isn't really even itself anymore. It's kind of blue instead of black, and it glows. I'd forgotten how much I can see under a full moon. It doesn't feel too scary to tiptoe with my bike through the grass in the opposite direction of the Jensens' yard, praying their German shepherds stay quiet. For some reason, luckily, they do. Maybe they can't hear me over the crickets.

Tai and I meet at the corner where Route 3 intersects with my road, just up from Maple Lake. We don't say much at all, pedaling as fast as we can toward the beach.

I'm glad I brought my sweatshirt; it's always chillier by the water. Tai and I stand side by side on the sand, looking out at the dark lake. The moon hangs over our heads, a silent jewel. Waves splash at our feet. We wait.

"So, clue number one," Tai says. "The drum sound. Not sure on your thoughts here, but so far it kinda still sounds like water to me."

"Shhh," I say. "Wait a little longer."

I close my eyes. That warm feeling spreads again, and then comes the pressure against my arms, reminding me he's there. I hold the warmth. *Listen*, says a voice inside, maybe mine or maybe Amos's. *Listen closely.* The waves tumble in one after the other.

———

A snatch of memory comes: Amos and I, when we were maybe eight, in the boat with Dad. We'd been holding our rods over the sides while Dad rigged up some jigs, hoping to catch a trout or two. Suddenly Amos's rod jerked down, and Dad rushed over to help him stay steady and reel in.

"*I've got it, Addie, I've got it!*" Amos yelled. "*It's really big too!*"

I set my rod down and went over to Amos's side. Silver fins flashed under the surface—a fish, fighting hard. *Why does Amos always catch the good ones?* I remember thinking.

Dad braced his feet against the boat, supporting Amos's back. The rod bent, then snapped up. "*More drag!*" Dad shouted. He fiddled with the rod as Amos pulled. Then the

176

line popped up and the rod straightened. Amos ricocheted back into Dad's arms. I looked into the water and saw a silver tail, flickering away into the deep.

"*I lost it*," Amos said, his voice full of hurt and wonder. "*It's gone.*"

Dad patted Amos on the shoulder. "*It happens, son. It's okay.*"

"*That was such a big fish too.*" Amos's voice started to crack. "*I could really tell.*"

Inside, I felt sour relief creep through my chest. "*You pulled up too fast,*" I said.

Amos wiped his hand across his eyes. His top lip quivered.

For one horrible second, I wanted him to cry.

But when he looked at me, I couldn't stay so mean. "*It's okay,*" I said. "*Don't feel bad.*" I wrapped my arms around him and, as the evening chill set in, felt surrounded by warmth.

⟋

I wrap my arms around my own waist now and pull, trying to lift myself off the ground like he used to. But it doesn't work. I squeeze until my fingernails pierce my sides and still my feet stick, stone-heavy, right where they are. Amos and I didn't get along perfectly all the time. But now that he's gone, I'd rather think about the times we did, instead of what I wish I could change.

I didn't mean to be jealous, I think now. I want to reach back into that memory, reset the drag on Amos's rod, keep that fish. Watch him lift it out of the water, thrashing and shimmering. Let Dad's pride drown everything else out, even me. If I'd known how little time Amos would have, I would have done that. I'd have done so much more.

The waves roll in. *I'm listening*, I think.

Another sound, then the smash of cymbals. I open my eyes. The waves look the same. But I'm positive there's something else in their sound.

I hear the low pound of a drum, hollow and round. There's a rhythm to it—first the splash of water, followed by those clanging cymbals, then a deep beat.

Tai pokes me. "I hear it." His eyes are wide open, staring at the water. "Look," he says, pointing.

Out in the middle of the lake, silver sparkles rise and fall. A shape seems to emerge—a tail?—then scatters apart and slips underwater. My breath catches in my throat.

Tai just shakes his head. "Wow."

I can't breathe. I can't move. All I can do is watch.

Until, all of a sudden, it stops. The water goes perfectly still. Even the waves fall silent, frozen in midair. I'm frozen too, waiting to see if it comes back.

"Was that it?" Tai whispers.

When I finally take a breath, the waves roll in again, but soft and quiet like before. The music's gone.

"That was it," I say, my voice flat.

———

Before we get back on our bikes, I pull the notebook out. With such a bright moon, I don't even need to use the flashlight on my phone to see it. I can't write fast enough.

"Don't forget to write about that silver pattern," Tai says. "That was really cool."

"Didn't it kind of look like a tail to you?" I ask. "Moving in and out of the water?"

"Definitely could have been a tail," Tai says.

I remember the fish Amos never caught, flashing through the water, the water closing over it. A lake can hold so many secrets.

Chapter 16

I guess I was paying too much attention to the cymbals, because I never felt my phone buzz in my pocket. When I reach for it, I see three texts from Dad, all sent in the last fifteen minutes.

Where are you

Calling Mama now

Mama's heading home, calling police, please answer

"No!" I shout, pressing my palm into my forehead. My heart races. I fumble with the phone—

Coming home now

Don't call police I'm fine

"Your dad woke up?" Tai says. "Wow. That sucks."

"You're telling me," I say. "My parents will be so mad."

Even though I'm annoyed, I feel guilty too. I know they have a right to be upset.

"You want me to come in with you?" Tai asks. "Try to explain?"

"No," I say. "Please don't come in." It's hard to think about the scene Mama will make when she sees me. "Let's just get back fast."

———

At home, I turn the knob quietly, even though I know Dad's awake and Mama's car is already in the driveway. I wonder if they'll dock her pay for leaving in the middle of a shift. I wonder what she said—*an emergency. My daughter.* Everybody must have been thinking: *Not again.* My stomach flip-flops, and I feel sick.

I tiptoe into the living room. Maybe some small part of me thinks that if I don't make noise, they'll forget I snuck out. Forget I scared them to death. I'll go into the living room and they'll be watching TV, eating microwave popcorn. Mama will scoot over on the couch and pat the warm spot next to her and tell me to snuggle in, here's a blanket. *Maybe it will be okay.*

But the first thing I see is Mama's face, wet with tears. Dad's sitting beside her, one hand on her back, the other over his eyes.

I stand perfectly still. When Mama sees me, she starts crying for real, and that makes Dad move his hand away from his eyes and stand up like he's about to say something. Instead, he sits back down and puts his face back in his hands. His shoulders shake.

It is so weird to watch my parents cry. The last time was at Amos's funeral. And that wasn't as weird because I was crying too. I can go back to the memory of that day, but I can't stay very long. It just comes in flashes. The casket, shiny polished wood. His face, unspeaking. Someone's voice telling me *It's okay, you can touch him*, and me wanting to hit the voice because this wasn't really *him*. The preacher opening his Bible, then closing it. Not saying anything for a long, long time. Muffled cries and tissues. So many casseroles afterward, and people telling me to eat even though I didn't want to, not ever again. And Mama and Dad, crumpled against each other.

"I'm okay, you guys," I say, and that makes Mama cry harder. She blows her nose and looks right at me.

"You don't get to do this," Mama says. "Do you have any idea what we—" She stops, buries her face in her hands.

"Okay, I'm sorry, but—"

Dad cuts me off. "If you're going to sneak out, shouldn't you at least have your phone on you?"

"I *did* have it, I . . ." But I stop then and look at the floor.

I know *having* it isn't really the point if I'm not going to listen for it.

"We bought you that phone for a reason," Dad says. "So we wouldn't have to wonder where you were, the way we had to wonder about—" Then he stops too, shakes his head. "What were you thinking, Addie?"

Dad, Mama, me, we all just sit there with springs and wires popping out of our bodies. Anger fizzles inside me, a spitting current. They're going to worry about me too much forever now. Maybe this is what happens when someone dies. A thing inside everyone else breaks and you just have to know you'll never really be able to fix it.

I feel the whale tooth cutting into my pocket, a reminder of everything I lost. And all I have left. And just then, I feel that warmth surround me.

I don't feel like I have very much to lose when I tell them about Amos and the creature. Maybe when Mama hears his name, she'll cry harder. Maybe Dad will clench his jaw and hold up his hand, tell me to stop talking. But then again, maybe they'll listen. Because it's either that, or keep on breaking.

I take a deep breath. "I was working on a project for Amos." The warmth gets stronger, holding tight.

Mama's face stills then and she looks up, the crumpled tissue rolling from her hand to the floor. Her eyes find mine.

It's hard to look at her—at her forehead, full of lines so deep now they look like the furrows in Uncle Mark's fields.

But I do look at her. I keep going. "He believed something about the lake—he thought there was…something living down there. He wanted to prove it."

"*Something?*" Dad says. "Something, like what?"

"Like a creature," I say.

"A *creature?*" Dad's voice cracks roughly. "What kind of creature?"

I squirm under Dad's gaze. "You know how we read those stories growing up, like about mysterious animals or…magical *things* living in the woods and the water? Amos thought there could be something like that in Maple Lake."

Mama looks up at the ceiling and sighs. "Nothing could beat his imagination," she says. Then she looks at me. "I suppose he thought only he could see it?"

"It had more to do with believing," I say. "I think he figured if you believed in it, you'd see it. He wanted me to help him investigate before he—" I swallow the lump in my throat. "Before he died. I didn't pay much attention at first, but now I'm kind of trying to go back and see if his clues were real."

"And that's why you snuck out of the house in the middle of the night?" Mama asks, shaking her head. "To find a magical creature?"

Then her eyes get really big. She doesn't have to say anything out loud; I see everything in her eyes. Amos sneaking out. The cold, the ice, the slipping and cracking. She knows now what he was looking for.

The air around us freezes, and I shiver in the summer heat. I need to keep talking, to just answer Mama's question like I don't know what she just realized.

"That's, um—that's most of it," I say. "I mean, I can see how it sounds kind of crazy. But it's not just about finding a creature. I think the pollution in the lake might be related. And I want to figure out how."

Mama just looks at me, and I can tell it isn't anger that makes her eyes flare like sparklers, then go dim. It's something else. Sadness, maybe.

"Well," Dad says, his voice hard and heavy. "You're grounded. All week. I bring you to the biological station, your mother or I pick you up, but otherwise you stay in your room. No library, no trips to the ice cream shop or Teddy's, no bike rides. And no calf. That's it."

"But Liza needs me!" I say. "Why do you want to punish her too?"

"Your cousin will be fine," Dad says. "She knows what she's doing. Besides, I don't think you've been going to the farm nearly as much as she expected you to."

I stare at the ground, my cheeks puffed out, my eyes

burning. Dad's right, and it's not like Liza's going to be sympathetic when she finds out I can't help with Rascal because I was out at Maple Lake.

At least I can still go to the biological station—I really need to get back to my research.

Dad stands up and puts his hand on my shoulder. Its heavy weight rests there. "Don't ever do that again," he says quietly. Then he leaves the room.

Mama surprises me then. She leans forward and takes my face in her hands. And even though her eyes are still wet, she smiles. It almost feels like that time in the lake when she held my face and said, "My little girl." Now, she strokes my hair. And then, so sadly I feel the rest of my heart flop out and slither away, she says: "Don't you know there isn't such a thing as magic?"

I look down at the floor, blinking back tears.

Chapter 17

Getting grounded meant I had lots of time alone in my room to go back over Amos's clues and my own notes. It helped soothe the sting of knowing that Mama and Dad didn't believe me.

Still, being stuck at home slowed the week down. I texted Liza to explain why I couldn't come to the barn, at least sort of, but I definitely left out some of the details. Like all the ones about Maple Lake. So basically, I just told her I was grounded. It took her a while to text back and when she did, she just wrote: OK. She didn't even ask why.

Now it's time for our Fourth of July dinner at her house, and I try to calm the flutter in my chest. Tai's coming with us and I just want things to go well.

"Addie, can you get the maple pudding?" Mama calls.

She's packing her work clothes in a plastic bag so she can leave for her late shift straight from Aunt Mary and Uncle Mark's.

Maple pudding's just as good as it sounds: maple syrup, milk, eggs, and vanilla stirred together and heated, then cooled to room temperature until it's light as air and creamy sweet.

As I carry the bowl toward the front door, I realize this is the first dish Mama's made for one of Aunt Mary's dinners since Amos died. She always used to bring something— chicken rice casserole, spinach salad when we could pick it fresh in the garden—but afterward, she just brought herself. And even then, just barely.

So I feel a lightness inside when I bring the maple pudding out to the truck and set it down carefully next to me on the seat. Dad turns the key and Mama checks her hair in the mirror, patting wisps into place.

When we pull in, Tai's already waiting outside. He jogs up to the truck, smiling.

I push the door open for him. As soon as he hops in, he shakes Mama's hand. "Hi, Mrs. Lago. I'm Tai." Then he shakes Dad's hand too.

"Good to see you again, son," Dad says, but he kind of chokes on the last word. Mama's eyes flash. I know how it feels to say something you didn't really mean to say, or didn't expect to hurt as much as it does. Leaves you feeling bumped and bruised.

We pull onto the road that bends around Maple Lake and up toward Liza's house. In late-afternoon sunshine, the lake sparkles like someone threw millions of coins right on the surface and made them float.

When we pull into Liza's driveway, DeeDee and Sammie run out. As soon as Dad puts the truck in park, they're on it, slapping their little hands against the windows. Aunt Mary rushes out, holding Baby Katy. "Girls, get away from there! Let Uncle Bruce out." Bumble howls.

"It's loud here," I say to Tai. "But it's fun."

"Looks like it." Tai hops out of the truck and the little girls stare.

"Who *are* you?" That's DeeDee, the outgoing one.

"I'm Tai." He sticks his hand out for DeeDee to shake. "Who are *you?*"

"I'm DeeDee. And this is my sister Sammie." Sammie's eyeing Tai suspiciously, arms crossed on her chest. She's always shy around new people.

"Pleased to meet you both," Tai says. "Do you know what I can do?"

"What?" DeeDee asks. She's got her hands on her hips.

"I can walk on my hands. Ever seen anyone do that?"

"You *cannot*," DeeDee says. "Feet are for walking, not hands."

Tai shrugs. "Well, watch this." And then he flips up into an easy handstand, moves forward a few steps, and flops down. "See?"

DeeDee and Sammie both stare, their jaws hanging open. Sammie's got her arms uncrossed now.

A split second later, they're hanging on Tai: "I want to do it! Teach me!" One at a time, Tai helps them flip over and steadies their ankles as they move their hands forward. He gently lowers their legs and they pop back up, shrieking. "Again! Again!"

Aunt Mary smiles. "You're pretty good with little kids," she says. But Mama just stares and clutches Dad's elbow.

"Come on, Laura," Aunt Mary says gently. "Get yourselves inside. Did you bring maple pudding? Oh, you *did*! Best news I've heard all day."

Mama turns to follow her. She moves slowly, like a robot, looking over her shoulder at Tai with DeeDee and Sammie.

I know what she sees. Anyone who knew him would. The only other person who made DeeDee and Sammie giggle like that, the one who always got them riled up with freeze tag and magic tricks and tickle-fests, was Amos.

It's so warm outside that Aunt Mary decides to move us all out onto her two big picnic tables in the backyard. Tai and I help her pin tablecloths down and set plates and cups out. I don't ask where Liza is or why she hasn't come out to say hi yet, because I'm pretty sure she's now officially one hundred percent mad at me.

Aunt Mary takes Baby Katy inside for a diaper change and Tai and I sit on the grass. Mama and Dad walk arm in arm at the edges of Uncle Mark's pasture, where the little stream of water that feeds into the Pine River begins. They're out of earshot, but I see their heads tilted toward each other, Mama's lips moving.

"So wait a second, Addie," Tai says. He's found a rubber ball in the yard and rolls it under his ankles, back and forth. "Your dad and your uncle Mark are brothers, right?"

"Yup," I say.

"So how did they decide who would get the farm?" Tai dribbles the ball a little.

"Oh," I explain. "My dad is older, but he actually didn't want to farm."

"Really?" Tai asks. "Why not? It seems fun."

"It *can* be fun," I say. "But not always. It's tough too. Uncle Mark and Aunt Mary work really hard."

"It seems like a lot to keep up," Tai says, looking around

at the fields spreading out past the lawn, at the barn and silo and implement sheds.

"Farming isn't even their only job," I say. "They always say nobody can make a living from a small farm anymore, that it's hard enough even with other jobs on top."

"Wow," Tai says. "So what else do they do besides all of this?"

"Aunt Mary's a teacher," I say. "Third grade. Uncle Mark grows hay and corn for feed, and runs the sugaring operation."

"What's sugaring?" Tai asks. "I mean, it sounds delicious."

"Making maple syrup." I point to the long blue sap lines running through the woods at the edge of the field. "Those all carry sap from maple trees to the sugarhouse, where it goes through an evaporator."

In the earliest part of spring, Uncle Mark likes to hang just one bucket from a tap in the trunk of the big maple in their yard and let us dip sap out of it with a ladle. The liquid runs clear and thin as water, but there's this hint of sweetness underneath. And you know that if you just wait, if you boil it long enough, the sweetness will grow.

"They sound...really busy," Tai says. Leaning back on his arms, he punches a foot forward to kick the ball my way, and I lob it back.

"I mean, my parents work really hard too," I say.

"Obviously. But my dad just always wanted to do something different. He likes building things. That's why he works for a builder. He can start with bare ground and make a whole house."

Tai's eyes widen. "That's awesome."

A little firecracker of pride sparks in my chest. "Yeah. It is."

I hear the screen door slam. It's Liza, holding her sketchbook.

"Hey," she says. "Long time no see." The air feels heavy, thick enough to cut.

"I know." I look down at the ground.

"Hard to keep this one out of trouble," Tai says.

Liza walks right up to Tai. "You got that right. I'm Liza."

"It's great to meet you," Tai says. "I'm Tai. And I happen to love art. Can I see what you're drawing?"

Surprise flickers in Liza's eyes. She flashes a shy smile, but holds the book close to her chest. "Um," she says. "I'm not finished yet."

"Oh, come on," Tai says. "I promise I'll like it."

The smile widens. "Let's wait till I'm done," Liza says.

"Can you at least say what you're drawing? A house? A tree? *Me*—your unsuspecting victim?" Tai's got his hands on his hips; he's keeping his distance.

But now Liza's laughing. "Okay, fine," she says, and

holds the sketchbook out. But she gives me such a sharp look I shrink back while Tai leans in to see.

He sucks his breath in a low whistle. "Nice," he says. "Very nice."

Liza blushes and snatches the sketchbook away before I can get a good look.

"Come on," I say. "You have to show me now too."

Liza narrows her eyes, but she folds a page back after all. I shriek a little when I see it: it's Rascal. Somehow Liza managed to get all her crazy patterns exactly right.

"It's perfect!" I say, and I mean it. "Are you entering this in the Shoreland Art Show too?"

"It doesn't have a whole lot to do with moon phases," Liza says. "So no."

Her voice crackles, jagged as broken ice.

———

In the barn, Tai recognizes Rascal right away.

"Those are some crazy-cool markings," he says. "It's almost like an artist designed her."

Liza smiles and hooks a halter around Rascal's head, leading her out of the stall. Then she hands the rope to me. "Want to practice?" she asks. Now her voice sounds cautious. Maybe a little hopeful. But as soon as she hands me the rope, she steps back, far enough to put some space between us.

I really need to. I didn't work with Rascal at all when I was grounded, and I know I wasn't going to the farm enough before that either. But maybe now is my chance to show Liza I can still help. I take the rope and pull, but nothing happens. Rascal stands still as a rock.

"Hold the halter rope right up next to her head," Liza says. "You have to do that if you want her to follow your lead."

I shift my hands up the rope, hold tight, and pull. Still, Rascal digs her heels in. I know I'll have to lead her during the fair, but I have no idea how. I should've practiced more. But with everything to investigate on Maple Lake, I just—haven't thought about Rascal as much as I should have.

"Don't pull so tight," Liza says. "Let it go a little."

I release some of the rope.

"Now bring back some of the tension, but not too much," Liza says. "And as soon as she takes a step forward, release it again. That will make her want to keep going."

Bit by bit, Rascal and I move forward.

"Nice!" Tai says.

"Okay," Liza says. "Now stop her, and pose her. Do you remember how her legs are supposed to look?"

I stop walking and gently nudge Rascal's back legs so they're evenly spaced.

"Not bad," Liza says. "I think you'll be ready for the ring pretty soon. Not like you have much time."

I wince. Hearing Liza say the words out loud, reminding me I've spent much less time with Rascal than I should have, stings.

"You're getting there!" I turn my head toward Uncle Mark's voice. I didn't even realize he, Aunt Mary, and Grandpa had slipped into the barn and were watching us work. Even Baby Katy's been quiet, sucking her thumb as she rides on her dad's shoulders. Through the open barn door, I see DeeDee and Sammie pushing each other on the tire swing outside.

I don't think I'll ever be too old to run over to Grandpa as soon as I see him, which is exactly what I do. "Addie Paddie," he says, then tugs my ponytail and smiles.

"Grandpa, Uncle Mark, this is my friend Tai," I say. "I wanted to show him the farm." Grandpa and Uncle Mark take turns shaking Tai's hand.

"We brought you girls a little something," Aunt Mary says. She walks toward us with her hands behind her back, and Uncle Mark follows; I can tell he's trying to squish his smile smaller than it wants to be.

I walk Rascal back to her pen and let her in, slipping the halter off.

"What is it?" Liza asks.

Aunt Mary brings her hands forward and shows us a beautiful box made of polished wood, with our names— *Addie and Liza*—etched with a wood burner on the front.

I let out a little gasp. Liza moves closer to me and squeezes my hand.

"It's your show box," Uncle Mark says. "For your brushes, polish, fly spray, clippers, that kind of thing." He scratches the back of his neck, his eyes on the floor, his smile still working to stretch past itself. I wish he would let it.

"Your uncle Mark made it," Aunt Mary says, "and I etched your names into it. Do you like it?"

"I love it," I say, and I throw my arms around Aunt Mary's neck while Liza hugs her dad. Then we switch.

There in the barn, for a second at least, everything feels okay. Liza doesn't wish I'd stay away from Maple Lake. I don't feel bad for not coming over as much as she thinks I should or for wanting to go look for clues instead. It even feels, for just a second, like Amos is there with us, squeezing our shoulders.

"Hey," Liza says softly, touching my elbow. "You'll come to the art judging, right? It's right before the calf show, so you just have to meet me a little early."

"I'll be there," I say. Liza lets herself smile then, and I feel my shoulders relax.

"Then afterward, we can go back to the animal barn," she says, her voice rising. She's letting herself get excited again, and I feel my insides churn with worry. What if I let her down? "The judges will come through there too during the afternoon and make sure our calves are well-behaved and the areas are neat."

"Good plan, girls," Uncle Mark says, and then he turns toward Tai. "Ready to learn how to milk?"

"Definitely!" Tai's so excited, he's bouncing on the balls of his feet.

"Well, let's go, then," Uncle Mark says. "Time for the tour."

We head over toward the big pasture, where the cows graze.

"They get lots of the green stuff," he says, "and fresh water, too." He points out the creek that runs right along the fence line. Amos and Liza and I used to sneak in there to cool our feet on the hottest summer days.

When we get into the milking parlor, Tai just stares. "Wow," he says. "I've never seen so many cows in one place." I blink, and the cows I've grown up knowing and watching and sometimes helping to milk look different somehow. New. I listen as Uncle Mark tells Tai about wiping down each cow's udder with iodine and water, then placing the prongs of the machines on them. The milking starts up with sucking, hissing sounds as the machines pull milk out of the cows and push it through tubes into the bulk tank, where it's cooled and collected and sent to a processing plant to be pasteurized, bottled, and shipped to stores.

"Addie said you wanted to learn to milk by hand," Uncle Mark says. "I saved a cow for you—Bess. She's a sweetheart." We walk down to the end of the milking parlor, where Grandpa places a small stool next to Bess and lowers himself onto it. She turns her head and looks at us with the deepest, brownest eyes.

Grandpa's been milking his whole life, and it's fun to see how fast his hands work. Quickly, he wraps his thumb and forefinger around one of Bess's teats, then squeezes the rest of his fingers down, letting the first few squirts of milk fall to the floor before placing a metal bucket underneath to catch the rest.

Then he gets off the stool and motions to Tai, who sits down. Grandpa guides Tai's hands, showing him how to position his fingers just right. It's not as easy as people might think; I'm not the best at it. Finally, though, after a lot of tugging, Tai gets his first few drops of milk out.

"This is so cool!" he yelps. Grandpa and Uncle Mark laugh.

I pull out my phone and snap a couple of pictures and a

short video. "What are your friends back in New York City going to say?" I ask.

"They're going to be super jealous," Tai says. "Guaranteed."

When we leave the milking parlor, I can smell the hamburgers Aunt Mary's grilling.

Tai leans in and whispers, horrified, "We're not going to be eating a cow they used to milk, are we?"

"No way," I say, laughing. "But they do raise steers—those are male cows, by the way, no udders—for meat. The hamburger you're about to eat definitely didn't come from a store."

"I—guess that's good," Tai says. "Kind of weird, though."

"Why?" I ask.

"Maybe I've just never thought that hard about what cows look like *before* they—you know. Become hamburgers."

"Most people probably don't."

A breeze carries the smells of meat and fire right over to us, and Tai shrugs. "I guess they should," he says, "but in the meantime—I'm hungry."

"Same here," I say. "They'll be ready soon."

Tai looks around, eyeing the fields and the mountains beyond. "Hey, what's that pond?"

Uncle Mark looks where he's pointing, just past the

barn. "Oh," he laughs. "That's not exactly a pond. Not one you'd want to swim in anyway. That's our manure pit."

Tai wrinkles his nose. "Seriously?"

"Well, we have to put it somewhere," Uncle Mark explains. "Where there are cows, there's manure. It actually comes in handy as a fertilizer. Lots of phosphorus in there—helps the hay and corn grow!"

Tai and I both stop walking. "Did you say phosphorus?" I ask Uncle Mark.

"Yup," he says. "Potassium and nitrogen too. Really keeps the soil rich. We just have to store it somewhere until we can spread it on the fields."

"Oh, um—okay. Right. Got it," I say. *Don't say anything, don't say anything,* I silently plead as I glance at Tai, who looks as surprised as I feel. I've known about the manure pit forever, and I knew it got spread on the fields, but I never knew it had phosphorus in it. I never even knew what phosphorus was until this summer. And how can it be bad for the lake, if it's good for the fields?

Maybe Tai and I are jumping to conclusions just because we heard the same word twice. Uncle Mark and Aunt Mary would never hurt Maple Lake, and their manure pit is miles away from the water. But suddenly, I'm not hungry anymore.

Chapter 18

The next day when I arrive at the biological station, I head into the break room and find Tai and Dr. Li sitting there, talking quietly. They don't look up; I don't think they see me.

Tai's looking at his mom while he talks. He's holding his hands out in front of him, palms open. I hear little snippets of what he says: "...*really want to do it*" and "*I like this too, but...*" And Dr. Li's listening. Nodding. She reaches up with one hand and gently smooths down a piece of Tai's hair that's sticking up.

Slowly, I back out of the room and head to the lobby. I don't want to interrupt their conversation, so I spend time studying the diorama of Maple Lake, surrounded by miniature versions of Bevel Mountain and Mount Mann. This version of the lake is perfectly flat and smooth. No waves. Nothing under the surface.

I hear footsteps and turn to see Tai heading down the hallway toward the lobby.

"Oh, Addie!" he says. "You're here."

"Hey, um—I was doing some more research last night." I really want to ask Tai what his conversation with his mom was about, but I'm also super worried about what Uncle Mark said... and what I read.

"So was I," he says. "Let's go to the computer lab."

We pull up sites we each looked at last night, and new ones too. Pretty soon we're tripping over each other's sentences.

"Did you see this one about agricultural runoff—"

"This one talks about industrial farms, though—"

"But this one talks about smaller farms too—"

"Wow, did you know one cow produces sixty-five pounds of poop a day? That means Uncle Mark and Aunt Mary have to deal with—"

We must have gotten a little loud, because pretty soon Dr. Li and Mr. Dale are standing in the doorway. "What's going on?" Dr. Li asks.

I want so badly to just say "Nothing." But Dr. Li might actually have a quick answer for the question I want to ask most—*Is this my family's fault?*

"We visited my uncle last night," I say.

"Yes," Dr. Li says. "Tai had a great time—thanks again for inviting him. I was sorry I had to work late, but I'm just pleased Tai's taking such an interest in local activities." Her voice sounds softer than it did in the beginning when I first would hear her talking to him, and I catch him smiling in her direction.

"The thing is—my uncle said something really weird." I twist my hands together, squeezing my fingers until I can barely feel them.

"What's that?" Dr. Li cocks her head to one side. Tai must not have told her. I'm thankful to him for that.

"Well, remember how you were asking us to research causes of phosphorus pollution?" I ask.

Dr. Li nods. In her eyes I see a tiny bit of worry, but she also seems so safe somehow. Like just the right person to talk to.

"Well, um...my uncle Mark said his cows' manure is great for spreading on the fields because it has phosphorus in it. Is that—is that the same kind of phosphorus you're saying is bad for Maple Lake?" My heart thumps against my ribs; I know that must be the dumbest question ever. *Is phosphorus phosphorus?* I just want so badly for her to say no. For her to laugh and say "Oh no, of course not, don't worry."

But instead, she sighs and looks at Mr. Dale. They both come in and pull up chairs next to Tai and me.

"We were concerned about this," Mr. Dale says.

"Yes," Dr. Li says. "This phosphorus from farms could contribute to the problem."

Heat rises in my face.

Maybe Dr. Li can tell I'm nervous, because her voice becomes even gentler when she continues speaking. "First of all, Addie, I want you to know that nobody's saying farms are the *only* cause of pollution in Maple Lake. People who don't live on farms can help prevent water pollution too, and Mr. Dale will have you research that."

"Okay," I say, but I can tell Dr. Li isn't quite finished. There must be some reason she's pinched her lips together, her eyebrows wrinkling.

"Still, this is a heavily agricultural area and there isn't as much urban development, so we do have to look at the role farms play," Dr. Li continues. She sighs. "Tasha and Jake have been pulling up articles about waterway pollution from farms in other parts of the state, and I hoped that wasn't happening here. I know how vital farms are to the local economy. But over time, under certain conditions, even smaller farms can have a negative impact."

"But my aunt and uncle's farm couldn't be part of the problem," I say. "It's so far away from Maple Lake."

Dr. Li unrolls a map on the table between us. "I know you've learned a little about watersheds, but have you ever seen a topographic map before, Addie?" she asks.

I remember Mr. Dale teaching us about different kinds of maps. This one's mostly green, with squiggly brown and blue lines running all over it, and the big blue blob of Maple Lake.

"You probably know, then," Dr. Li says, "that topographic maps show physical features in a landscape—like lakes and rivers. They also show elevation, which is important in a place like this that has so many mountains."

I can see how the squiggly brown lines seem to lift Mount Mann and Bevel Mountain up from the page, showing their height above the lake.

"Can you find your aunt and uncle's farm on this map?" Dr. Li asks.

It takes me a little longer than it would on a regular map, because it's harder to see the roads and the town names, but eventually I find where the farm would be. Dr. Li leans over with a pencil and lightly circles the spot I've pointed out.

"Jake and Tasha have analyzed the numbers we've found so far," she says, "and it looks like the highest phosphorus concentrations in the lake are found near the mouth of the Pine River. Can you find the Pine River on this map?"

It doesn't take me long to locate the point at which it

spills into Maple Lake, and I begin tracing my finger up the winding blue line.

"Keep following that line," Dr. Li says gently. "Where does the Pine River originate? Can you find the smaller creeks that feed into it?"

I know where this is going. I can already see it. Part of me just wants to take my finger off the map, but I know that if I do that, it won't stop what's happening to Maple Lake. It's better to know for sure.

I can feel my heart tighten as the Pine River narrows into the skinniest blue line, no wider on the map than a strand of my hair: Black Creek. The same Black Creek that starts way up in Uncle Mark and Aunt Mary's pastures. The same creek the cows drink from.

"But that doesn't have to mean anything," I say. "There are lots of other farms. The manure pit Tai noticed isn't right by the stream."

"It doesn't have to be," Dr. Li says. "Phosphorus attaches to the soil or is consumed by plants during the growing season, and rain can carry soil to the creek bed."

"But lots of farmers have manure pits," I say, my heart racing.

"You're right, it's not just your family's farm," Dr. Li says. "And I realize theirs is smaller than many of the farms in the county. But the Pine River does originate up near where many of Shoreland County's smaller farms are located, and it flows into a part of Maple Lake that's shallower."

"Shallow isn't good, right?" I ask. "My parents always said Maple Lake stayed clean because it was deep."

"Yes," Dr. Li says. "Those shallow parts I mentioned are also warmer, supporting more plant life, including algae that thrives on phosphorus."

"This still doesn't make sense, though," I say. "The farms have been there forever—well, for a long time. Why would this just be happening now?"

"Well, you're right about Maple Lake being mostly deep," Dr. Li says. "That depth helps it stay clean. It takes a long time for phosphorus to build up. But as some of the farmers increase the size of their herds, and struggle to keep pace with crop demands, it gets worse."

"So we'll just put up a fence," I say. "That can keep the soil from going into the creek."

"A fence wouldn't be quite enough," Dr. Li says. "But there are a variety of different strategies a farmer can use." She talks about something called a buffer zone of grass that sits between a farm field and a stream. She says that tilling fields less, covering manure and keeping it far away from water, and installing biodigesters to compost manure can help. While she talks, my mind clouds. Some of her words sound like static. Should I even have mentioned the farm? But then again, wouldn't Dr. Li have figured it out anyway?

"It's really about changing a larger system," Dr. Li says. "As we make more demands of the land, we have to put practices in place to protect it."

"That sounds like a lot," I say. My tongue feels thick, my throat dry. "I mean—how much will it all cost?"

Dr. Li clears her throat. "That's a great question, Addie. Some state funds do exist to help farmers implement environmentally friendly practices. But—" She pauses and looks at Mr. Dale, who then clears *his* throat.

"It's...well...it's not necessarily going to be easy," he says. "We can't promise the changes won't cost farmers anything."

Mr. Dale leans forward and makes a steeple with his hands. "Addie," he says, "I know news like this would be a big deal not just for your family, but for lots of families in Shoreland County. I take that very seriously." He looks up at Dr. Li. "*We* take that very seriously."

Dr. Li nods. "We really do."

I slump back in my chair. All kinds of feelings swirl around inside. I feel ashamed that my family has probably played a part in hurting Maple Lake, but I'm scared too. I've slept over at Liza's house enough to hear Uncle Mark and Aunt Mary in the kitchen, talking about bills after they think everyone else has fallen asleep. I watched Liza once, straining to hear their voices through a heating vent. Her lips pinched up in a straight line; her eyebrows nudged together. I knew it was the same face I made, lying in my room at home, listening to different voices saying basically the same things. Maybe everyone gets that look when they run up against a problem they can't quite solve.

"How about you head out to the lake for one more sample?" Dr. Li asks. "You could go out to the mouth of the Pine River and bring back a bottle; I could analyze it for you, and show how the numbers compare to other parts of the lake."

Leaving the office sounds great. Even though Dr. Li's being really nice, everything she's saying about phosphorus and farms feels like it's closing in on me, and I can barely breathe.

The room spins, but I put my hand on the back of a chair and take a shaky breath. *Just walk out the door*, I tell myself.

Tai and I had planned to look for clue number three, but right now I feel like I'm walking through deep sand, stuck and sliding. I squeeze my eyes shut tight.

Out the door, I tell myself again. *Get out on the water.*

Now that we know what could be causing Maple Lake's pollution, Dr. Li probably won't need to send us out on the boat anymore. Now might be our last chance.

Chapter 19

Phew," Tai says, leaning back in his seat on the boat, "I'm so glad we're out of there."

It *does* feel good to be back on the water. But also, when you feel gray and cool inside and the sun's so bright it clusters in crystal pools on the water, it feels cruel. It's supposed to be so hot today, we both put our swimsuits on under our clothes so we could swim later.

I let the wheel slip in a circle through my fingers, guiding the boat in a gentle arc so the water sprays up around us in little beads.

"When you traced your finger up from the Pine River to Black Creek," Tai says, "you got all pale and looked like you were about to fall over. You okay?"

"I just can't believe this is happening to Maple Lake," I say.

I slow down, then cut the boat motor. An image of Amos splashing in the shallows wavers into focus, and tears pool in my eyes. "I don't want it to be different than it's always been," I say, my voice cracking. It's not just because I love being on the boat, or because I want to keep fishing. It feels like keeping Maple Lake just the way it is lets me keep Amos too.

"I'm upset about what's happening to the lake," I continue. It's hard to explain this to Tai, but I need to try. "Except it's also that...I don't want to believe that this could really be my family's fault. We've been on Maple Lake for so long, you know? Generations of us. Part of me feels like we must know the lake better than Mr. Dale or your mom or anyone else—"

"Wow, you kind of sound like Darren," Tai says.

My heart drops into my stomach. "No, no, that's not what I meant—" I begin, but Tai holds up his hand and speaks quietly.

"Darren didn't want to believe that someone who wasn't from here belonged here, or knew anything about Maple Lake," he says. "Right?"

I don't want to admit it, but I nod.

"Well, maybe he has a point, in a way," Tai says.

I shake my head. "No he doesn't. I think even he realized that."

"I just mean, sometimes people don't want to look at what they might be doing wrong," Tai says. "Sometimes it takes someone with a different way of looking at things to be able to see what needs to change."

"Are you saying that just because I've grown up near Maple Lake, I can't help fix it?" I look out at the water, toward the opposite shore.

"No way," Tai says. "I mean, obviously you care about the lake. But hasn't it been kind of hard too? When my mom first told you Maple Lake was polluted, did you believe her?"

"I didn't even believe Mr. Dale," I admit. "I didn't want to."

"But you do now, right?" Tai says.

I nod. Of course I do. I've seen the evidence.

"So if you know what's wrong, you can help fix it." Tai looks at me, his eyes patient and still. "That's the way it works."

"But I love my family," I say. "And also, I love the farm. It's hard to think about it hurting Maple Lake."

Tai reaches out, his palm open. I reach back and squeeze his fingers.

When we let go, Tai speaks again, softly. "You're doing your best," he says. "You know?"

I hope that's true.

There's so little wind today I don't have to worry much about drifting. The boat rocks just a little, then leans hard to one side as Tai bends over, sample bottle in hand. He steadies himself on the edge of the boat, then rinses and fills the bottle.

"It makes sense that you're worried," he says. "Isn't your uncle's manure pit right near that stream in the pasture? Seems like there's a lot he might have to do differently. What do you think?"

I shudder. I don't feel like talking about phosphorus anymore. Words from the articles we read have been jumping around my head all morning. *Crop cover. Downslope surface water.* I picture Grandpa, his big shoulder pressed against Bess's side, hands moving quickly as he showed Tai how to milk.

"I think—" I stop, watching the trees along the shore flash by. I push the throttle and turn toward Bear Rock, letting the boat's edge cut the water clean, a dark wave rising against the side, clear water droplets spattering. About ten feet out from Bear Rock, I slow to a stop and look at Tai.

"It's definitely a lot," I say. "Changing where they put the manure. How they store it. Not using it on the fields as much. Planting different stuff. Not tilling as much." I feel my heart pounding. I look away from Tai, toward the dark green mountains jutting toward the water.

Tai puts his hand on my shoulder. "It'll be okay," he says. "Mr. Dale said there were ways to help pay for the changes. And besides, isn't it worth it to protect Maple Lake?"

I definitely want to protect Maple Lake. I just want to protect the farm too.

"We'll figure it out," Tai says. "And hey—" He points past the boat. "We're just about at Bear Rock. Should we check out clue number three? The shape in the water?"

Amos's magic doesn't make perfect sense. But right now, I'd much rather be thinking about the creature, and how to find it if it's really out there, than about where Uncle Mark's manure pit is, or what he might have to do to fix it.

"Okay," I say. "Can you give me a hand with this anchor? I don't want to get too much closer—it gets shallow kind of fast, and rockier. We have to swim."

"Uh, I thought we were swimming later," Tai says. "Like, from land. Remember what Mr. Dale said? Stay inside the boat?"

I shake my head. "I know we're not supposed to swim," I say. "But we can't stay in the boat this time. Not if we want to look for that clue." I lift the anchor, and there's a soft *thunk* as it drops into the water. Will it hold this time? Part of me hopes it does, but the other part wants to have another reason to believe in the creature. "We'll keep our life jackets on. Nothing to worry about."

"If you say so!" Tai sounds excited; he heads to the little platform at the back of the boat and balances there, bobbing back and forth. Then he cannonballs into the water, shrieking. Water sprays up around his body.

I catch my breath as Tai bobs on the surface, sputtering. "That was awesome!" he yells. "Your turn!"

I hang the swim ladder over the side of the boat and start lowering myself in, step by step.

"Oh, come on!" Tai yells. "You gotta *jump*!"

I bite my lip and hang on, little waves tickling at my heels. This is the first time I've been back in deep water, really swimming, since last summer. When Amos was still alive.

"No thanks," I say.

Swim ladders are supposed to make it easier to get in and out of the water from a boat, and they technically do, but they're just attached to the side with a hooked top and the pressure of your own arms pulling them tight as you climb. They wobble a lot, so if you let go with one hand, the ladder sways to one side and you get all off-balance. There's this moment where you just have to let go with everything you have and let the water take you.

The cold makes me gasp.

"C'mon!" Tai says. "Over here!" He takes a few strong strokes toward Bear Rock.

I suck my breath in now and spin onto my back, staring

at the white-hot sky. The water holds me. For a second, I can pretend Amos is there, floating on his back just out of sight.

"Come *on!*" Tai yells again. "You're lagging, Addic!"

The nice thing about swimming is I can rub my eyes hard and pretend it's just water. "*Coming!*" I yell. "Geez!"

I take a deep breath and spin back onto my front, then swim toward the rock. When I stop just past Tai, his mouth's hanging open.

"You're fast," he says.

"Not with this bulky life jacket on," I say, lifting my shoulders in an awkward shrug. "But I've been swimming here my whole life."

"Still," he says. "Impressive."

Bear Rock is huge and flat, pinkish brown and filled with sparkling bits of crystal that catch the sun. Tai and I haul ourselves up and sit, breathing hard.

"So where should we look?" Tai asks.

"I don't know." I'm hoping I'll recognize what I'm supposed to find when I see it. "Somewhere in the middle of the lake was all he said."

"I guess we'll figure it out," Tai says.

The sun's hard and bright; I hold my palm up to shield my eyes. Out in the center of the lake, light collects in a wide band.

"Have I ever told you about Sparkle Island?" I ask.

"No," Tai says. "Where's that?"

"Right there." I point to the light, so thick on the tiny waves it looks like we could hop out and walk on it.

"Is that one of Amos's clues?" Tai asks.

I shake my head. "No, my dad's the one who told us about Sparkle Island. It's not an actual thing—well, I mean, most people wouldn't think of it as one anyway—it's like a mirage. Anytime there's so much sunlight shining on one distant part of the lake that it makes the water start looking like a solid thing, that's Sparkle Island. So it can be anywhere, on any lake. It could even be on Lake Tianchi."

"Huh," Tai says. "I can see where Amos got it, I guess."

"Got what?" I ask.

"His taste for magic," Tai says. "Sounds like your dad has it too."

⁓

Then memory surges, bright and strong: Amos and I, really little, in the boat with Dad, and Mama there too, her head tipped back against the prow to catch sun.

"Is it a real island, Daddy?" I heard Amos ask.

Dad's mouth twisted into a little smile. *"What do you think, son?"*

I'd been looking out at the water, shading my eyes like I was doing now. Wondering what it would feel like to step out onto all that light.

Amos nodded slowly. *"Go over there,"* he said. *"I want to walk on it."*

Dad laughed then, and ruffled Amos's hair. *"That's not how Sparkle Island works, buddy."*

Mama sat up and reached for Amos, smiling. *"Your dad's right, honey,"* she said. *"The closer you get to Sparkle Island, the harder it is to see it."*

"If it's real," Dad said, *"there's no way to know. Because it breaks apart as soon as you get close to it."*

Amos shook his head. *"I think it's real,"* he said. *"I'll go find it when I'm bigger."*

Mama laughed. *"Not till you can tread water for five minutes straight and swim at least halfway across Maple Lake without stopping,"* she said. *"I'll time you. Then you can go find Sparkle Island."*

Usually Amos would've smiled then, given Mama a high five. Game on. But that time he didn't. He squeezed his face up, thinking hard, then leaned against the boat and looked out toward Sparkle Island, his chin in his hands, his head cocked to one side, like he was listening to something far away.

———

Even now, I think I know a little how he felt. There's a way of being empty that can fill you right up when you want something so bright, something that slips away the closer you get.

Tai taps my shoulder. "Hey, Addie," he whispers hoarsely. "Hey."

I realize I've had my eyes closed, the memory filling them.

"Look," he says, louder.

I open my eyes. And the Sparkle Island I see then is different from the one Dad pointed out, from all the ones I've seen growing up on Maple Lake. And what's different is the shape in the middle. I open my mouth, but no words come out.

"Is that it?" Tai asks, not taking his eyes off the water. "What Amos saw? Is that the creature?"

Still, I can't say anything. I just watch as a pocket of deep blue, glowing like a star, emerges through the sparkles. At first the silvery-blue shape seems to spread, but then it gathers itself and rises slowly, held up by the water. Pinpoints of light shimmer around it, zigzagging like fireflies.

Even though I can't explain what I'm seeing, I'm not scared. I remember when Amos tried to show me this once, but it looks different this time. It's bigger, and it glows. It has a shape, curved and smooth. A neck? It moves so gracefully, like a dancer. It dives, plunging into the sparkles. But this time it doesn't disappear: it rises again. Then it seems to turn, as though it's looking at us, and I see two dark points on either side. Eyes? Before I can decide for sure, it dives again, and then the sparkles cover it. I count five deep breaths, waiting for it to come again. But it doesn't. Sparkle Island moves back into place, as real as an illusion can be.

"Yes," I say finally, so softly I'm not even sure I've spoken out loud, but Tai whips his head around to look at me, so I know he heard. "That was it."

Tai nods. "I thought so," he says. "That was beautiful. It kind of reminded me of a Chinese New Year celebration— on mute, maybe."

"Really?" I've heard of Chinese New Year before. It happens later than the one we celebrate in the United States, and I really like that it's based on the cycles of the moon.

"Oh my gosh, the fireworks are like nothing you've ever seen before," Tai says. "Tons of colors and lights, just shooting every which way. It's amazing. If you could be in a city in China, watching from an apartment window, you'd just feel like the whole world was one big awesome light show. It's so...happy."

"I really hope I can see it someday," I say. "But those lights just now—they weren't loud, like fireworks. And they were just one color. Maybe two."

"I know." Tai still sounds like he's seen something he can't quite believe. "But they felt just as big, somehow."

Then we both sit quiet for a moment, looking at the water. I'm waiting for the shape to come again, but I did see it once, and maybe that will have to be enough.

Once we've swum back to the boat, I get in the driver's seat and stare at the water, trying to make sense of everything.

"I can't believe it," Tai says, shaking his head, his eyes wide.

"Me neither." My heart pounds. "I don't know what exactly they prove, but the clues Amos wrote down—he's not the only one who could see them."

"You're going to record it, right?" Tai asks.

Slowly, I pull the notebook out and start writing. Then, I flip back through all the pages of my notes alongside Amos's, his handwriting next to mine. It's almost like we're talking.

"So, I was thinking about the creature," Tai says, breaking the silence. "And everything my mom said, and I wondered…do you still believe the creature could be related to the pollution somehow?"

"I think…I think if the creature exists, it's a part of the lake," I say. "A really important part. But it's also a mysterious part. Not everyone will know about it. Even your mom says it's hard to know *everything* for sure."

"I get it," Tai says. "But remember my scientific method? Do we *share* the information we have, or not?"

It's hard to know how to answer. At first, I'm quiet, letting my thoughts churn. Finally, I say the only thing that makes sense to me so far. "What happened on the boat, with the creature…I still think that should be our secret. Sharing—isn't that so people can have a chance to fix problems?"

"Pretty much," Tai says.

"If there's really a creature," I say, "it isn't a problem. If anything, it's just trying to *show* us a problem. So I think we need to share what we know about the pollution. The creature—" I pause. "The creature, or whatever it is—it's just ours. Something between me and Amos…and now you too."

"That doesn't sound very scientific," Tai says, his voice teasing. "What is *happening* to you?"

"I know, I know," I say. "But why does a person have to be just one thing?"

Tai shrugs. "I never said they did," he says. "I mean, as you know, I've never been that into science. Always thought it was kind of a drag. But doing all this research has made me actually think it's kind of cool. I guess it just took me a while."

What took *me* a while was realizing that I could believe in science without giving up on magic.

Chapter 20

Tai and I tie the boat up and step onto shore, our feet making soft imprints in the sand. We already toweled off, put our clothes back on over our suits, and stayed out long enough in the sun to dry our shoulders and the little bits of our hair that got wet from splashing water, even though the life jackets kept us afloat.

I take a deep breath. "Let's not go in yet. Can we just stay here for a little bit?"

"Of course." Tai sits down on the beach and hooks his elbows around his knees. I sit right next to him.

You're really friends with someone when you realize you're okay being quiet with them. Listening to the sound of water with Tai, I feel okay again.

When Tai breaks the silence, I know the words have been coming for a while.

"I talked with my mom earlier," he says.

"Yeah?" I try not to let on that I already know—I'm just glad he's telling me about it.

"I told her the truth," Tai says. "About soccer." His voice sounds calm and strong.

"What did she say?" I ask.

"It was actually cool," Tai says. "She really listened. She told me I was doing good work this summer. She…didn't say no. To the team, I mean. She even said she wants to watch me play sometime."

"Tai, that's great," I say. "That seems like a really good start."

"It was," Tai says. "I guess my dad might have been right after all."

I'm happy for Tai. Mama and I are probably due for a conversation like that.

I wish I could sit here forever. But there's work to be done. I stand up, brushing sand off my legs.

"Time to face the phosphorus," Tai says grimly, as though he's reading my mind.

When we get back to the lab, lugging the cooler, Mr. Dale motions us into Dr. Li's office. "Let's have a quick meeting," he says.

Dr. Li, Tasha, and Jake look up from the stacks of papers spread out around them. "Hello there, Tai and Addie," Dr. Li says. "How did the sampling go?"

"I successfully collected it without falling into the lake," Tai says solemnly, clearly leaving out the part about *jumping* into the lake.

"Well, thank goodness for that." Dr. Li squeezes Tai's shoulder. He looks up at her and smiles.

What would Dr. Li think about our investigation of the creature? On the one hand, I'm using the scientific method. I just happen to be using it to maybe find something magic too. But even Dr. Li believes that science can't always explain *everything*.

Then I realize Dr. Li's talking again, and I straighten up in my seat. "...too much publicity," she's saying. "But raising awareness will be important." Mr. Dale is nodding. He looks over at me and Tai.

"How does that sound?" he asks.

"Er—" Tai says, clearly stalling. "I'm going to leave this one up to Addie."

"Sorry," I say. "I, uh—didn't hear you."

Mr. Dale leans forward. "We're looking at the last stage in the scientific method," he says. "What Tai cleverly referred to as *Share*. Now that we have a solid set of findings, we do feel it's important to release some of them. It will help kick-start solutions while Jake and Tasha continue pursuing some other hypotheses and monitor locations in the Maple Lake watershed."

My mind stumbles until I realize he's talking about speaking up. All I can do is turn his last few words into a question: "Release some findings?"

"We'd like to run a piece in the *Herald* that explores phosphorus pollution," Dr. Li says. "It could explain different causes, and what people need to do to help the lake. We actually feel it would be powerful for the Young Scientists— both you and Tai—to share your perspectives."

My hands clench. The *Herald*'s the only paper in the county, and it's a good one too. It's won awards. Whatever gets printed in the *Herald* is something basically everyone I know is going to end up reading, or at least hearing about.

"Will we have to write about the pollution from farms?" I hope Dr. Li can't hear the tremor in my voice.

"That would certainly be part of the piece," Dr. Li says. "It would fit nicely in the section of the newspaper dedicated to 'Youth Voices.'"

Mr. Dale steps in. "You've seen that section before, Addie, right?"

Of course I have. Usually it's someone's creative writing, or artwork, or an opinion piece or song. One of Liza's sketches ended up there last year.

"This would be a great way to wrap up the work you've done," Mr. Dale continues. He looks steadily at me, his voice careful. "As a scientist, Addie, you do need to think about that last step in the process—sharing—and what you want to do with the information you have."

I stiffen. Can anyone tell my fingers feel like they're filled with ice water? Just thinking about attaching my name to an article in the paper makes me want to swim out to Bear Rock and stay there until Dr. Li and Mr. Dale forget they ever asked me to do this whole Young Scientist thing in the first place.

Mr. Dale's looking at me, his head cocked to one side. He opens his mouth again, then closes it. Maybe he knows about the ice water—and maybe he knows why it's running all through my body. You can't take back what gets printed in the *Herald*. And it's in everyone's living room. *Everyone's.* Mr. Dale knows that. If I write an article talking about pollution from farms, the whole county will think I've chosen Maple Lake over my family. Have I?

"Sweet!" Tai says. "When the paper comes out, can we sign autographs? Like outside Teddy's?"

My jaw clenches. "I'm not doing it," I say. I know I've been feeling like I want to talk about what's going on with Maple Lake, but now that I'm hearing how that might actually play out for people I know, people in my family, I'm not so sure.

"It'll be okay, Ad." Tai's leaning back in his chair, spinning the soccer ball on his fingertip. "We've been reading so much about this phosphorus stuff, we can write something up for the paper in, like, T-minus *nothing*."

"Easy for you to say!" My voice shakes. "You'll just go back to New York City at the end of the summer and forget it. Meanwhile, I actually *live* here."

Dr. Li places her hand on my shoulder, gentle and strong at the same time. "It's not easy," she says. "I know it isn't. Believe me. But think about the end goal. We want to help Maple Lake, and we care about the people who live near it too. There is a way to balance those two desires, but it must start with information."

Most of the time, I don't think about Tai and me coming from different places. Having different lives. Most of the time, it's enough to just be where we are: on a boat, watching the lake, laughing about something, or just being quiet. But right now, I feel a big space pushing its way between our chairs. And wedged into that space is this single fact: Tai *didn't* grow up here. If he had, he'd know that what Dr. Li and Mr. Dale are asking us to do is everything except easy.

Mr. Dale clears his throat. "Addie," he says, "I know writing for the *Herald* feels like a big deal, but we need to raise awareness. It's a great way to begin working toward solutions. You have a unique opportunity here to really advocate for farmers, and show your support, while still talking about how to help Maple Lake."

Tears prick my eyes; even if I don't write the article for Youth Voices, I want to know what's going to happen to my family once all of this becomes public. What will these new rules the government could put in place mean for Uncle Mark and Aunt Mary? Will they have to stop farming? Whatever happens, I'll be right in the middle of it because I was part of this project. We followed the scientific method, but it seemed to move too fast, and I have to decide something I'm not ready for. All I know now is that I have to leave. I run as fast as I can out the door, down the short staircase to the beach.

The sun's still hot enough, and the memory of water fresh enough on my skin, that it doesn't feel totally crazy to leave my T-shirt, shorts, and phone on the sand and walk right into the lake in my bathing suit, up to my knees. Still, my skin prickles with cold. The water's so soft, curling around my legs. I remember Mama from before, smiling, splashing. *Melted is good enough for me.* I close my eyes, lift my arms up in a V, and dive in. As soon as I'm under, the cold spreads. But it feels good too, surprising. It feels like waking up.

Above me, the water has already closed over the space where I plunged in. Like I was never there. *Did you realize that, Amos?* I think. *Did you know you would just disappear?*

That you would sink too deep for me to pull you out? Then leave me all by myself, trying to solve your mystery plus another one on top of it?

I burst back through the surface of the water, suck in air. I'm crying now, wiping water and tears out of my eyes. Underwater, everything was dark. But up here, the sun's so bright, and it just keeps shining.

They had to dive in to find him. Thick wet suits and oxygen tanks. A yellow rescue raft hovering on thin ice. Hands pounding his chest. Blue skin. Mama kneeling, wailing. Dad's face in his hands. *I'm so sorry, but we were unable to*—My head shaking and shaking, forever.

I choke on my sobs. *Where are you, Amos?* I think. *You left me all by myself.* I can't stand that he's gone. That he did something that could make him gone. That I'm standing here in Maple Lake, shivering all alone, with a problem I don't know how to solve.

I just want him to be here, and not only because he would know what to do about Uncle Mark, about the phosphorus, about everything. It's also because times like this—when I need his help—remind me that without him, I feel like half of a person.

My teeth chatter. Suddenly the cold is too much. I start walking toward shore, the lake pulling against my skin, filling in all the spots where I used to be as I move forward.

My feet drag on the sand at the bottom of the lake, fighting the pressure of water.

Tai's waiting on the beach, a towel tucked under his arm. He hands it over without saying a word. I don't want to take the towel, but I feel goose bumps prickling up and down my arms. I wrap the towel around my shoulders and sit on a dead log, my teeth chattering so much they sound like bowling pins falling down, over and over again.

Tai sits beside me. He's as still as the glaciers before they started sliding away, changing the face of everything. All I can hear is my own ragged breathing, and the soft *whoosh* of little waves lapping the shoreline. They sound so gentle, but I know that's only part of the story.

"Addie," Tai says.

I wipe my eyes with the corner of the towel and look at him.

His voice softens. "Do you want to tell me how your brother died?"

I look up at Mount Mann, tall and green, covered in cedar and rock. I picture the glacier pushing its way through, so slow but so strong. Then I picture it melting, drop by drop.

"He drowned," I say. "Four months ago. Right here in this lake."

Tai nods, like he knew it all along. He doesn't say anything, but he scoots closer to me on the log and rests one arm over my shoulders. We sit there like that while the waves come in, again and again. I feel a warm squeeze, and I can't tell if it's Amos's or Tai's arm, pulling me close.

"You love Maple Lake, don't you?" There's a heaviness in Tai's voice, but it's not unkind. "You want to be able to swim in it whenever you feel like it, right? Don't you want your *kids* to be able to swim in it too?"

"Of course I do," I say.

"Listen," he says. "You should see China. It's such a beautiful country, and I love visiting. I want to live there for a while too, someday." He takes a deep breath and looks out at the lake. "But you wouldn't believe the water pollution. I think one of the reasons my mom works so hard on fixing it here is so she can maybe get some ideas to help clean up the waterways there too."

"Really?" I ask.

"It's pretty serious," he says. "Over half the groundwater in China got a bad rating recently, like it wasn't fit for human consumption or something. Mom told me."

Tai pulls out his phone and taps the screen. "Look at this," he says, scrolling through pictures. "This is Beijing, the capital of China. My parents lived here for a few years before they moved to the US. We always fly in there first when we go to visit my grandparents, and it's a pretty amazing city, but there's also stuff like this."

My jaw drops. I see lakes clogged with trash, pools of dead fish.

"There are so many people in China," he says. "New buildings going up every day. This is what happens. And now people are trying to backtrack, figure out what went wrong and how to fix it."

I shake my head. "I've never seen water like that."

"And it's not all like that," Tai says. "But Vermont's like this little bubble. There's barely anyone here—and don't get mad, I don't mean that like I did before when I talked about 'nothing.' I think it's beautiful here, and I like the people." He pokes me lightly on the arm.

I poke back.

"But anyway," he continues, "having lots of space and not many people doesn't mean you don't have an impact on the land and water."

"I know. I saw the map, but...it just doesn't feel right. How could a farm like Uncle Mark and Aunt Mary's hurt Maple Lake?" I say. "Your mom even said it was small."

"That just means it might take longer," Tai says. "You want to be a scientist. Well, scientists stick up for nature. Someone has to."

Maybe I can't do this after all.

"Your aunt and uncle will want to help," Tai continues. "If something's really going on with their farm, or anyone else's, they will be so *on* it."

"But it needs to be fair," I say. "Maple Lake matters to them, but the farm does too. And farms are important for this whole state. Remember I told you how hard it is to make a living farming?"

"Yes," Tai says. "And I know a lot of dairy farms are being sold because of that. My mom told me."

"It's hard," I say. "Vermont needs farmers, but the harder we make it to farm, the fewer farmers we'll have."

I just didn't know how difficult this would be.

My phone pings, and my stomach clenches when I see it's a text from Liza.

Two more weeks! she writes. **You coming over to practice with Rascal tonight?**

I know I should, since the fair's coming soon, and maybe seeing Rascal would clear my head. But I can hardly stand the idea of going to the farm right now. Telling Liza and her parents about the phosphorus or not telling them sound equally awful.

I know my response isn't great. But it's all I can manage.

Maybe, I write.

235

Chapter 21

As we pull into the fairgrounds, Tai's eyes widen. I guess there's a lot to take in for someone who's never been here before: big muddy trucks parked side by side in the field, people milling in and out of red barns in a row, a giant Ferris wheel spinning, a chain saw buzzing and wood chips flying over at the sculpture contest, the occasional ribbon-decked rider pointing her horse toward the gymkhana arena.

"I'm headed to the tractor pull," Dad says after we park. He nods toward the grandstand.

"I figured," I say. It's Dad's favorite. "But I think we'll hit some rides."

The tractor pull's never been my thing. The way the engines pop and growl, the smoke billowing into the air, the stench of gasoline. Amos liked it, but I always snuck off to get cotton candy instead. Dad looks down, and guilt stabs: he shouldn't have to go alone.

But he seems to read my mind. "I'm meeting some guys from work there," he says. "Pretty sure they already found a spot." He winks at me. "Have fun. See you for the dairy show in not too long, right?" He checks his watch. "Eleven? But you'll be heading to the art show just before?"

Dad's kindness makes my heart ache a little. "Right," I say. I watch him walk away, his broad shoulders bent.

"You don't look very happy about the dairy show," Tai says.

I went to Liza's last night, but late. I told her I only had fifteen minutes to practice because Dad needed to get going. But I told Dad Liza only had fifteen minutes too. My stomach churned the whole time as I went through the motions with Rascal. I looked at her a little differently. She's just a baby, but Uncle Mark and Aunt Mary promised that one day she'd be part of their herd. Does that mean she'll just end up being part of the problem too?

"You're acting weird, Addie," Liza said, peering at me through narrowed eyes. Right now, Tai's giving me the same look.

"I'm fine," I tell Tai. But I'm not really prepared for

the dairy show, and the weight of everything I haven't told Liza is bearing down. I decide to totally change the subject. "Have you ever had fried dough?"

"Maybe once before, in Coney Island," Tai says. "This place reminds me a little bit of that, actually. Except it's a lot less crowded, even though there are more animals around. I can actually breathe."

Ms. Pierre's fried dough is the best; she sets up her stand every year, and I never miss a chance to go. Everybody else knows how good it is too, so we have to wait a little bit in line. By the time we get to the front, my mouth is watering.

"Hey there, Addie!" Ms. Pierre says. She's known me since I was really little; her daughter and I are only a grade apart in school. "How's it going?"

"Hey, Ms. Pierre," I say. "I'm good." It's funny how that one word can make all the complicated things feel simple.

"What have you been up to this summer?" she asks.

"I'm actually working out at Maple Lake with Mr. Dale," I say. "And with some scientists, like Tai's mom." Tai waves, and Ms. Pierre gives him a warm smile.

But she raises her eyebrows when she looks at me. "The lake, huh?" I know she's thinking about Amos.

I nod and try to figure out how to squirm my way out of this conversation. Ms. Pierre's brother and his wife own one

238

of the bigger dairies in town, and I don't even want to think about the phosphorus on their place.

Ms. Pierre saves me. "Good for you, kiddo," she says, her voice gentle. "So what'll it be?"

"Two fried doughs with maple syrup, please. Thanks, Ms. Pierre." I watch her scoop a few extra fried dough bits into the little paper container.

Tai looks pretty happy when he pops a maple-syrup-drizzled piece in his mouth, closing his eyes in some kind of blissed-out trance.

"Got any Ferris wheels around here?" he asks. His eyes are still closed, which is probably why he hasn't spotted the huge one about a hundred feet away.

"Let's go," I say, laughing. "You can see Maple Lake from the top."

I've turned to lead him in that direction when I literally bump into Darren walking the other way.

"Oh, um—hey," I say. Darren nods at me, and then at Tai.

"How's it going?" Darren asks.

"We were just heading to the Ferris wheel," I say. "Are you and your brother doing the Demo Derby this year, Darren?"

"Yup. Got a good one this year." Bits of hay stick to his shirt, his boots. He's been haying, and from the time or two

I helped Uncle Mark and Aunt Mary I know it's hot, sticky work. Endless work.

The Demo Derby is one of the most popular events at the fair. People get old cars and take all the glass out and paint them, and then they go onto this big dirt track and just ram their cars into each other. The one whose car lasts the longest wins.

Maybe it sounds dangerous, but people love it. Darren's too young to drive, obviously. But he really likes helping his brother get the car ready. I remember going to his house with Amos a couple of years ago and he showed me how his brother had given him a whole section of the car to paint. He looked so proud.

"Hey, Darren," Tai says. "Addie's told me you spend a lot of time on Maple Lake, not just for the Derby."

I look quickly at Tai, trying to hide my surprise. I don't remember telling him that at all.

Darren turns a little red. "Yup," he says.

"Well, I think it would be kind of cool to go out in the boat with you," Tai says. "You could show us some of your fishing tricks, and we could tell you more about the pollution on Maple Lake. Just so you knew what you were looking at."

Darren's eyes widen. I wonder when the last time was that someone invited him to hang out.

"Sure," he says, almost smiling. He kicks at the ground

and then says something else so soft I barely hear it: "I used to go out in the boat with Amos sometimes."

I remember that. Days when I'd hang out with Liza and Dad would take the boys.

"My rod wasn't very good," Darren says, a little louder. "Just kind of a cheap old one from a tag sale. Amos always made me trade with him. He said he was getting sick of his rod anyway. He said it bored him to use it every time. He wanted a challenge."

Darren laughs to himself, then takes a deep breath. Tears blur my eyes.

When he starts talking again, his voice sounds raw, like the words hurt to say. "That rod was super nice. Not the kind of rod anybody would ever get bored using."

My throat thickens and burns.

Darren swipes a hand across his eyes and looks away. "I always caught a lot of fish on those trips," he says. "Can't remember if Amos did. He always spent the whole time telling me how good I was doing."

That sounds like Amos. It's not easy, hearing people who also knew him tell stories like that. It probably isn't easy for Darren, telling it. Or being around me, when it just makes him think about Amos all over again. But at the same time, the story's like a present. I want to unwrap it slowly and save it forever.

I punch Darren's home number into my phone and promise to invite him out on the boat sometime. After we say goodbye, Tai touches my arm.

"Darren really misses your brother," he says.

"I know he does," I say. "We all do."

A fire engine bell signals the start of the parade. Tai and I dash across the track before enough antique cars, floats, horses, and kids throwing candy will pass by to block us from the Ferris wheel.

We don't have to wait long in line, and the wheel starts moving almost before we're done buckling ourselves in.

"Get ready," I tell Tai. "The view of Maple Lake's coming soon."

I like the way my stomach lurches up with the Ferris wheel, almost like it's shooting its way toward my throat and leaving that empty, bottomless feeling below. This one's moving kind of slowly, and Tai cranes his neck around to catch the first glimpse of the lake.

"Hey, there it is!" he says. Then his jaw drops and he nudges me. "Addie. Look." He reaches up and points down toward the mouth of the Pine River.

Most of the lake looks flat and glassy blue, but when I look over at the river, I see it: the water dark and churning, and a silver shape rising up, then diving down. Over and over.

I know the lake's so far away, but this shape seems like

it's right in front of my eyes. It seems like it's rising, rising, getting closer—

I lean back in my seat and grip the edges of the bar in front of us. Before I can look again, we're swinging back down.

"I think it'll take us up two more times," I say. "Look closely, okay?"

"Do you have the notebook?" Tai asks.

I pat my back pocket and little fizzy bubbles start to pop and collide in my head; it's not there. My brain skitters back to this morning. *Darn*, I realize.

"I left it on my desk." I hope Dad doesn't notice. "Can you take notes in your phone while I describe what I see? If I try to mess around with mine, I'll get distracted."

Tai reaches into his pocket for his phone and opens the Notes app, ready to go as the Ferris wheel moves up again and a sliver of Maple Lake starts poking through the trees.

As soon as we get to the top, I train my eyes onto the exact spot by the Pine River where we saw the shape before. Sure enough, the swirling darkness next to the river churns, but now it looks like it's spreading, creeping farther and farther across the flat blue. Is nobody else seeing this? The people in front of us don't seem to notice anything; they're leaning toward each other, laughing about something, not even looking at the lake. I don't hear anybody behind us exclaiming with any kind of surprise either, as we glide back down to the bottom.

I describe everything while Tai types, and before we know it we're on our way up one more time. I feel my hands shaking as we crest the top, but when I look at the lake this time, there's nothing. It's just blue, with little ripples of white waves poking through.

"Hey," I say. "There's nothing there anymore."

Tai cranes his neck to look. "Huh?" he asks. "What happened?"

"Look," I tell him. "It's just—normal."

Tai scans the lake and scratches his chin. "That's so weird."

Too fast, we're back on the ground again, slowly unbuckling our seat belts, trying to process what we saw.

"We need to go back up," I say as soon as we exit the gate. "That was just too strange. Do you think we imagined it?"

"I don't know," Tai says, "but if you want to go up again, I will. Aside from that one spot at the mouth of the Pine River, did you see anything else that looked weird?"

I shake my head. "Nope. It was just that spot. What's interesting is . . . that's the spot your mom showed me on that map."

The line seems to move more slowly this time around,

but it might just be because we're so anxious to get back on the Ferris wheel and figure out what's going on with Maple Lake.

Tai bounces on the balls of his feet, cranes his neck. "This is so crazy and cool," he says. "I wonder if we'll see anything different."

Or anything at all, I think.

We get up to the top, and Tai and I both whip our heads right around to the mouth of the Pine River. At first, it's just blue. But then, little points of darkness, almost greenish black, start popping, swirling in a widening circle right at the river.

"Here it comes," I say. Little firecrackers start popping around inside my head, and I take a deep breath so I can keep focusing on the swirls far below.

The dark keeps moving and then, from the center, the silver shape gracefully rises. The tightness in my chest starts to loosen, like a rope unwinding itself. Up the shape comes, and down it dives again into the deep. My heart seems to move with it, beating hard. Whenever the shape dives, it cuts through the dark, and blue circles of water emerge. Then darkness skitters into it until the silver comes back.

I can't stop watching.

"Hey," Tai says suddenly, breaking my trance, "are we stuck or something?"

I guess we have been up here for a while.

Almost on cue, a voice crackles through a microphone from the ground. "Uh, ladies and gentlemen," the voice says, "my apologies, but there'll be just a slight delay here. Little glitch in the system. Thanks for your patience."

Her words barely register; I'm still staring across the landscape toward the river. "I want to see what happens here anyway," I tell Tai.

The silver shape moves away from the Pine River and swirls around the whole of Maple Lake. The little white-capped waves go still, making room for the shape as it rises up, dives down.

"What do you think it's doing?" I ask. "Do you think it has to do with what your mom showed me with the topographic map?"

If there really is a creature, is it trying to help Maple Lake too?

"I don't know," Tai says. "What do you think?"

I think Amos didn't understand the whole story. I think maybe I'm starting to.

Watching the dark and the silver and the blue, and the river that looks so tiny from up here trickling down into all of it, I'm so mesmerized that I don't realize how much more time has passed until other people's voices cut into my thoughts. "Think we'll have to climb down?" someone's saying. "I hope they deliver lunch up here," someone else says.

Lunch? Wait a second—what time is it? I reach into my pocket and fumble with my phone. *10:50 a.m.*

Oh *no*. No no no. No! I missed the Shoreland Art Show. And I'm supposed to be in the ring with Rascal in ten minutes!

I nudge Tai with my elbow and point to the time on my phone, which, now that I look at it again, is clogged with missed text messages from Liza. His eyes get wide. I know he understands right away, but there's nothing he can do. This is my fault.

"Here we go, ladies and gentlemen," the voice from the bottom says, and finally the Ferris wheel lurches down.

This time, Tai and I can't scramble fast enough to unbuckle our seat belts.

"Follow me," I say. I grab his hand and start to run.

Chapter 22

I see Dad first. He's in the stands, watching the line of kids waiting to lead their calves into the ring. Liza's close to the back. When he looks at me, I think I'll dissolve under the hurt in his eyes, but somehow I stay in one piece, even though I can feel my legs shaking. Uncle Mark and Aunt Mary sit next to him, and they're watching me like they've never seen me before and can't quite figure out who I am. Or who I've become.

The gate opens, and kids start filing into the ring. I can reach Liza before she steps in, but it'll be close. I sprint up to her, leaving Tai behind.

If Dad's eyes dissolved me, Liza's shrivel me. There's a calmness in them that's a little scary. But underneath that calmness, she's shaking. "Forget something?" she asks.

"Liza." I catch my breath and try to say something else, but the words lock up in my throat. I reach for Rascal's lead rope, but she pulls it away. At the front of the line, someone's calf is balking. It buys me a little extra time, but what can I even say?

"I did great, by the way," Liza says. "In the Shoreland Art Show. First in my age category, and everyone else was older because—you know—only high school kids ever bother entering."

"Liza, I—" But she lifts a hand.

"You've been busy," she says. "I get it. Busy out on that lake, which, by the way, *of course* your parents didn't want you out there—but I didn't actually think you were so busy you'd forget to be here for—" She stops, and I see her lips pressed tight together, ready to say *me*. But instead, she opens them and lets out a breath. "For Rascal."

I look down at my feet. She's right. There's nothing really to say. "I'm sorry," I whisper.

Liza's eyes fill with tears. "I've got this," she says, and leads Rascal into the ring.

And she really does. They're perfect. I stand there and watch as Rascal does everything she's supposed to do. She follows Liza. She stops and stands when Liza stops. She turns, and backs up, and stays perfectly still while the judge looks her over.

That's supposed to be me, I think. But is it? Should I be showing calves when I didn't work as hard as Liza did? And when I know full well that even sweet, silly calves like Rascal, who rubs her knobby head against my side and sticks her tongue out and actually likes to be brushed now, could one day contribute to the pollution in Maple Lake?

A fist squeezes my heart so hard I think maybe there will be nothing left when it lets go. I hear people clapping in the stands, and I see the judge handing Liza a ribbon. I see Rascal nodding her little head up and down.

I want to pull Liza back to me, make her listen to something, some explanation I'll hopefully come up with that will mend the rips and tears I made. But I also think I should leave. Images flash into my brain, searing me. I see Liza's eyes, at the Shoreland Art Show, scanning the crowd for me. I see her in the animal barn, arranging Rascal's brushes in the show box Uncle Mark and Aunt Mary made for us, and looking around, wondering where I am. Not finding me.

I walk back to Tai. "We need to go," I whisper. "Let's wait by Dad's truck. He'll find us there."

What was it Liza said back when we were drawing the moon in Mr. Dale's class? That the darkness had a shape too? Right now, standing in the heat of the fair, I feel all the time I *didn't* spend with her, all the things I didn't say, taking shape and swelling inside.

Losing Amos taught me how emptiness could fill a room. The second I saw Liza step into the ring with Rascal, I knew why I'd avoided her, why I'd let her down. She lost Amos too. She knows what darkness feels like. And being with her makes me feel it all over again.

Chapter 23

I take a deep breath before knocking on Liza's door. When Dad dropped me off and helped me unload my bike from the back of the truck, I didn't say how long I planned to stay, and he didn't ask. He barely said anything to me, the whole way back from the fair, dropping Tai off and then going to Liza's. When Dad's upset, he just gets quiet.

"Hey, Liza," I say when she opens the door. "I, uh—I need to talk to you."

Liza looks at me for a long time. "Do you?"

"It's about the lake," I say, "and the research we've been doing."

"I'm not really interested in hearing about the lake." Liza's voice is cold.

"I know I messed up," I say. "I wasn't there to help with Rascal."

"Help." Liza shakes her head. "Help with Rascal."

"I should have come over more often." I'm fumbling over my words. "I tried—"

"You think I really needed help with Rascal?" Liza asks. "I've been showing calves since I was ten."

Suddenly I know what she's saying, and I can't believe I didn't realize it before. It makes me wish I could disappear.

"I did this for *you*," she says. "Mom and Dad thought it was such a good idea. They said it would give you something to focus on, something to feel good about."

For just a second, I close my eyes and picture Liza and her parents sitting around the kitchen table, their voices quiet, making a plan. A plan for me.

At first, thinking about it feels like draping a blanket over my face and trying to breathe through thick cloth. I squirm, wanting to pull it away. But the blanket slips down to my shoulders and holds me close. Then it's just warm. Safe.

"I didn't even want to show a calf at all this year!" Liza says. "I was going to focus more on art. Spend more time on my portfolio." Her voice shakes. "But I didn't. I wanted to help *you*."

"You did help," I whisper.

"It's really not just about Rascal, though. Or the Shore-land Art Show." Liza's voice strengthens, evens out. "You haven't been around at all. My entire summer has consisted of trying to keep DeeDee and Sammie from stealing my pencils and Baby Katy from eating my sketches."

"I know I haven't been around as much," I say.

"Mom and Dad said I needed to let you be. And I wanted to, but—it's really hard." Her voice cracks on *hard* and she buries her head in her hands.

"Liza?" I should reach out and touch her shaking shoulders, but she feels so far away.

"It's just... it's like I lost you both." Liza looks up, her voice small. "It's like I have to miss you both."

Both. My mind reels. *Amos.* Liza still misses Amos. Obviously she would, but I've never really asked her about it. I mostly thought that her full house and her loud sisters would fill up every space in her heart.

But they can't. She has a space that will always be empty now too. Just like I do.

It might not be the exact same space. Amos wasn't her twin. But he was her cousin, and she loved him.

"Can I come in?" I ask.

At first, she doesn't move. Her outstretched arm blocks the door. She shakes her head.

"I just don't get where you've *been*, Ad," she says. "It just doesn't feel like you're ever with me anymore. And I don't just mean at my house. I mean, like—are you with me *in here*?" She points at her heart.

"I'm here now," I say. "Can I please come in?"

Liza breathes in, out. Then she moves to the side, lets go of the doorframe. And I step inside. Finally.

Up in her room, we sit on the floor, our backs against her bed.

"I let you down," I say.

Liza doesn't argue. And she doesn't look away either. So I know it's true.

"I really did," I say. "And I'm sorry, Liza."

Maybe she's been waiting to hear me say that for a while. To show her that I see what's happening, that I see *her*. Because once the words come out, the air in the room changes. Liza's shoulders sag a little, and she wipes her eyes.

"I just wanted to make things as good as they could be," she says. "As much like before as I could. But nothing's the same anymore."

"I know. But Liza…it also can't be." What else can I say? It's true.

"*Why*, Addie?" Liza asks. "Why did you want to go back to Maple Lake, so soon…so soon after Amos died? I don't understand how you could miss that place."

"It's who I am," I say. "And honestly? I liked being around a few people who didn't know me as just...someone who was a part of Amos."

Liza nods, her eyes shining.

"But I also think Amos is still here in a way," I say. "Even when he's not. I feel it all the time, Liza. Not just at Maple Lake. But here too."

"Here?" she asks.

"Right here, between you and me." The warm feeling comes back again.

"He'd be proud of you," she says softly. "For going back on the lake. He was brave like that."

"He'd be proud of you too," I say. "With your art. He would have been there for the Shoreland Art Show."

"Well," Liza says. "Now you can be too. If you want to. I have my portfolio right here." She reaches under her bed and pulls out a bound book of sketches, the blue ribbon still attached.

I flip through the pages, catching my breath.

Liza is such a good artist. Once when Amos and I were little, we watched the original *Mary Poppins* because Mama loves everything ancient. At one point, Mary Poppins's friend is drawing beautiful pictures with chalk on the street, and he and Mary Poppins jump right into the pictures. Once they jump in, they're really *there*—in a totally

256

different world, made by the pictures. That's what Liza's sketches feel like.

She stuck with the moon phases, but she added something new: landscapes. They feel dark, but beautiful—heavy gray and black lines giving way to gray shadows. There's Bevel Mountain and Mount Mann, thick with trees. There's Route 3, curving along the water. There's Maple Lake, shimmering. I don't know how she makes it shimmer, since she sketches in pencil. But it just does. And there's a moon in every picture, so put all together, the sketches show all the phases we learned about in class. They also show places—all of our beautiful places.

"Wow," I say.

Liza covers her face with her hands. "You don't have to say anything."

"No, these are really good, Liza."

"Urgh," she says. "I don't know. I just wanted to try something different. Like you, I guess."

"Well, keep trying it," I say. "It obviously worked. No people, though?"

Liza shrugs. "I don't know. I wasn't really thinking about people when I drew them."

I reach over and squeeze her hand. She doesn't let go.

I take a deep breath. "So, there's something I need to explain to you . . . And then to your parents."

Liza's eyebrows knit together. "Yeah?" she says, a half question.

"The thing is…" I twist my hands together, rubbing my knuckles. "I don't know how to say this."

"Just spit it out." Liza laughs. "How bad can it be? After everything we talked about?"

Then the words just tumble; I don't hold them back anymore. "Maple Lake is polluted," I say. "Like, you can't tell, unless you see the harmful algal blooms, but it really is. There's a lot of phosphorus in it. Tai and I drove all over the lake and measured it, so I know it's true. Too much phosphorus hurts wildlife, and… and phosphorus can come from a lot of different places, like chemical treatments on lawns, or construction, or—"

"Whoa, slow down," Liza says. "Phosphorus. Okay."

I take a deep breath. "But a lot of the phosphorus is flowing into Maple Lake from farms."

"Farms like ours?" Liza asks.

I have to work really hard not to look away when I answer. "Farms like yours."

"It's not really that big of a farm," Liza says. "What about the Pierres' place?"

"Bigger farms have had to do things differently for a while, to prevent pollution," I say. "But small farms haven't, so some of them can actually cause issues too. We have to try to figure out what people could be doing differently."

Liza nods slowly. "So... that's what you want to talk to Mom and Dad about?"

"What Mr. Dale and Dr. Li found out means that farmers here will probably have to make some pretty big changes in the way they do things," I say.

"Like what?"

I explain what Tai and I have learned. Liza's eyes narrow and she starts chewing her lip. When I stop talking, there's just silence. We both sit there in it, waiting.

"I mean..." Liza begins. "Mom and Dad know what they're doing, though, you know?" She doesn't sound mad, just worried. "They've been doing it forever."

"I know," I say. "That's part of what I want to explain. Maple Lake is really deep, and that keeps it more protected from pollution, and it didn't seem to me like small farms would be a problem. But the phosphorus buildup has happened over time anyway—it just took a while."

Liza nods uncertainly. The longer I wait to talk to Uncle Mark and Aunt Mary, the worse I feel. I'm putting off something I have to do. "Look, I just really need to talk to them."

"They're probably in the barn," she says, her eyes worried. "I told them you were coming over, and they told me not to worry about babysitting or helping with chores. I think they figured we'd need to talk." Liza tucks her sketchbook between the bed and the wall.

Guilt must pass like a cloud over my face because Liza links her arm in mine and sighs. "I'm sure it'll be fine," she says.

Out by the barn, we find DeeDee and Sammie taking turns pushing each other on the tire swing hanging from one of the old maples. When Amos and Liza and I were little, we did the same thing.

"I'm going to stay out here with DeeDee and Sammie," Liza says. She probably realizes that I need to handle this conversation.

The barn is dark and cool, quiet except for the milking machines, steadily hissing and pumping. I walk into the milking parlor and find Aunt Mary and Uncle Mark moving between and around the cows, wiping udders, attaching machines. Grandpa's there too. Baby Katy's shaking a rattle in the playpen they have set up near the door to the milk house.

I pull a stool over to Baby Katy's playpen and watch everyone work. They move quickly, confidently. Baby Katy reaches for me and I lift her up, bounce her on my knee. "Any suggestions?" I ask her. She purses her lips and blows a raspberry, drooling down her shirt. "Okay," I say. "Thanks."

When milking's over, Uncle Mark starts moving the cows back outside, Grandpa sweeps the aisle with a long-handled push broom, and Aunt Mary looks in my direction. She hesitates for just a second, then walks over and wraps me in a hug.

"You get a chance to talk with Liza?" she asks.

"Yeah," I say. "We…we figured a lot out. Aunt Mary, I'm "

But she shakes her head. "Don't be," she says, cutting me off. "Your uncle Mark and I, we understand." Baby Katy reaches for her and Aunt Mary picks her up and gives her a kiss. Then she pulls a different rattle out of her pocket and sets Baby Katy back down where she can play safely.

Uncle Mark comes back in, brushing his hands off on his jeans. "Hey there, Favorite Niece," he says. He ruffles the hair on my head and winks, but it just makes me feel worse. Maybe they forgave me already for missing the 4-H show, but they're really not going to be happy when I start talking about phosphorus.

I tell them everything. About driving the boat all around Maple Lake, taking water samples. About reading until our eyes hurt. About Dr. Li and Jake and Tasha and Mr. Dale and the article they want us to write.

When I'm done, Uncle Mark whistles under his breath. His eyes flash.

261

Silence fills the barn, drowning out the hiss of the milking machines.

Aunt Mary finally speaks. "Guess they weren't kidding about the pollution in the lake."

I shake my head.

"Honey," Aunt Mary says, "this is . . . a lot."

"A lot!" Uncle Mark breaks in. "You can say that again." He sticks his hands in his pockets, looks at the ground. Not at me.

Then it's quiet again, except for Baby Katy's rattle. Nobody seems to know what to say.

"Addie," Uncle Mark finally begins. "Are they going to talk to us? To farmers?"

I squirm under his stare. I know Dr. Li and Mr. Dale have talked about needing to communicate with farmers, but I don't know when they're going to.

Grandpa's voice is calm. "Nobody wants to pollute Maple Lake," he says. "Addie, honey, we love the lake."

"I know," I say, biting my lip.

"It's not the farms anyhow." Uncle Mark is talking faster now, his voice hard. "They know about everything else that goes into that lake? All the construction runoff from that Walmart everyone thought would be so great?"

I can feel my cheeks flush hot. "Well, those could be problems too—"

"The changes you're talking about," Uncle Mark interrupts, "they're big ones. Expensive ones." He looks over at Aunt Mary. "Who's paying?"

At this exact moment I really wish I could just melt into the floor.

"I'm sorry," I say, miserable.

Uncle Mark won't look away. "When you weren't there for the show with Rascal," he says, "I thought—*It's okay. She's going through a lot.* But I never thought it would be this."

I hang my head.

"You know," Uncle Mark says, "your brother used to follow me everywhere." I've never heard Uncle Mark's voice sound quite this way. Husky. Cloudy like a sky about to rain. "All over these fields. This barn. Knew every corner. And now you want to change it?"

I followed you too, I want to say, but don't. *I only want to change it to save it.*

Grandpa puts his hand on Uncle Mark's shoulder, but he moves away.

"Do you remember what year your grandpa's grandpa came here from Quebec, honey?" Aunt Mary asks.

I shake my head. I've never been great with dates.

"In 1840," Aunt Mary says gently. "We've been here a long time. Now, honey, I know you've worked hard—"

"This state needs farmers," Uncle Mark cuts in. "Look how many farms like ours have disappeared. And here we are, still trying as hard as we can to make it work."

"She knows," Grandpa says. He looks down at me with eyes so kind they make me want to take everything back.

I can feel myself shaking. I knew Uncle Mark and Aunt Mary wouldn't be happy about this. I just didn't know that when it finally came down to it, I'd have the strength to keep telling them what I believed. Turns out I do. "But this state needs clean water too," I say in a voice that's not mean, just honest.

Uncle Mark opens his mouth like he's going to say something else, but then he looks down, turns on his heel, and pushes through the door leading to the milk house. He lets it swing shut behind him.

"Addie Paddie," Grandpa says. "I know you're doing what you need to do. We can figure this out." He wraps his arms around me.

My tears melt into his scratchy shirt.

Chapter 24

I ask Aunt Mary to drop me off at the beach. We load my bike into the van's crowded trunk, pushing a row of seats down to make it fit.

She's quiet at first, but then she reaches over and ruffles my hair. "Don't let Uncle Mark get to you too much, honey," she says. "He's just worried."

I blink back tears and turn to the window so Aunt Mary can't see.

"Okay, actually we're both worried," she continues. "But like Grandpa said, we really don't want to pollute Maple Lake either."

"I know," I say. "But Dr. Li and Mr. Dale are being careful, Aunt Mary. They don't want to hurt farmers."

"Are you sure?" Aunt Mary asks. "Do they understand

how farmers would be affected by some of the changes they want?"

"I told them they needed to think about cost," I said. "They are. They said the state would help."

Aunt Mary's face is still knit all over with worry. "But are they sure we're even causing most of the problems in the first place?"

"They're still doing more research," I say. "But science is about doing the best you can with the information you have." Which sounds weird coming out of my mouth, because a few months ago I thought it was always easy to know what was true and not true.

Aunt Mary nods. "So what information do they have, honey?" she asks.

"It's called non–point source pollution," I say. "That means it can be hard to trace."

Aunt Mary looks so sad, but she's listening. "How does that tell you for sure that farms are an issue?" she asks.

"Well, they're not the only issue," I say. "People living in neighborhoods can do things differently to help the lake too. But we tested samples and found out there was phosphorus feeding into Maple Lake from the Pine River." My voice trembles. I don't want to say the next part. But Aunt Mary deserves to know. "And we know that the creeks up by your farm and the neighbors' farms feed into that river. I tested the water myself, and I read the maps. At least some of the pollution has to be coming from farms."

"Okay," Aunt Mary says. "I mean, this is hard, but I can see it makes sense."

This isn't the end of the story, I think. *Just because this happened to Maple Lake, doesn't mean it needs to keep happening.* "If there was a chance you could help Maple Lake," I ask, "would you?" My voice sounds stronger now than I thought it would.

Aunt Mary looks toward the lake and takes a deep breath. Then she smiles, and she takes hold of both my shoulders.

"I would," she says. "Absolutely. But just remember, nobody can do it without help."

"I know," I say. "That's fair."

"You've always been so smart, Ad," she says. "I'm proud of you, you know. Uncle Mark is too. But he isn't going to want to change, at least not fast. And not if he's treated like an enemy."

I think if I spoke, I'd start crying again. So I just wrap my arms around Aunt Mary and bury my face in her neck.

"You sure you're not headed home?" she asks, rubbing my back. "It's almost supper. You could've stayed, you know."

I shake my head and pull away. "I'm just going to sit here for a little bit."

"And your mom and dad won't mind?" Aunt Mary looks uncertain.

"Tai's meeting me soon," I say. "My parents told me we could bike back together." The lie slides out, smooth as water. I'll just text them later.

Aunt Mary squeezes my hand, her eyes gentle. "Be safe," she says. She watches in the rearview as I unload my bike, then pulls the van away and heads back up Route 3. Now it's just me and Maple Lake.

The water's quiet, no wind. I listen to the soft lapping of it, pushing against the sand, then breaking away.

People always talk about the smell of the ocean, but I'd choose this instead.

I breathe in. It's fish and sand and froth and stones rubbed soft, but underneath, there's a hint of ancient ice. The scent of clean. Water so clear, at least away from the harmful algal blooms, that you can open your eyes underneath and barely have to rub them when you get out. A brightness.

A seagull caws overhead, a lonely, cold sound.

Memories of Amos fill my mind. They run together, they gather in pools.

I remember one day he dragged me out of school right at the bell and made us get on the bus first. And he just couldn't sit still. He kept jiggling his leg so hard I could feel the seat vibrating. I could tell he was excited.

He was always excited about something. I remember

the way his knee would pound up and down like a jackhammer on the bus when he couldn't wait to get home and hatch some plan.

We were going to fish with Dad that night and he couldn't wait, because it was finally close enough to summer to head out with the boat, and we hadn't had much of an ice fishing season that winter. He wanted to get back out on the water, frozen or not.

Tears well in my eyes.

And then he said, *"I just want to fish that lake forever."*

Forever, I think. *Long after I'm gone too. Long enough so my great-grandkids and their great-grandkids can fish in the Maple Derby.*

I think if the creature's in Maple Lake, it's supposed to stay there forever too. Amos thought it was the last one, and it wasn't supposed to die. I know technically every living thing does, but Amos's creature would have to be different. It might be part white whale, but it's part magic too. And it needs the lake to stay alive.

I hear a car pull up in the small parking lot behind me and turn to see Barbara Ann's Subaru. She rolls down the window.

"Hey there," she calls. "I was just headed to Teddy's and saw you. You don't need a ride or anything, do you?"

"Hey, Barbara Ann," I call, wiping my eyes. "Thanks,

but I have my bike. I just wanted to be at the lake for a little bit."

She snaps her watermelon gum and looks out toward the water. "I understand," she says. "We all need the lake now and then. You know what's kind of funny?"

"What?" I ask, walking up to her car.

"This is exactly where I found that tooth," she says. "I was taking one of my beach walks, and there it was. Just right where it was supposed to be."

The lonely seagull caws again. We both follow the sound with our eyes and watch him ride the air.

"I've kept it safe," I say. "I always will."

Barbara Ann smiles, her eyes still on the seagull. "I know, honey," she says. "That's why I gave it to you." Then she starts the car back up and pats my hand. "Take care now," she says, and pulls away.

Another gull joins the first one, diving in wide swoops over the lake. *Caw. Caw.* Water crashes softly to shore, muting their screams.

It's time for me to investigate clue number four. I'll stop by home to grab some food, then head out. I was supposed to text Tai a plan, and I don't want to hurt his feelings, but I need to do this one alone. I think later he'll understand.

Chapter 25

It's not even close to sunset when I get to my front door. But Mama and Dad are on the front stoop, their foreheads all wrinkled up.

"Was just about to come looking for you," Dad says gruffly.

Darn. I forgot to send that text.

"I don't know where to start," Mama says. "The fact that you missed the 4-H show and left your cousin in the lurch—that's one thing. But the rest?" She shakes her head, her lips pressed tight together. I wonder what she's heard.

"Your aunt Mary called and said she dropped you off at Maple Lake," Dad says. "Guess she wanted to make sure we really did tell you it was okay to go."

My cheeks burn. They don't need to remind me it wasn't.

Mama's eyes flash. "She told us a few other things," she says, her voice sharp. "About how those researchers are planning to tell farmers that they need to fix things for Maple Lake."

There it is. The burning in my cheeks slips down and I feel something hot and wild begin to churn inside.

"Aunt Mary understands," I say. "And the researchers aren't trying to bother anyone. They're just trying to help the lake."

"Your aunt Mary probably just didn't want to worry you." Dad rubs his hands together, trying to bring some softness back. But he doesn't look at me. I can tell he's nervous. "Neither do I. But that farm—it's not just a place. It's where I grew up. That land has been in our family for generations. And it's how Uncle Mark and Aunt Mary put food on the table."

"I already know that, Dad!" A lump rises in my throat, but I force it back down. "I was the one who *told* the researchers that. I told them they need to talk to farmers too, and think about their side of things."

"Their side of things?" Mama says. "Isn't that the side that really matters? How long has Dr. Li been here anyway? How can any of them know what's best for our lake?"

"Now you sound like Darren too!" I say.

"Darren?" Mama asks, puzzled.

"He didn't think people from somewhere else could help Maple Lake. Well, maybe *you* don't know what's best for the lake." I feel my voice rising. "You can't just ignore what's there. Telling yourself the lake isn't polluted won't change the fact that it *is*."

I'm just shy of yelling, but I manage to keep my voice steady. "Aren't you supposed to already *know* that anyway?" I point my eyes right at Mama and I feel a sneer twist through my lips. "Didn't you want to be a scientist too? Before you gave up?"

"Don't speak to your mother that way." Dad's voice has taken on the super-deep, quiet tone it gets during those rare times when he's actually, truly mad.

But I keep going. "It's true. You guys just want to give up! You think you can hide from Maple Lake? Pretend it doesn't exist? Never go out on it again, even if you drive past it every day?"

Mama's voice comes in cold. "Maybe I won't. I don't see a need to go out on that lake ever again. And neither should you."

"You don't trust me." I can feel my voice billowing up now, like stormy waves. "You don't trust me to know what I'm doing, even when I've proven myself." I clench my hands at my sides. My heart thumps in my chest. "I had to lie to Mr. Dale just so he'd let Tai and me take the boat out ourselves and look for Amos's clues, because even though I *know* how to drive a boat, I knew you wouldn't trust me to keep doing it."

"What?" Dad stares at me, openmouthed.

"You've been going out on that lake without any adult supervision?" Mama's voice shakes. "The Maple Derby was one thing, when I knew your father and Mr. Cooper and all those other fishermen would be watching. But *this*?"

"See, you don't know what I've been doing! You don't even *know* me. Whenever you look at me, you just see— him. Or you wish you could." My throat thickens. I grab my iPhone out of my back pocket and toss it in the grass. "I don't need this phone! I don't need to tell you where I am every second." When it lands, I see Dad flinch. I start to shake, but it's too late to stop.

"You're all we have left." Mama's voice trembles. "Think about your brother, and what he would do. Don't you know how much he loved working with your aunt and uncle? How much he loved that farm?"

"See, that just shows how little you know *either* of us. *I* love the farm too! And Amos would have wanted to save the lake!" I'm screaming now. "If he'd known what was wrong, he would have wanted to make it better. He would have done anything for it!"

Mama's eyes dampen, unbelieving. In them, memories

shine. I see us there, splashing each other in the lake. I feel her brushing my hair, rubbing my back after she gets home from work, when she thinks I'm still asleep.

Then I see her looking closely at me, her forehead wrinkled, her eyes full of questions. Doubts.

"I'm going to do what I can too," I say. "Dr. Li and Mr. Dale want us to write an article for the paper, about what people—including farmers—can do to stop the pollution."

Dad's eyes widen, and Mama's mouth falls open. "What?" Dad asks, his voice just a little on the loud side.

"You're going to put your name on something saying that farmers need to change?" Mama asks. "That your own family needs to change?"

"My own family has *already* changed," I say. I feel the chill in my voice. I push past Mama and Dad into the house, where I grab Amos's notebook, then stuff my swimsuit and an empty water bottle into a plastic bag. Back outside, I hop on my bike and start pedaling as fast as I can, my hair blowing back like wings.

I don't look back. And if Mama and Dad say anything else, I don't hear them. There wasn't much of a breeze to start with, but the faster I go, the more I make my own.

Chapter 26

My legs should be tired by now. But they aren't. They just keep going, pedaling so hard they burn. And the burning just makes them want to go more.

I have to look for Amos's piece of evidence—the gold flecks in the water—and the water bottle will give me a way to preserve it, as long as I can find it.

This would definitely be easier with a boat. And I should've brought a life jacket. But there's no way I can sneak into the biological station right now, and I might not have much time before one, or both, of my parents decides to follow and try to stop me. It won't take them long to find me; I'm going to Amos's favorite fishing spot—not Dad's, near the Pine River, but one much closer to shore.

I tuck my bike into the bushes next to the trailhead.

This is one of my favorite paths; it winds all along the bottom of Bevel Mountain, hugging the water. I jog along the rutted dirt, ducking tree branches, until I get a good way past the sandy beach that's always crowded on hot days.

Once when I was out on the ice, I saw something. . . .

I don't want to wait until winter to investigate clue number four. Besides, I don't think it's about the ice. Maybe Amos didn't notice this clue until winter, but if the creature's in Maple Lake, the evidence will be there; the season doesn't matter.

And even though I know it, I still want to see it. To see if the last clue is true. To finish Amos's work and my own too.

Amos always started out fishing at this spot. He said the fish there waited just for him, and once they heard him cut his motor, they started biting. But his good spot was about twenty yards out. I know it's deep there. Really deep. I bet that's why the creature likes it too. And I'm a good swimmer.

The sun's slipping lower, bleeding reds and oranges into the sky. But it's still shining; it hasn't given up its warmth yet. So I have light, and I have just enough time. Carefully, I step past the path onto the big rocks that jut into Maple Lake. I leave my T-shirt and shorts on the rock and lower myself down; then I'm halfway in, balancing on a slimy underwater rock. Once I push off from here, it's all swimming. I take a deep breath and dive through, letting the dark water hold me.

Even when I come up for air, I'm still not tired. I push through the water, my arms churning, my hand grasping the bottle. I count strokes—*one, two, three, four, breathe!*— and move slowly, saving my energy, just like Mama always said to. Before long, I'm there. I'm right where he was. But instead of slipping, my legs tread water, keeping me in place.

I remember Dad, running. Mama, falling onto the ice, closer to shore. Me, screaming. I close my eyes, tell my mind to stop. *Find the flecks of gold*, I say.

I look down. My head's so close to the water, I'm not even sure I'll be able to see anything.

Come on, Amos, I think, even though it's the creature I'm looking for. *I swam all the way out here. I'm here for you, and I know we don't have forever. Now show me something.*

A little wind starts to pick up, which is strange at sunset. It sends waves flitting across the surface of the water like little dancers. But I'm calm. My legs feel strong. I look down again.

From the deepest parts of the dark water, I start seeing little points of light. They're so tiny at first, I think I'm imagining them. Are they fish eyes? Tricks from the setting sun?

They spin up and up, coming closer, coming up larger. The wind picks up a little more. Waves rock me back and forth; I stop treading water and spin onto my back, catching my breath, resting. But I don't want to lose the light.

When I pop back over and start treading water again, the gold flecks are everywhere, and they're big—like scales. They seem almost alive, tiny little muscles pushing back and forth. I reach for them, scoop the bottle down into the water. But when I lift it up, the scales melt away before my eyes.

"No," I say aloud. "Don't melt. Please don't melt."

I'm breathing hard now. The wind races, ripping the bottle away before I can tighten my grip. I know I need to start back to shore, but I think I have energy for just one more try. If I can dive down, scoop with both hands, maybe they'll stick—

I hold my breath and go in, reaching everywhere. Underwater, it's like all the light seeped away from the sky and came into Maple Lake. I feel the gold all around me.

I pop back up, gasping, my fists clenched. I'm not going to open them until I get back to shore, until I can show someone—

Swimming with fists instead of hands is hard. I take a few strokes, then stop to tread water. A few more strokes— maybe I'm starting to get a little tired now. And cold. I shiver. The sun slips farther down, its last tiny sliver shimmering. Then it's gone.

I know I can make it. The shore's not far. But oh—I *am* tired. So tired. I kick my legs, but it gets harder to stay high above the water.

All of a sudden, there's a *whoosh!* that rises up from the very bottom of the lake and catches me. It can't just be wind. It's bigger than that, and it's coming from everywhere, pushing me toward shore. I feel the biggest, smoothest weight reaching from down deep to hold me up. I sputter, fists still clenched, water droplets blinding me—

"Addie! Addie!"

I can't tell where the voices are coming from—above or below. If it's Amos or the creature. My chin drops below the surface and I panic, clawing my way back to anything, letting one fist open but keeping the other closed tight for as long as I can.

But then that big smooth weight from below pushes me even higher and I breathe air, real air, and then it drops away so fast I can feel the pressure rush away below, speeding down like a roller coaster, and now there are hands instead, from above, reaching under my shoulders, pulling me up. My knees knock against the hard side of a boat on the way up.

It's Dad.

I'm in the boat then, and Mama's reaching for me.

They're both still saying my name, over and over, and I realize it was their voices I heard, high above the water when I was in it.

Mama hugs me to her and wraps me in, holding my bones together. I lean against her shoulder. My fists are still clenched so hard they're white. Slowly, I let my fingernails release pressure from my palm. Holding my breath, I curl them back. There's just skin. Nothing else.

"They're gone," I sob. "They melted."

"What?" Mama asks. "Addie, what are you talking about?"

But I can't answer. "They all melted," I repeat. *But it was there*, I think. *It was there, and it saved me. It held me up long enough for you and Dad to find me.*

Tears slip down my cheeks. *Why didn't it save Amos too?* I ask. It's the question I haven't been able to answer. But just because the creature is strong, doesn't mean it can do everything. I do know Maple Lake needs help, and maybe the creature does too. Maybe it can't do all the saving.

"You need to get warm," Mama says. She reaches under Dad's seat on the boat and pulls out the thick blanket that's always there, then wraps me up in it without taking her arms away.

"Tai called you," Dad says. "On your phone."

281

"I'm sorry, Dad." I choke on the words.

"He thought you might be heading here. Something about a fourth clue?"

I'm so tired. There's nothing left in me to hide.

"Yes," I say. "Amos's clues."

"The creature," Mama says, shaking her head. But there's no anger in her voice. It's the old Mama now. She's still holding me.

"I needed to help him." I choke on the next part. "Because I didn't help him before," I say. "Not enough. When he died, he was—"

I bury my face in the blanket.

Dad rests one of his big hands on my shoulder. "It's okay, Addie," he says. "It's okay."

I don't know why he says that. It's never okay. But in that moment, I just decide to believe Dad. And I tell them that Amos died trying to prove the fourth clue because he wanted to get evidence that I demanded. That it was my job to prove it for him now, not just to finish his work but to add to it—to use science to help Maple Lake *and* the creature. Finding the fourth clue became my way of showing Amos I believed, and cared. And I did—I *did!*—but the clue melted away, right out of my hands.

Mama's stroking my hair.

"That boy really did love this lake," Dad says, his voice

282

thick and strange. Tears slip quietly from his eyes as the boat spins through darkness, its lights pointing to shore.

Mama sighs and lets her arm fall around my shoulders. "Do you know," she says, "when you were toddlers, how much I hated this lake? I thought it would steal one of you for sure. You were both so curious, wading out too deep. Whenever I had one of you in my sight, the other would slip right out of it. I never thought I'd be able to relax again. I remember once—" She starts to laugh, then wipes her eyes. "You were two. Amos was toddling too fast, and he went right past you. You just looked at him, and I thought I could see the wheels turning; you were thinking, *Watch out.* And then, of course, he fell right in the water."

"Really?" I ask. "How deep was it?"

"Not very," she says. "But it doesn't take much for a toddler to get in trouble with water. Of course I started to rush over. But you know what you did, Addie?"

"What?" I ask. I obviously don't remember; I was only two.

"You got to him first." Mama rubs my shoulder. "Bumped right over, slow and steady. And you started grabbing at him with your hands. By the time I got there, you had him half out of the water. Not sure how you did that, since he was heavier."

I laugh, then sniffle.

"You were always more careful," Mama says. "Always

watching. I never worried as much about you. But that doesn't mean it would hurt me less to lose you."

She readjusts the blanket around my shoulders and holds me tighter.

Then Dad clears his throat, cuts the motor, and moves close to Mama and me. "It's true, honey girl," he says, his fingers light on my shoulder.

"And it's scary," Mama says. "It hasn't been easy this summer, you know. You've felt...far away."

"I've just been at the biological station," I mumble. "That's not far." But I think I know what Mama means. I've *felt* far from them. I've *wanted* to be far from them. And they can tell. Then again, Mama has felt far away too. She hasn't been the Mama Before in a long time. None of us will ever make it back to *before*.

Dad opens his mouth to speak, then closes it. He squeezes my shoulder and when I look up at him, I can see his eyes shining.

"Before," Dad says, "before, you told us we couldn't look at you without seeing him."

I blink and look up at Dad, trying not to cry.

He kneels in front of me. "It's not true," he whispers. "Look at me, Addie."

Slowly, I raise my eyes.

"I *do* look for him everywhere, Ad," Dad continues. "I

look for him in the truck. In the boat. At the empty seat at the table. It's still hard to believe he's gone."

I nod. I know how it feels to want him back. I feel so close to Amos when I'm in the water, and if I let the creature slip through my fingers, I'll let the last of him go too.

"But when I see you, Ad, I just see *you*," Dad says. "You are strong, and bullheaded as anything sometimes, and smart, and you're —you're just *you*. That's it. And that's enough."

Then Dad wraps his arms around me, and around Mama, and I'm stuck in the middle so tight I can't move, but I don't want to anymore. We stay there like that, the boat rocking a little in water that calmed back down.

"Shhhh," Dad says, stroking my hair. But he's not really telling me to be quiet. He's just trying to show me he's there.

"Our family is not the same as it was," Dad says. "But we are still a family." Mama nods and tightens her grip on me.

Their love feels so good, but strange too, so much of it pouring out on just me. I'm not used to that. I'm still trying to figure out who I am without Amos. And I almost don't want to say the next thing. But I have to. I pull back just a little.

"I'm writing the article," I say. "Maple Lake has been here since the glaciers, Mama—you told me that. I want it to be here for a lot longer. I know Amos would too."

Mama stiffens a little bit, but she doesn't loosen her grip on me.

"The scientific method says you have to look at everything from lots of different sides," I say. "And Dr. Li and Mr. Dale and Jake and Tasha, and even Tai, keep talking about pollution from farms, and they say they're worried about helping the farmers too, but so far I think I'm the only one who's talked to farmers—Uncle Mark and Aunt Mary."

I see Dad smile, just a little, as he releases his hold on me and starts the motor back up. "You'll figure it out, Ad," he says.

Mama opens her mouth like she's about to say something, but then closes it and rests her chin on the top of my head. Dad peels the boat away in an arc, water rising up from the dark. The lights on the boat guide us all the way back to shore, and from there, we go home.

Chapter 27

Tai digs in his pocket and pulls out a wrinkled square of newsprint. It's the article we wrote for the *Herald*. "My mom saved it for your parents," he says.

"Thanks," I say. "I'm pretty sure they already got one. Plus, I read it on my phone and saved the screenshots."

"I figured," Tai says. "But you know old people. The more printed copies, the better."

I take the newsprint and unfold it. And, okay, it *is* kind of cool to be able to hold our words in my hands.

YOUTH VOICES: LET'S PRESERVE MAPLE LAKE, AND FARMS TOO

After collecting and analyzing water samples throughout Maple Lake, we have found evidence of high phosphorus levels. Phosphorus is an important mineral that helps keep us strong and healthy. However, high amounts of it can be dangerous for our local waterways because it changes the ecosystem. It creates harmful algal blooms that can hurt drinking water and keep people from being able to use the lake. It also hurts fish and other wildlife.

Phosphorus pollution can come from many different sources, such as new construction projects and lawn treatments near Maple Lake, septic systems that malfunction, and wastewater treatment plants. To help, people can install rain barrels, maintain their septic systems regularly, and stop doing their laundry when it's raining so that less water goes into the treatment plant. When they mow their lawn, they can let lawn clippings decompose so the grass roots grow strong and absorb more water.

But in addition to some of the more urban causes of pollution, farms within the watershed also contribute to high phosphorus levels. These farms all have streams on their property that flow into Maple Lake. Since farms are such an important part of Shoreland County, and farmers are so helpful to our community, we need to make sure we support them as they care for their farms and the lake.

There are things farmers can do differently to help clean up Maple Lake. For example, they can build new manure pits in different places. They can create buffer strips, which are wide sections of plants between streams and pastures that help collect runoff. They can create a nutrient management plan and apply manure only during certain times of year. They can also use cover crops.

But these changes cost a lot for farmers. And we need farmers for our economy and our land. Local dairy farmer Mary Lago says: "We all love Maple Lake. But changing how we farm can be difficult, and expensive. We are hoping for help, and time, from the state so we can see this lake clean for our grandkids."

We think the state should set aside money to help farmers. That way, they can make improvements that would help the lake. Also, farmers should be asked to help with making new environmental rules. They know the most about what it is like to work with the land because they do it all the time and they care about the environment, so we should listen to what they say and trust that they will help. This way, we can keep Maple Lake healthy forever, or at least until another glacier comes through.

Addie Lago and Tai Jiang

Young Scientists, Maple Lake Biological Station

"You going to show it to your aunt and uncle?" Tai asks. "They've probably already seen it," I say. "Uncle Mark and Aunt Mary have gotten the paper for, like, ever. And obviously, I had to call Aunt Mary for that quote anyway."

The last time I saw Uncle Mark, just after the article came out, I thought he'd walk right past me. But instead he handed me some grain buckets and asked me to walk out and feed the cows, which were milling around the big feeder in the lot outside the barn. He didn't say much and neither did I. But he did still call me Favorite Niece. And we worked together all afternoon, side by side.

Tai and I are at the biological station for one last afternoon, cleaning the boat and storing files, helping to close up. Tai's leaving to go back to New York City tomorrow, where his mom will continue analyzing all the data we collected. And before too long, I'll be back at middle school. But Mr. Dale came through with his promise—he's letting me join the Science Club, and I'll go to the high school to do experiments every week.

"I can't believe you're leaving," I say.

"Can't get rid of us that fast," Tai says. "Mom has to come back this year to check in at the university. Who knows? Maybe I'll be able to come along. I never did that boat ride with Darren." He smiles, his eyes dancing.

"I hope so," I say. "What will you think of, when you think of your favorite parts of Vermont?"

"Hmmm," Tai says. When he speaks again, he's quiet.

"Your grandpa and Uncle Mark being really patient when I squirted milk in all the wrong directions. Teaching me how to do it right."

"Yeah." I smile. "They're good ones to remember."

"And you," he says, "kicking the soccer ball back to me in the office. I know it probably didn't seem like a big deal but...that's when I knew you were going to be my friend."

Tai hugs just like Amos always did—full of bones and angles, but warmth too.

I thought I'd feel sad saying goodbye to Tai, but instead I feel okay. It's not like I'll never see him again. I just know I will.

Dr. Li and Mr. Dale come in, hauling stacks of folders that they set down on the table with a soft thud.

"Addie," Dr. Li says. "It's been a pleasure working with you. You've done an excellent job this summer."

I blush. "Thank you, Dr. Li."

"You've been through a very hard time, from what Tai and Mr. Dale have told me." Dr. Li's kind eyes shine. "Yet you've worked incredibly hard. You're determined. Knowledgeable."

"Um, thanks," I say. "I mean, you're welcome. I mean... I'm really glad I did this." I turn to Mr. Dale. "I can totally help whoever becomes the Young Scientist next summer, by the way. You'll probably have more research to do on the lake. I could show them the ropes before they start."

Mr. Dale and Dr. Li look at each other with these weird smiles on their faces. Then Mr. Dale laughs kind of awkwardly and claps his hands together. "Yeah," he says. "About that... there probably won't be a different Young Scientist next summer."

"Why not?" I ask. "Did I do something wrong?"

Mr. Dale shakes his head and laughs. "Not at all," he says. "But—I should probably just go ahead and tell you this, but I don't want you to get upset. We sort of—made the position up. For you."

"Huh?" I ask. Now it's Tai and me looking at each other, confused.

Mr. Dale smiles so big I forget to be embarrassed.

"I saw so much potential in you," he says. "And I knew what a hard year it had been for you, and that Dr. Li had a son your age that you'd probably get along with..." He trails off.

I can't believe Mr. Dale made this all up. No wonder Liza hadn't heard him talk about it in class. I cringe at first; it's kind of weird to think about somebody doing all that just for me.

"I know I told you I was really interested in science back when I was your age," Mr. Dale says. "And there wasn't anybody telling me to go for it, showing me I could do it. All that's true. But I don't think I told you how much time I spent fishing with my little brother on Maple Lake."

He takes his wallet out of his back pocket and reaches into one of the slots.

"Look at this," he says, "from back in the days when we actually used rolls of film."

It's a picture of a younger Mr. Dale, probably around the age I am now, and a little boy, probably about eight. They're in a boat, and Mr. Dale has his arm around the boy's shoulders. The boy's holding a perch and smiling about as big as a kid could.

"I know a Maple Lake fan when I see one," Mr. Dale says. "And Addie, I knew you'd want to help."

I think about how it felt heading out on the boat with Tai, the sun on my face and the wind in my hair; and about how much I *needed* to learn everything I did, no matter how hard it was, if I wanted to save Maple Lake.

And I smile at Mr. Dale. "Thanks," I say.

"Addie wasn't the only one who stood to benefit from working as a Young Scientist, though," Dr. Li says, winking at Tai. "When Mr. Dale proposed the arrangement to me, I thought it sounded perfect."

"*We know*," Tai says, rolling his eyes, but he's smiling too.

"Let's just say it worked well for everybody," Dr. Li says.

"And Addie, Mr. Dale's been telling me more about your professional goals too. Did you know there's a word for an aquatic biologist who studies freshwater ecosystems? You could be a limnologist."

Limnologist. The word feels smooth and round on my tongue.

"I'd love to host you in the city next summer," Dr. Li says. "There's an intensive weeklong science camp I'm trying to convince Tai to do...if it doesn't conflict with pre-season soccer practice, of course. You'd be the perfect candidate."

She might notice my blushing and looking at my hands, because she adds: "There's funding available for talented students like you."

"It would be so cool!" Tai says. "You'd really like the city. I could show you my neighborhood, take you to Central Park...even teach you how to ride the subway!"

My heart leaps with the thrill of seeing a new place. Still, a week away from Maple Lake in summer—I'd miss Mama and Dad. And I don't know if they'll even let me go in the first place. But after that night on the boat, Mama asked me if I wanted to go walk the lake trail with her. Maybe when we do, I can ask her about Dr. Li's science camp. I'm pretty sure she won't say no right away.

Chapter 28

Mama and I are quiet, tightening our boot laces and sticking water bottles into our hiking packs at the trailhead. She and Dad and I have come a long way since the night in the boat, but they haven't said much about the article since it came out. Dad's given me hugs and winks, and once even told me he was glad I was helping to find a way to help Maple Lake *and* farmers. But it's been harder to tell where Mama stands. She just hasn't said much, so the article feels like a big rock squeezed between us, at least to me. When Mama actually asked me to get my hiking boots out of the closet and meet her at the car, I was surprised. Nervous. I'm not Amos, and he's the only person she hiked this trail with before. I still feel fluttery inside, wondering how it will go.

She walks just ahead of me. It's a steep, skinny trail, and

I watch the tracks her boots make in the dirt. Birds sing around us, chickadees and red-winged blackbirds talking to each other in music. Light drifts through weepy cedar branches and towering ash trees and splotches the ground.

Then we turn a corner where the path widens, and Mama stops, breathing hard. She reaches behind and motions for me to walk closer. I jog a little to catch up, and we fall into step together.

"Barbara Ann mailed me a copy of the article," she says.

"Oh really?" I try to keep my voice light.

"I don't know why she sent it." Mama pauses, but I can tell she's not quite finished. Some thoughts are still bubbling there, waiting to come out. "Okay, I can probably guess why. She wanted to make sure we'd really read it."

She doesn't seem upset. Her voice sounds almost soft. Mine is too when I ask: "So did you? Dad told me I did a good job, but—I was wondering what you thought."

She stops then, looks at me. "I did read it," she says. And then she smiles. "You're a good writer, Ad. I don't think I ever knew that about you. I'm not sure I was paying attention."

Pride flickers inside. "Thanks."

"And—you talked about farmers," she says. "How important they are."

"I told you I would," I say.

She puts her hand on my shoulder. "You did tell me that. Dad says he hopes the researchers listen to you."

I laugh. "He told me that too."

"He's so proud of you," Mama says. "We . . . we both are."

"Why didn't you trust me, then?" I ask. "I mean, in the first place?"

Mama sighs, then pulls me over to one of the big rocks sitting between trees. I didn't even notice that we'd reached the lookout point, with the whole of Maple Lake unrolled below, so far away it looks as small as my hand. Mama and I sit on the rock, our knees touching, our eyes focused on all the blue.

"There's something I want to explain to you," Mama says. "Do you remember what you said about me, that day you ran off to the lake by yourself?"

I feel my cheeks flush hot. I don't really want to think about everything I said.

Mama's voice cuts gently in. "You said I'd given up. And I want to say—you're right. I did give up. What you don't know is why."

The air's so still now, I can't hear the birds sing anymore. It feels like the whole forest is waiting for Mama to speak.

"Addie, you know that all your life I've been telling you about Maple Lake," Mama says. "About the science I remembered from high school. I was a good student, you know. Or maybe you don't know. But I was."

I nod. "Liza told me."

"Going away to a four-year college wasn't an option for me," she says. "You know, when your grandpa and grandma got sick, they needed me, and money was tight anyway. I don't regret staying home for them, but I did want something different too. At one point. So I never stopped reading. Environmental science articles, studies focused on local water sources, books about aquatic ecosystems."

Mama takes a big drink from her water bottle. When she starts talking again, her words tumble together a little faster, like she's working toward an end she doesn't want to think about. "Then, in the last couple of years, I started seeing journal articles about lake pollution in Vermont," she says. "Nothing about Maple Lake, not yet. It's such a unique lake, you know, like I always told you—so deep and cold, and Shoreland County is so rural. I know we got the Walmart and the condos, but there's not nearly as much development here as in other parts of the state."

"You told me to look at construction," I say. "Back when I first started."

"I know I did," she says. "And it was worth looking at. But honestly, I had also read about some regulations the legislature was considering for small farmers based on other parts of the state where water pollution was worse, and I started to worry about what could happen to Uncle Mark and Aunt Mary. I knew Maple Lake was shallowest where the Pine River feeds it, and I just...I had a bad feeling."

Mama takes a deep breath and points out at Maple Lake. "Look how blue that is, though. Doesn't seem like anything could be wrong with it, does it?"

"Not from up here, I guess," I say. But I've been in it. And I can't go back anymore to not knowing, not seeing.

Maybe Mama can't either. "I started seeing the harmful algal blooms. Just here and there, out walking."

My jaw drops open. "You knew about the blooms? You never told me!"

"I didn't want to believe it," Mama says. "I didn't want to think it could really happen here. Because if it could, if the lake I knew so well could change, then everything could change. And of course...everything did."

I don't know what to think. All the stories Mama told us about the lake, about glaciers, white whales, the names of trees—she's probably the reason I want to be a scientist in the first place. But she did what Tai says scientists never should do: she had information and she didn't do anything about it.

"And then your brother..." Mama pinches her lips together, then presses her forehead with her fingers. "Last winter. Your brother came to me wanting to tell me something…about the lake."

"Amos talked to you about Maple Lake?" I wrap my arms around my waist and shiver even though I'm not cold.

"He told me he was looking for something in there," Mama almost whispers. "Begged me to tell him how scientists prove things, so he could too. But I kept putting him off. I didn't want him investigating the lake. I didn't want to know what he'd find."

My jaw drops open. "He told you about the creature?"

"No, he didn't tell me any specifics," Mama says. "And I guess I didn't listen very closely either. I didn't want to. I was thinking of the harmful algal blooms, I guess. I wasn't looking past what I could see. Eventually, he stopped asking." She wipes her eyes with one hand, then holds me at arm's length and looks at me. "When you told us about the creature, I realized what he'd been trying to tell me. I wish I had listened to him. And to you."

The whole forest holds its breath. Not even the tiniest breeze ruffles the cedar branches. At the same time, I feel my shoulders sink down. And I do breathe. I take a big, shaky gulp of air.

So Mama knew something after all. She didn't know about the creature, but she knew Amos saw something in the lake. Knew he wanted to talk to her about it. She probably felt as guilty as I did.

"Is that why you didn't want me to do the Young Scientist program?" I ask. "Because you knew what was wrong with Maple Lake, and you didn't want anybody to find out?"

"That's part of it." Mama looks down at her hands. "But after your brother died, I wasn't just worried about finding out what was wrong with Maple Lake. I was worried about the lake, period. I didn't want it to take away the only thing I had left—you."

"But I love Maple Lake, Mama," I say. "And it's like Barbara Ann said—that makes me want to stay close by. I mean, I might leave for a little bit. I want to go to this summer camp Dr. Li told me about. Later I *do* want to go to college and learn more. I want to visit China someday too; Tai's told me so much about it. But I also want to come back."

Mama hugs me close again, and we both look out at the water. From way up here, usually it's hard to see waves. But all of a sudden they start coming, little points of white spiking up everywhere, bumping against each other, folding over and under. And then, in the middle of the lake—a shape, round and glowing, starts diving and swirling in the deep. As soon as it came it's gone, and like a blue sheet, the lake folds back in place.

I turn to look at Mama and her mouth is hanging open. "Did you see it?" I ask, even though I know she did.

She nods slowly. "Is that what Amos was talking about?" she asks.

I nod. "Amos believed there was more to Maple Lake than what we could see on the surface, or—or what we could explain," I say. "I didn't want to even look for it at first. But honestly, the more time I spent out there, doing the research Dr. Li and Mr. Dale asked me to do, the more I just realized that even though there's so much I can understand about Maple Lake, so many numbers and charts and things we can figure out, there's just so much I'll never understand."

Words keep pouring out, and Mama nods, urging me to keep going. "There's this—this *feeling* out there," I say. "It's like when we're fishing, and you can feel the fish bite, and you can even see them swimming while they fight the line, but you pull them out of the water and you can't see the world they came from at all, not really. And no matter how much you measure it, there's just—something more there. Something wild."

"Well, when I saw those harmful algal blooms," Mama says, "all I felt was scared, Addie. I didn't know what to do. That's the difference between you and me."

"No," I say. "I was scared too. I was especially scared to

talk to Uncle Mark and Aunt Mary. And then to tell Dr. Li and Mr. Dale that we needed to listen to them too."

"But you did it anyway." Mama reaches around my shoulders and pulls me close again.

We sit there awhile, quiet again, but not the same kind of quiet we were before. Now it feels like we're finally breathing the same air. Mama sighs. "Every parent hopes their child will be better and braver than they were," she says, resting her chin on my head. "And you are."

I can feel her tense up then, and she takes a shaky breath. "Amos was too."

I can feel Mama's quiet tears soaking into my hair, and mine drip onto her knuckles.

"Will it always feel like this?" I ask Mama. She pulls away a little and looks at me, swiping her hand across her eyes.

"Like what?" she asks.

How can I describe what hangs between us? The air that's supposed to have a shape, a breath?

"Like he's gone." I look into her face for an answer. But instead, she smiles and shakes her head. She pulls a strand of hair away from my eyes.

"Oh, honey," she says. "He *is* gone. But at the same time, he's not. Don't you see?"

I know that all I see around me—the shivering leaves,

the spicy pine needles on the ground, the flutter of wings, the sheet of water—reminds me of him. But it feels empty too, because of the empty spaces where he should be.

But Mama puts her palm against my chest and smiles. Her eyes sparkle now. "He's right here," she says, her voice cracking. "And I don't mean that you're him, or even that you have to be like him. You just hold him in your heart. You always will."

I put my hand over hers and close my eyes. When I open them, I see Mama looking right at me. And I feel the warmth, the pressure around my chest, the arms I can't see pulling me close.

"When I look at you," Mama says, "I see my Addie. My brave girl."

I think I finally do too.

Chapter 29

I ended up showing Amos's notebook to Liza, and telling her about the creature. I guess I finally realized that there wasn't any point in trying to keep secrets from someone who loved Amos too. And I know now that I don't need to make myself more alone than I already am. I *need* Liza. She's not just family; she's my friend.

On the mountains around Maple Lake, some of the leaves are already starting to change color. I see them popping, tiny bursts of orange and red holding their own in all that green.

People get nervous when the leaves turn, even though it happens every August. They start talking about frost, and fall. But I'm not worried. It just means there's more beauty coming—a different kind. No use trying to hold on too tight. Everything keeps moving, just like mountains, whether we want it to or not.

I tap my back pocket, where the whale tooth Barbara Ann gave me at the beginning of the summer sits, wedged deep in the corner. *My first clue*, I think. *The first one I added to the notebook.*

Next to the tooth is a folded piece of paper. I pull it out. I've folded and unfolded it so many times since Liza gave it to me, I'm worried the creases will tear it apart. But I open it again anyway.

She must have been listening when I asked her where the people were in her drawings, because she drew two into this one: a boy and a girl. They're looking at the lake, so you can't see their faces, and they're holding hands. I didn't have to ask; I knew she'd drawn Amos and me.

I fold the picture back up and stand with my toes in the lake. I won't be able to do this when the ice comes.

～

It always took Amos a while to stop going barefoot on the beach. *"Just one more time,"* he would say. *"It's still warm enough."*

Just once, he convinced me to run in with him. I think we were ten, and it was mid-October. All the summer people had packed up and closed their camps. We were the only ones on the beach.

"Trust me, Addie," Amos said. *"It's soooo warm."* He was

trying to sound convincing, but he was cracking up, tugging at my hand.

"*You're so bad!*" I yelled. "*I know you're lying!*"

"*No, I swear!*" He laughed, doubled over, tears streaming from his eyes. "*It's like a warm bath!*"

I don't know why I gave in. "*Okay, fine!*" I yelled into the wind. "*I'll race you!*" I started running, but it didn't take Amos long to catch up. And we didn't just dip our toes in. We belly-flopped, flat on our faces, in our clothes. We shrieked with laughter.

And the strange thing was, even though the water *was* cold at first, even though it made us gasp, there was this tiny piece of warmth left. This sliver of summer, hiding under the surface. It's like the lake was reminding us: *I was warm once. And I'll be warm again. Just wait.*

When we came up, dripping, too out of breath to keep laughing, feeling the cold all over again, Amos hooked his arm around my waist. I leaned into him. And we trudged back onto the sand.

———

Now, alone, I catch my breath. I open my eyes as wide as I can, take in the lake, its rough waves, its steely blue. I wade in to my ankles and feel the water on my skin, clear and cold. *I miss you so much,* I say. *I always will.*

Does he whisper back then, *Press your hand to your heart?* The words hang in the air, clear as water. His voice feels so close, my ear vibrates from the sound. *It can't be*, I think. *How can you be here?*

But I put my hand where he tells me. And when I pull it away, and turn up my palm, I see it. A bright golden scale, wider than my thumb. I stare, drinking in that light, then quickly close my fingers up in a fist. I feel the scale still underneath, warm and smooth.

Maybe it will melt away when I open my hand. But I know for sure it was there.

Acknowledgments

Writing and publishing a book is part science, part magic. I'm grateful for everyone who helped shape Addie's journey on Maple Lake.

Special thanks to my agent Katie Grimm, who not only believed in this story, but connected with my mission to continue writing about the magic of nature. Katie, you've worked tirelessly on my behalf and provided exceptional guidance; I'm grateful for your wisdom. Thanks also to Cara Bellucci, who read and gave insight.

To Lisa Yoskowitz, the most thorough and thoughtful editor I could hope to have: thank you for breaking your own rule and taking a chance on a sad story. You appreciated what this manuscript already offered, and clearly saw what it needed. Thanks to Hannah Milton, Barbara Perris, Annie McDonnell, and the entire team at Little, Brown Books for Young Readers for connecting with Addie and turning *The Light in the Lake* into a real book. I'm also in awe of the beautiful cover illustration and design by Ji-Hyuk Kim and Karina Granda.

All writers benefit from mentors who believe in them, and the late Vermont author Howard Mosher was mine. He patiently read, gave feedback on, and encouraged me in revising this story. He was not only an inspiring role model for many writers, but also a wonderful neighbor to me. Phillis Mosher, thank you so much for reading and providing support and friendship. I miss you both more than I can say.

Many other early readers of this book shaped it invaluably. Amy, Cole, and Quintin Janssens, I appreciated your wise and loving feedback. Nicole Goldstein, you are the world's most responsive, helpful critique partner. Rose Daigle, your enjoyment of the story helped me believe it was worth telling, and I relied on your ideas to make it better. Leslie Rivver, Liz Greenberg, and Lisa Higgins, thank you for providing such helpful suggestions and support. Zoe Strickland and Jeni Chappelle, I'm grateful for your excellent editorial feedback. Taryn Albright, thanks for your early confidence. Jim and Nancy Rodgers, your bed-and-breakfast in West Glover, Vermont, was a lovely place to write. The Vermont College of Fine Arts' Writing Novels for Young People Retreat run by Sarah Aronson gave an enduring gift of creativity and knowledge.

Judy Lin, thank you for reading and bringing your

extensive expertise to my characters. I'm very grateful for your help.

Two issues that fuel this story—water quality and farming—are rooted in places I love. Vermont's Northeast Kingdom, where I used to live, has a big piece of my heart and always will. This book would not exist without it. I'm originally from Michigan, the Great Lakes State, so living near and playing in the water is a way of life for me. We are all affected by water quality, whether we live in an urban, rural, or suburban environment, and everyone bears a responsibility to help keep our waterways clean. If you're interested in learning more, one great step you can take is to investigate your local watershed. Start with the National Environmental Education Foundation's Watershed Sleuth Challenge at neefusa.org/watershed-sleuth.

As much as I care about conservation, I'm not a scientist. Therefore, special thanks go to Dr. Kris Stepenuck, Extension Assistant Professor of Watershed Science, Policy and Education at the University of Vermont's Rubenstein School of Environment and Natural Resources, for reading the scientific portions of this book and giving me so much information about phosphorus, watersheds, ancient oceans, and more. Thanks also to Ralph Tursini, Forest Lands Manager and Facility Coordinator, for providing clarity about forest management. I appreciate Laurie Carr, science teacher extraordinaire, who let me discuss my story with her class at Lake Region Union High School.

My grandparents Aaron and Irene Reinhard were dairy farmers. Their dedication to caring for animals and land made a significant impression on me, and I wrote more short stories than I can count in their farmhouse. I'm grateful to my father, Donnie Reinhard, for drawing on his own experience raising prizewinning 4-H calves to verify the accuracy of Liza's; and to my mother, Sharon Reinhard, who patiently listened to the whole book read aloud. I also appreciate the help of Megan Webster and Jim Dam, who generously shared their experience and knowledge about dairy farming, and read portions of this book.

I couldn't have written much at all without the support of my wonderful husband, Matthew, who always said "Of course" when I needed a day of drafting or editing, and who never stopped believing in me, even when I wanted to. I'm ever grateful for our two amazing children, Aaron and Joan, who inspire me daily, and remind me why I write in the first place.

**Turn the page for a sneak peek
at Sarah R. Baughman's
breathtaking next novel:**

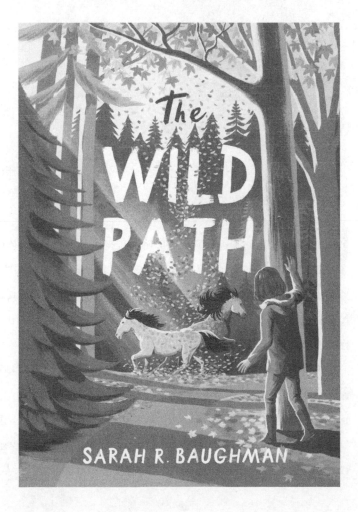

CHAPTER 1

Walking to our mailbox always feels longer than walking back. I take the same path both ways, past fields and fence line, but steps can't measure how fast I want to get there. It's the wanting, not the distance, that matters.

Everything around me is set to change. The maples covering the mountains started to pop, little bursts of red, yellow, and orange poking through green. I saw my breath this morning, a puff of smoke. The wind smells almost like snow.

And when I wrap my sweatshirt tight, the envelope pressed to my chest crinkles like dry leaves.

Dear Andy,
Guess what?

That's how my letters always start. They're not like texts, where you get right to the point. There's more waiting. Not only in the time it takes to stretch whole sentences across a blank page, but in the trip that page takes from my desk to our mailbox and all the way to the Starshine Center in New Hampshire, where Andy can pick up a pen and write back.

I can't text him anyway, even though Mom and Dad got me a phone for my birthday this month, one of those simple ones with no apps at all, only their numbers and my best friend Maya Gonzalez's already programmed in. Andy doesn't have a number anymore. His cell phone's just one thing they took away, and they won't give it back until he's done with what they want him to do, until he figures out how to get better. "Getting better" is probably like walking to the mailbox—wanting to reach somewhere so bad but no matter how hard you try, you feel like you're wading through fallen leaves.

Still, I like Andy the way he is—how he wears his baseball cap crooked and sets up a tent in two minutes flat and pretends to steal my nose with his finger and thumb even though I'm twelve and he just turned eighteen. Will he still do those things once the Starshine Center has made him new?

Mom thinks Andy's homesick, even though he never says it. "He misses things we take for granted," she tells me, knotting her fingers together, her eyebrows pinching into that space above her nose that's always wrinkled now. "Tell him about those things." So I write: Sunny sneezed while I was brushing her face so now I have horsehair AND snot all over my shirt.

I write what I know will make him smile. Because even though he wasn't doing much of it by the time he left, Andy loves smiling.

Proof: His letters back always start with a joke.

WHAT DO RACEHORSES EAT?

He hides the answer, written upside down at the end, to keep me reading. It's not like he has to—I already hold each of his words in my head as carefully as I hold Dad's homemade anise candies on my tongue, trying to make them last.

LOVE,
ANDY

P.S. Fast food!

It's bright today, and a little cold; stalks of corn shiver and shine like the sea. But the air feels good too, so I tip my head back and squint into the blue. I was born on a morning like this. That's how I got my name: Claire. In French, it means "bright and clear." "That's what you were from the beginning," my parents always say. "You still are."

They don't see how my insides flutter when I think about Andy, or school, or how to keep Sunny and Sam safe in our barn instead of sending them to a new one.

They don't see the birds in there.

Sparrows that soar over our barn can actually fly to the tops of clouds, then plunge back to earth. And that's exactly what my flutter feeling is like: It sweeps in from a place beyond me and gets under my skin, shaky as wings.

I don't know exactly where my sparrows go when they leave. But they visit more and more now that Andy's gone.

By the time I get to the mailbox, my hair's tangled under my chin. I brush it back, pull the metal door until it squeaks open, slip the letter in. Next comes my favorite part. It was Andy's favorite too. He was the one who explained we had to tip the red flag up with our fingers so that Mr. Meyer, who's been driving mail around our back roads since Mom was my age, knew he needed to stop and take what we'd left inside.

Dad says we used to fight over who got to put up the flag, but by the time my memory kicks in,

Andy was already letting me do it every time, lifting me at the waist so I could reach as high as I needed.

I raise myself a little on my toes now, even though I don't need to anymore, and push the flag up myself.

Dear Andy, I wrote this time.

Guess what? I miss you.

CHAPTER 2

"Back from the barn already?" Dad's frying eggs and potatoes at the stove. He doesn't need to turn around to know I'm on the front porch, stamping driveway dirt from my boots.

"Just mailed a letter. Came back for my hat." I grab it out of the basket by the door and tuck it over my ears.

In the living room, Mom pushes her chair back from the desk. She's spent a lot of time there lately, staring at the computer, looking for jobs. But now she bends her head around the doorway to the kitchen and wags her finger at me. "Told you it was cold."

I hold up my hands. "You might have been right. *This* time."

Mom laughs, then wraps her hands around the mug of coffee Dad offers. She sighs, and the wrinkles that scrunch up her forehead go soft and smooth. "Just what I needed," she says. Dad kisses her on the cheek.

"Ugh." I push the door halfway open. "See you guys later."

"We know not to wait." Dad stretches a set of metal tongs toward me, and I grab the strip of bacon hanging from them before heading back outside. Saturday breakfasts are always the best because Dad uses cooking as a way to procrastinate before settling into his living room chair with stacks of history essays to grade. He says food always turns out just the way he expects it to, unlike most other things in life.

Still, I'd rather keep my plate warm in the oven and take my time with morning chores. I can't ever squeeze enough minutes out of school days to groom Sunny and Sam with the currycomb plus both the hard and soft brushes, or to smear baby oil over the burrs tangled in their tails. But on weekends, time widens somehow.

Now I want to stretch it even further. Ever since Mom lost her accounting job when Kroller's Auto closed last spring, she and Dad have been worried. He teaches, and does tutoring in the summer, but it doesn't feel like enough. They both say it doesn't make much sense to keep horses anymore.

Dad says he's sorry. Mom says it will hurt her too. But they still hope to sell before winter comes, so they must not see how Sunny and Sam hold my skin and bones together, all in one piece. They don't see my heart quiet and calm when I'm braiding manes and picking hooves and squeezing my heels against soft flanks, pushing to go faster, cold wind in my hair.

There's always warmth in the barn. I slip into the hush of it and let my eyes adjust to the gray light of the big, airy entry that holds our hay wagon and tractor. From behind the latched door leading to the separate area we call the "horse stable," lined with stalls and a tack room, I hear Sunny and Sam shifting on their bedding, pushing wood shavings into piles with their big hooves.

When I walk past their stalls, they swing around to face me and hang their heads over the doors. I twist the strands of their chestnut forelocks in my hands and bring both my curved palms to their noses. Their whiskers tickle my skin.

Sam's a little bigger than Sunny, and a little sweeter too. When I move into his stall to get his feed bucket off its hook, he sways to the side, ears flopping, eyes half shut. Sunny has more opinions. She nods her big head up and down and noses my palm.

"Don't be rude," I say. I push my shoulder against hers until she scoots and I can pull her bucket out too.

The fact is, I love them both.

Today I'm riding Sam. A few days ago I worked Sunny on the lunge line, guiding her in circles, making her trot and canter. If I don't give her enough practice out of the saddle she gets prickly, shy. Holding a horse's attention while you're standing on the ground makes riding sessions work better.

But it's easy to get lazy and skip lunging Sam. No matter how many too-busy weekdays keep us away from our trails in the woods, Sam stays calm. If anything, he needs an extra nudge to get past a walk. When Maya comes to visit, she likes to ride him. She can't have a horse at her house in town, but she says being friends with me is close enough.

"Sam's more my style," she told me last time. "I bet he even likes to sleep in, just like I do." Then she leaned back, closed her eyes, and fumbled around for an imaginary snooze button. Maya always knows how to make me laugh.

I shake dust from a thick woven saddle pad, then bring out the saddle and bridle. Each piece has a name: horn, cantle, stirrup, cinch, headpiece, broadband, throatlatch, bit. Leather locks with metal and fits just right.

Sam follows me out of his stall, his nose at my elbow. Once I fasten cross-ties on either side of his halter I brush his thickening coat. I'm hurrying, filled with a tremor that's nothing like the sparrows. Instead of feeling like I'm going to break apart, I'm putting myself back together.

I work my fist between the saddle pad and the bony ridge of Sam's withers like Andy showed me, making a space where nothing pinches. Then I hook the right stirrup over the horn, swing the saddle up and set it gently down, pull the cinch swinging under Sam's belly, then tighten it. Next the bridle: bit slipping between teeth, reins gathered in my hands.

And then we're ready, gone, out into sunshine made more blinding by the barn's dimness. I blink slashes of light away and lead Sam down the path to our arena. It only has two walls front and back, with open-air sides, but the roof keeps too much rain and snow from getting in. We have a tiny circle I can ride in by myself well into the winter if I can't convince anyone else to trail ride, since I'm not allowed to do that alone. It's better than nothing. Every time I start moving Sam around the arena, I can see the hoofprints we left from last time leading the way.

"Ready, Sam?" I tighten the cinch one more time, then latch my left foot into the stirrup and swing my right over his back. Settle in. Here we go.

From the saddle, I see so much: the middles of

mountains, the mailbox a little speck in the distance, its red flag the size of a pinprick. Everything on the ground looks smaller, matters less. My shoulders roll back, my muscles shift. Inside, I'm warm and strong.

Heels down, reins clutched in my gloves, eyes pointed straight ahead to where I'm going, I can do anything.

When I lead Sam back into the barn, I see Mom there, brushing Sunny. She's been coming to the barn during my chore time more often lately.

"Hey, you," she says. "Thought we could exercise both horses together, head out into the woods a bit. That way you can eat breakfast sooner."

Mom knows I can wait for breakfast. She's here for the same reason I am: because the barn's dark enough to make dirt look pretty, quiet enough for a crowded brain to think, softer to look at than a glowing screen. Because problems sink through the grooves in these wood-plank walls and get swallowed whole.

My heart swells a little. Maybe riding Sunny and Sam will remind Mom that they need to stay here.

Mom must see the hope rise into my cheeks, all rosy and warm, because she's gentle when she says, "We talked about this, Claire. We need to take care of Sunny and Sam as long as we still have them, and that includes exercise."

I feel the sparrows race in then, pecking my swelled-up heart. They tickle my throat, making it hard to talk. *I'm losing everything that matters*, a voice inside me whispers. *And I'll never get it back.*

Sunny and Sam aren't supposed to belong to anyone else. They're ours. And I don't care if Mom says I can still ride her friend Marcy's horse anytime. It's not the same.

"I already rode Sam," I mumble. "In the arena."

"It can't have been for very long, though," Mom says. "A little more won't hurt. And Dad's got so much grading to do. I'll never be able to drag him out here. You'll come, right?"

I always want to go into the woods. This is the best time of the year for it, the bugs finally gone and the damp smell of fresh leaves turning all around, mixing with the spice of cedar and pine.

When crisp air fills my lungs, it stills the sparrows too. I smile just thinking about it, and Mom sees.

"I'll take that as a yes." She rubs Sunny's neck and unclips the cross-ties. "This girl's all set. Ready to go?"

Mom leads Sunny toward the door, and I turn Sam around to follow.

"When do you think Andy will be home?" I whisper against his neck. "Not too long, huh?"

It seems like he's been gone forever, but Mom marks the days with Xs on the feed-company calendar she tacked on the barn wall, so I know it's really only been a month. August 27. That day, I followed Andy out of the car and up the steps of the Starshine Center, my tongue a block of ice refusing to melt in all that summer heat, keeping words too far down to speak while everything inside—my throat and ribs and flip-flopping stomach—screamed at him not to go. I knew why he was there. We had already sat down as a family the week before and I'd listened to Mom and Dad explain. Andy's voice cracked as he told me himself that there was such a thing as too much medicine, that he needed help to stop taking the pain pills a doctor had prescribed after he hurt his back snowmobiling. He'd taken too many, for too long. I understood what the therapists told us, that Andy has a problem he'll need to work on, that it's called *addiction*. I remembered how empty Andy's eyes had started to look, how he'd been staying out later and later at night and sometimes didn't come home at all. But I also knew that wasn't the real Andy. It couldn't be. When we camped on Pebble Mountain, he brought graham crackers and marshmallows and bars of chocolate. He lit fires without matches and whittled sticks to sharp points. He didn't need pills.

Sam looks at me from sleepy eyes, his ears flopping every which way. He's relaxed. I cup my hands under his nose, and he breathes into them, his whiskers tickling my palms.

He doesn't have any answers for me.

But with horses, and questions, you have to be patient.

Ashley Cleveland

Sarah R. Baughman

is the author of *The Light in the Lake* and *The Wild Path*. She taught middle and high school English in the United States, China, Bolivia, and Germany. After six years in rural Vermont, Sarah now lives with her husband and two children in her home state of Michigan, where she spends as much time as possible in the woods and water. Sarah invites you to visit her online at sarahrbaughman.com.